NORWICH BOOKF
Rice, Patricia,
Formidable Lord Quentin /

MAY 0 1 2015

FORMIDABLE LORD QUENTIN

0= Never
1copy

THE REBELLIOUS SONS

Patricia Rice

Guernsey Memorial Library
3 Court Street
Norwich, NY 13815
www.guernseymemoriallibrary.org

Copyright © 2015 Patricia Rice

All rights reserved, including the right to reproduce this book, or portion thereof, in any form.

This is a work of fiction. Any references to historical events, real people, or real locales are used fictitiously. Other names, characters, places, and incidents are the product of the author's imagination, and any resemblance to actual events or locales or persons, living or dead, is entirely coincidental.

Published by Rice Enterprises, Dana Point, CA, an affiliate of Book View Café Publishing Cooperative
Cover design by Killion Group
Book View Café Publishing Cooperative
P.O. Box 1624, Cedar Crest, NM 87008-1624
http://bookviewcafe.com
ISBN 978-1-61138-444-4 ebook
ISBN 978-1-61138-445-1 print

OTHER BOOK VIEW CAFÉ BOOKS BY PATRICIA RICE

MYSTERIES:
EVIL GENIUS, *A FAMILY GENIUS MYSTERY,* VOL 1
UNDERCOVER GENIUS, *A FAMILY GENIUS MYSTERY,* VOL 2

HISTORICAL ROMANCE:
NOTORIOUS ATHERTON, *THE REBELLIOUS SONS,* VOLUME 3
FORMIDABLE LORD QUENTIN, *THE REBELLIOUS SONS,* VOLUME 4
THE MARQUESS, *REGENCY NOBLES,* VOLUME 1
ENGLISH HEIRESS, *REGENCY NOBLES,* VOLUME 2
IRISH DUCHESS, *REGENCY NOBLES,* VOLUME 3

PARANORMAL ROMANCE:
TROUBLE WITH AIR AND MAGIC, *THE CALIFORNIA MALCOLMS*
THE RISK OF LOVE AND MAGIC, *THE CALIFORNIA MALCOLMS*

One

Late July, 1809

"I HATE TO ABANDON you in this horrid hot town, Bell," Abigail Wyckerly, Countess of Danecroft protested. In her traveling gown and bonnet, she descended Belden House stairs, trailing her gloved hand over the banister. "The Season is over and you'll be all alone in this old house. I wish you would come with us."

Isabell Hoyt, dowager Marchioness of Belden, in hastily donned morning gown, declined the use of the rail, following her friend with naturally graceful poise. Both in their late twenties, the countess's more matronly, but properly draped figure played counterpoint to Bell's slender one in dishabille.

Despite Bell's worldly ennui, Abby's wisdom found its target.

Not acknowledging a pang of loneliness at the reminder of the empty months ahead, Bell languidly waved away her friend's suggestion. "Dearest Abby, I am not the sort to pamper your charming menagerie of children and pets. The country has been bred right out of me, I fear. I will be fine. There will be enough of us left in Town to sit about roasting those who abandon us."

Bell's words rang hollow, even in her own ears. Once upon a time, her life had been built on children and pets. She'd outgrown that infantile phase, she assured herself.

"Gossiping with a bunch of old biddies," Abby declared with scorn, much too perceptively. "You are in dire danger of becoming one of them. You are too young to bury yourself in trite nattering."

"Boredom trumps the constant hullabaloo I once lived with," Bell countered with a trace of aspersion.

Undeterred, Abigail beamed at her former mentor. "You are too clever to live so idly. You need another project. I will think on it. But in the meantime, I must confess that I'm eager to return to my menagerie. Should you change your mind, we'll put you up in our highest tower, and you may descend only when the children are out of the way. The stable is yours, and you know it."

Bell's investment had helped Fitzhugh Wyckerly, the earl of Danecroft—Abby's husband— to build his stable so his impoverished estate could start producing an income.

Bell considered money to be something one invested in

happiness. Just seeing how happy Abby and Fitz were together had paid off better than she'd dared hope.

But the mention of horses reminded her of why she would never return to the country, where animals were a way of life. "Perhaps if there is a pleasant day, I might take the carriage out. We'll see," Bell lied politely.

A sharp rap at the townhouse door sounded from the foyer below, bringing them to a halt on the upper stairs.

"Were you expecting company at this early hour?" Abby asked in surprise. "Or have I lingered longer than I thought with my farewells?"

As if in answer, the tall clock at the base of the stairs chimed ten in the morning. Bell was most generally not out of bed at this hour.

"I thought you were the last to leave town," Bell said, leaning over the rail to be certain a servant had heard. "A puzzle! Let us spy and see who it might be."

A sturdy footman wearing a stiff mien of disapproval hurried down the hall below to unlatch the massive entrance doors. Stepping out of sight, Bell gestured for Abby to join her in the shadows of the landing.

"Perhaps a new protégée?" Abby asked teasingly. "It's time for one."

"Nonsense, you saw all the pleas Belden ignored, as he ignored yours." Bell was still incensed over that cache of unanswered letters in her late husband's files. "I believe I have succeeded in finding and aiding all the impoverished relations he abandoned. There are no more who need introductions to society."

Bell diverted her interest to the opening door below.

A disheveled boy of roughly six years rushed in, then skidded to a halt and gazed in shock at silk-covered walls, gilded mirrors, and polished Chippendale. Behind him followed a young woman wearing a black, baggy gown ten seasons old, and a hooded bonnet so large, her face couldn't be discerned. She carried a wriggling infant of indeterminate sex and stopped woodenly just inside the door.

Bell had to grab Abby's arm and hold her back. The big-hearted countess loved babies and would have run straight down to welcome the strangers with open arms and coos and cuddles. Bell, on the other hand, had learned to fear surprises. This was why she hired large, reliable footmen. A woman living alone needed security.

A more slender female with the yearling gait of an adolescent bounced in. She, too, was garbed in sackcloth and virtually invisible. Bell had just started to wonder if they came from one of those exotic countries that hid their women behind walls when two black crows followed them in.

The man wore the most hideous flat black hat that had ever afflicted Bell's gaze. He was dressed entirely in ebony except for his neckcloth. The woman with him was large and buried in enough dark broadcloth to dress an entire orphanage.

"This is the home of the marquess of Belden?" the man intoned in a broad American accent.

The home of Lachlann Hoyt, the *current* marquess, was in Scotland. Belden House was the home of Edward, the *late* marquess, but the footman had been trained not to divulge the slightest bit of information to strangers. He stiffly held out a silver salver to deposit a card on.

The stranger laid a rectangular packet on the tray. "Then our charges have been safely delivered." He turned to the youngsters. "Godspeed, children."

He was about to turn and usher out his companion when the boy broke into wails. Bell could no longer hold Abby back. The countess flew down the stairs to hug the child and rebuke his elders.

With amusement, Bell listened to the petite countess scold like the farmer's daughter she'd once been and the mother she was now.

"It is utterly rude to simply abandon children like errant parcels! Let the servants fetch the marchioness. Go sit in the parlor. Young man, stop the crying. If something is wrong, you must use words, not wails."

Laughing silently as the tall Americans were herded by a nagging banty hen into the visitor's parlor, Bell waited for the footman to run up the stairs to deliver the packet. He startled a bit at finding her hiding on the landing, but he made a dignified recovery, bowed, and held out the tray.

"Have cook send up tea and biscuits," she said, gesturing carelessly and trying not to reveal her eagerness to discover if this missive contained a new challenge.

Abby had been right. Bell always dreaded the loneliness of Town after everyone had fled to the cooler countryside. During the busy months, Bell didn't have time to miss the fields of her childhood. In summer, however... She plotted. Only this summer, she had run out of ideas, and weeks of boredom stretched ahead.

Bell's dislike of boredom had been the reason she had spent her first summer as a widow searching through her late husband's files in hopes of discovering the whereabouts of her family, a fruitless search, as it turned out.

Instead of finding her father's whereabouts, Bell had learned to her disgust that the husband she had once admired as all that was superior in men— had entirely abandoned his many impoverished female relations.

That had given her a new mission to mask her loneliness and disappointment at not finding her sisters. Giving her husband's money back to his deserving family members had kept her entertained these last years and been well rewarded by friendship with the late marquess's many and scattered relations, like Abby.

Bell hid her anticipation until the servant had run back down the stairs. Biting her bottom lip, she opened the oilcloth packet, and frowned at finding only a single sheet of vellum inside.

As executor of the estate of Glendon Boyle, recently of Boston in the state of Massachusetts, I have been requested to deliver the deceased's worldly possessions to the Marquess of Belden. Guardianship of his unmarried descendants under twenty-five is hereby bequeathed to the marquess in deference to all that gentleman has done for the family.

Bell's vision blurred, and light-headed, she grabbed the stair rail. It could not be so. *The estate of Glendon Boyle...*

She struggled to comprehend the rest of the verbiage, but she could not read past that first sentence.

Daddy was *dead*?

In all those years of not knowing, she had hoped and prayed...

She clutched the rail and tried not to shatter. She'd had a decade to develop a formidable control over her volatile emotions, and she desperately employed those measures now. Her eyes remained dry. She didn't wail like the child below. She didn't call for smelling salts she didn't own.

Still, she couldn't shut out a sudden rush of images of Irish skies and emerald fields, a laughing lilt, and strong hands holding her on her first pony... Unwelcome tears threatened. She hadn't cried in eons—probably since the last time she'd seen her family. She'd cried buckets then. Cried and cried until she'd been certain her soul had shriveled to a dried-up walnut.

Those had been futile tears. She refused to waste more. Stiffening her spine and taking a deep breath, she re-read the missive, hearing the sarcasm as her father consigned his heirs to the man he most despised. There had always been method to her father's madness.

Hands shaking, Bell proceeded downward, listening to the voices carrying up from the parlor. Could this letter possibly mean... Despite her despair, her heart dared to pound harder in anticipation.

Perhaps sensible Abby could make sense of the gibberish in this missive. Her father, *Glendon Boyle,* had been the *Earl of Wexford,* but there was no reference to his title. Perhaps the letter was from a fraud.

Yes, with the aid of her late husband, her father had run off to hide in the Americas after a series of disasters, but...

She couldn't think further than that. Recalling the young people below, she felt hope thumping like a drum in her ears.

Impostors, her head said scornfully.

Tessa, Syd, her lonely heart cried.

Impossible, said her cynical head. *Never. Tess and Syd here?*

Oh, please, Lord...

She'd thoroughly crumpled the letter by the time she arrived at the door to the visitor's parlor. Abby had the boy and the toddler in hand and had been about to lead them from the room. Bell scarcely noticed. Her gaze traveled directly to the two younger females, who had quite improperly thrown aside their hideous bonnets.

Two heads of chestnut-red hair lifted expectantly. Two identical sets of velvet-lashed emerald eyes flashed. They'd been born with their father's coloring, so similar to Bell's own. The last time she'd seen them, they'd barely been older than the boy who accompanied them— but she'd recognize her sisters anywhere.

"Tess, Syd," she whispered, and tears flowed despite all she'd done to defeat them.

"Isabell?" they asked in unison, standing uncertainly.

"Is it really you?" the elder asked. Tess had been almost ten when they'd parted, the more likely of the two to remember her.

Swallowing the huge lump in her throat, Bell glided towards them, eagerly drinking in every aspect of their grown-up faces. Gently, she touched a tiny scar on Tess's hairline. "It still shows," she said in wonder. "I'm so sorry."

Openly weeping, Tess— Lady Teresa Boyle— flung her arms around Bell. "It's you, it's really you! I didn't think we'd ever see you again!"

Bell held out her arms to include her younger sister, who was still stunned to speechlessness. With both her sisters in her arms again after ten long years, she could scarcely breathe from joy and weeping.

"You smell the same," Sydony whispered in wonder. "Any time I smell lily of the valley, I remember you. You just don't look like you anymore."

Since the eighteen-year-old girl her sisters remembered had worn her hair hanging to her waist and roamed boldly about her father's lands wearing a stable boy's gear, her baby sister had reason to complain. Bell laughed and choked on tears at the same time, hugging them harder.

"You don't know how much I've missed you!" Bell cried. "I cannot believe you're here. Papa never wrote. I didn't know where you were. I didn't even know you were alive!"

"Papa said the marquess forbade him to write ever again. He said he'd be ruined all over if we tried to write to you." Tess hugged her tighter, then stepped back. "I did try a couple of times, after we moved from Virginia to Boston, but I never received a reply. We didn't know if you were alive either."

Bell cursed her parsimonious husband for the thousandth time. Edward must have destroyed *her* letters! He'd kept all the other pathetic begging letters he'd received from his family, but not the ones that would have reunited her with her sisters. Had he even opened them or just cast them directly upon the fire?

Remembering the angry man who had saved her and her sisters from her father's debtors, she had a glimmer of understanding of why he'd keep her from her drunkard of a father. But to keep her from her sisters...

It was too late to castigate the clutch-fisted old goat now. She'd thought she'd loved Edward once. He'd bought her gowns and jewelry, offered her entrée into the highest society, and given her a marvelous new life. He really hadn't owed her or her family more. Bell understood that better than her younger self had. She didn't have to like it.

Looking uncomfortable and out of place in the airy pastel room, the grim black crows rose stiffly from the blue brocade sofa. "We'll be going then. Our job here is done," the man said.

The boy in Abby's hands began to wail again.

Bell hid her impatience with the odd couple who had safely delivered her most precious dreams. "Don't be foolish. We haven't even been introduced. May I have the pleasure of the acquaintance of the generous protectors who have returned my family to me?" With the practiced decorum learned in a decade of London society, Bell released her sisters and held out a welcoming hand.

"Thaddeus and Lucretia Gibbons." Tess hastily introduced them. "Daddy's lawyer recommended them as they were coming this way anyway. Mr. and Mrs. Gibbons, this is our half-sister, Lady Isabell

Hoyt, the Marchioness of Belden."

Isabell was proud to know that her little sister remembered some of her etiquette, even if she hadn't quite got the introduction right. Americans didn't have titles, so Tess might be excused her small lapse until Bell had time to brush up their memories a little.

The Gibbonses didn't accept her hand but stiffly nodded.

Abby whispered, "The little ones need a water closet. I'm whisking them away. I'll return shortly."

"If you will show me the way, I'll help you, my lady," Tess said politely, taking the youngest child in hand. "Beebee is only just two and barely trained."

Still lightheaded, Bell dropped into the nearest chair, finally acknowledging the younger children. She was not maternal, like Abby. "Beebee?" she asked faintly as a maid entered with a tray of tea and biscuits.

"Short for Beatrice. Tess is a widow," Syd explained as the little ones were led away. "We thought she was safely settled, then Dawson—her husband— caught some fever and died in Jamaica not long after the babe was born. Tess was devastated. She still cries."

Syd, the younger of Bell's sisters, studied an embroidered, bow-legged chair, then lowered herself into it as if fearful of sullying the cloth. The Gibbonses finally gave up and settled back on the sofa.

Hands shaking too hard to lift a teapot, Bell indicated that Syd take charge. The girl did so awkwardly, as if unaccustomed to using one of the major skills young ladies her age were proud to show off.

They were the daughters of an *earl*. Bell didn't wish to contemplate what kind of life her sisters had led in her scapegrace father's care. She forced a smile and waited for her guests to sip their tea before asking one of the ten thousand questions buzzing through her exceptionally light head.

"You were an acquaintance of our father's, Mr. Gibbons?" she asked politely.

"Only indirectly, my lady," Mr. Gibbons said, sampling one of Cook's strawberry tarts.

"He means the Methodists sometimes brought Daddy home from the tavern," Syd said without an ounce of shame, as if a father who got too drunk to walk was a common occurrence. "Daddy took our step-mama's death hard."

Bell bit her tongue. Glendon Boyle, the scapegrace Earl of Wexford, had taken *her* mother's death hard and his second wife's death even harder. And there were some who said his drinking had led to their deaths in the first place. But their father was dead, and the girls didn't need a loving memory tarnished. Bell was the one who had learned the hard way to scorn the weaknesses of the male of the species.

"Your step-mama?" she inquired in trepidation. He'd killed off *three* wives?

"Kit's mother. Papa had to find someone to look after us when we arrived in America. Charity was our nanny, and then they got married. You would have liked her. She was from Ireland too."

Bell kneaded her brow. She didn't know a great deal about children, but she knew quite a bit about the ways of men and the laws of inheritance. She would very much like to ask how old *Kit* was and how long ago her father had married the nanny, but she already knew the answer. Her father had always wanted an heir. He'd marry any female he got in the family way.

The grubby urchin that Abby was leading back to the parlor was now the Earl of Wexford.

Two

LORD QUENTIN HOYT, fourth son of the current marquess of Belden, handed his lathered gelding to a stable hand. He checked his pocket watch as he strode down the mews to his back gate. Satisfied at the time he'd made, he handed his hat to a footman who hurried to greet him. Still wearing his muddy boots and the filth of the road, he eagerly took the stairs two at a time to his study.

In a house blessedly quiet and now free of the twittering females his family foisted upon him during the Season, he could finally settle in and tend to neglected tasks. Work was the reason he rose in the morning. He whistled as he entered his book-crammed study.

Acton Penrose, an old friend and his newly hired aide, appeared as soon as Quent dropped into his desk chair. "You made good time, sir."

"Leave off the 'sir' bit. You're the one with society connections, not me." This was mainly because Quent's impoverished Scots family had scorned England, their English relations, English schools, and even the title his father now possessed. That was water well under the bridge and never a source of regret. He had little use for society except as a means of making money.

Quent lifted a stack of new leather books from his chair, their pages uncut and beckoning to be read. He looked around and found a stack on his shelves that wasn't quite full yet. He sneaked a peek at a map in one particularly tempting volume before reluctantly stashing them away.

"I don't know why you keep ordering books you never read," Acton complained.

"It's August," Quent said in satisfaction. "I have no sisters to escort about, everyone is out of town, so I have few meetings. I can spend my evenings with books I've only heard about all year."

Acton wrinkled up his nose in distaste but wisely held his tongue. From good family, with the sound education and social acquaintances that aristocratic relations and Cambridge brought, Penrose had lost his small inheritance to a scoundrel. He'd nearly died at Trafalgar attempting to earn a living as a naval officer. He still limped and favored his injured arm, but his mind was sharp, and he was always eager for action. Books weren't action in Acton's young mind, Quent understood.

Quent loosened his wilted neckcloth and unfastened his waistcoat as he flipped through the correspondence waiting on his orderly desk. "Do we have the information on that steamboat investment yet?"

The tall, ginger-haired ex-officer slid one set of documents out from beneath the others. "In here. It looks promising."

Quent had only just hired him but had found his friend's insight invaluable already. With luck and Penrose's aid, he could double his accomplishments. He'd need to. Now that his father had inherited the title of marquess of Belden, the family responsibilities were seemingly limitless, while their fortunes remained quite confined. Quent's older brothers had chosen farming to cover the estate expenses. They depended on Quent's business acumen and London acquaintances to generate the capital needed for major improvements.

"Excellent." Taking the papers, Quent lit a lamp to better read them. The steam engine had an auspicious future, the kind of imaginative investment he enjoyed.

Unfortunately, it wasn't the kind of investment that generated quick cash. His father's aging fortress needed a new roof, if his many siblings and extended family weren't to drown this winter. Quent grimaced as he read. The design of this engine looked promising, but manufacturing experimental engines would drain more cash than he had and might not generate income for decades. Damn.

"What will happen in the future if we begin traveling about by steam?" Acton ventured to ask, distracting Quent from his numbers. "Think of all the stud farms and stablemen who make horses their business. And sailors—how will they earn a living? It seems impossible to imagine."

"And it will happen many years after we're moldering in our graves, I should think," Quent said, setting the papers aside and reaching for the next batch. "Unfortunately, now that my father is responsible for both the Belden and Hoyt properties, he needs more wealth than Croesus possessed. So I can't afford to take risks on that future."

Painfully aware of the vagaries of fortune, Acton couldn't argue. "It is a shame the late marquess left his wealth to his widow instead of to his estate. Then you could enjoy investing as you'd like, and your family would be provided for."

"Edward was a miserable miser and made that fortune on his

own, albeit with the aid of Belden coal," Quent said, speaking of the late marquess. "The error was on my great-grandfather's part in not demanding that his heirs sign an entailment on the mines as well as the farms. Edward was within his rights to leave his funds anywhere he liked."

"Marry Lady Bell and reunite fortune with land," Acton suggested with a grin, knowing he hit a sore point. Lady Isabell Hoyt, dowager marchioness of Belden, enjoyed spending the fortune her husband had left her.

"Your diplomacy needs work," Quent said dryly. "But you remind me... Send round a note to the lady telling her I'm back and at her disposal."

It didn't hurt to remind Lady Bell that he existed, just in case she should grow bored with her empty bed after these years of widowhood. Marriage wasn't his goal, but the lady was.

"Ah, I was saving the best for last," Acton said with a self-important nod. "Lady Belden's sisters have arrived from the Americas. They're currently on the hunt for a nanny."

Quent dropped the documents on the desk and stared at his aide. "Her *sisters*? What about her father?"

He'd made it his place to learn Lady Bell's history. Quent's family had been horrified when Edward, the old marquess, had come home with a new wife. As long as Edward had no sons, Quent's father had been his only heir. A new wife had meant the potential loss of estate and title. At the time, Quent had wanted to believe that Bell was no more than a fortune hunter.

But Bell's credentials had been impeccable, even if her father had been a dissolute gambler. She'd doted on her husband while he was alive and behaved with perfect circumspection in the years since his death—except for spending Edward's wealth as generously as Edward had hoarded it.

Personally, Quent suspected the old marquess had married Bell just to spite his irascible Scots heir. The Hoyt family wasn't known for its loving generosity.

But Bell had been grateful to the old curmudgeon for saving her family from disgrace and had never said a word against him. So it was Quent's own jealousy at the old man's good fortune that colored his views now. He'd only been twenty-five at the time Edward had married Bell. Quent had been living on luck and looks then and couldn't even earn a glance from the vivacious young Irish bride.

Over this past decade, Bell had grown more beautiful—and

sophisticated and cynical. The wide-eyed young innocent was gone, replaced by a dignified marchioness who commanded the small portion of society she deigned to acknowledge. Quent preferred the sensual widow to the naïve child.

If she had lovers, she was damned discreet about it. The men at his club had taken to calling her the Virgin Widow. That was a challenge he was prepared to meet—should she give him the slightest hint of interest. Which, admittedly, she hadn't. Perhaps, now that his sisters were out of the way, it was time to escalate his pursuit.

"Her father has apparently died," Penrose explained. "He must have left an estate sufficient for his executor to ship her sisters back to Lady Bell. I've only heard the news third hand, so I don't know all the facts yet."

Quent peeled off his riding coat and headed for his chambers and a bath. Business could wait a few hours. "Send word round to the lady that I'm on my way over."

He ignored Acton's knowing grin.

BELL HAD SETTLED at her private desk to dash off correspondence to her circle of friends about the latest developments, when her maid delivered Quent's note. Her first reaction was one of relief that he'd called on her so quickly. And then she scolded herself.

"He's simply poking his nose where it doesn't belong. I will not rely on him or any other man," she vowed, folding the note into a square. But she rose and checked her mirror and found a prettier shawl to go with her gown. It had been a decade since she'd undertaken the study of the most distinguished ladies in society and learned to create an elegant style and air of her own. She wasn't truly worried about her appearance.

She was nervous for reasons beyond her looks. Her father's trunks had arrived this morning. She'd had time to peruse his documents before sending them to Summerby, her solicitor, with queries. She wished Quent had stayed in Scotland long enough for her to find answers.

She could hope that if she gave him a simple task, he wouldn't have reason to look deeper. Yet.

Quent arrived immaculately dressed, as if about to set off for a night on the town. His blue superfine fit his broad shoulders to perfection, but the tailored elegance didn't suit him. London gentlemen needed shoulder padding to achieve anything half so impressive as Quent's yeomen's shoulders. He stood taller than any man in any ballroom she'd ever attended. His muscled legs in tight stockinette had caused delicate females to gasp and fan themselves. He belonged on a destrier, wearing a suit of armor, at the very least. He always made her blood race a little faster, but she'd learned she needn't act on rash urges anymore.

Wearing the cloak of civilization, she knew how to behave. She doubted that Quent was capable of misbehaving.

Bell led him to Edward's study, where she could pour him a brandy. "I see you're already off to discuss business at Lloyd's. You didn't need to stop by so soon after returning."

They'd known each other too long to stand on propriety. That she didn't require a servant while entertaining him spoke of their long-accepted roles. She was grateful for her worldly widow status. It simplified so much. She would never have fared well as a simpering maiden. That Quent acted as the Hoyt family representative in London gave them a family connection to quell rumors. That he was the most formidably proper gentleman in town aided her cause.

"I take it your sisters have gone back to Scotland. Since I have no protégée to marry off to your bachelor friends at the moment, I cannot think you needed to hurry over," she said insouciantly, pretending this was an informal call.

Quent merely nodded acknowledgment of their ongoing wager. Bell had dowered Edward's unmarried female relations so they might have choices she'd never had. Quent had steered his group of impoverished younger sons in the direction of her well-dowered protégées. Bell was adamant that her protégées needn't marry. Quent's friends had still swept them off their feet. Bell had agreed to sponsor Quent's sisters in society in payment of her losses. Since she would have done so anyway, she'd been quite entertained and thought the outcome fair.

"How can I help you?" she asked when he merely accepted his brandy.

More polite and better dressed than Brummell, with glossy black hair, rugged cheekbones, and a stubbornly square jaw, Lord Quentin Hoyt was a man who caused ladies to swoon when they spoke of him.

Unfortunately, all society knew he was a younger son of a crude Scot and that he'd made his fortune in trade, so the marriageable maidens swooned in private.

He sipped his drink and studied her. Bell couldn't tell if the appreciation in those sinfully lashed eyes was for her or Edward's French brandy, but she wasn't the sort to swoon in any case. Men could be pleasing to look upon, but she knew their danger and kept her distance, even if this one made her blood race.

"You think I shouldn't be eager to gaze upon your rapturous beauty after so long a time apart?" he asked, his damned whiskey-brown eyes dancing in amusement.

Quent's normal mien was businesslike, efficient, and often impatient. He seldom laughed. That he did so now, however discreetly, stirred Bell's wish that he could be anyone but who he was. Lord Quentin Hoyt was... all sumptuous male. He was hard not to notice.

He created urges that Edward had seldom generated. She resented that.

"If you truly admired rapturous beauty, you'd escort that bird-brained but gorgeous Lady Edith about town and adorn your home with gilt and murals," she retorted. "Do not tease, Quent. I am out of my depth and in dire need of masculine knowledge. Would you set your circle of friends to helping me find a tutor? All my friends are either elderly or out of town, it seems."

"A tutor?" He raised a skeptical eyebrow. "You plan on learning Latin and Greek?"

"Stop it," she ordered in annoyance, pouring sherry for herself. "You collect gossip worse than any old biddy. Fitz will have told you about my sisters' arrival."

She wasn't entirely certain she should mention Kit, but Quent would know soon enough, and she had no better way of explaining her need for a tutor. "My father apparently arranged to keep his title and our wretched plot of Irish countryside out of the crown's hands by finally producing an heir. I'll not have the boy grow up as ignorant as we did."

"I had an excellent education," Quent reminded her, amusement still flitting about his lips. "But I take your point. I assume you're saying that the next Earl of Wexford will be as dependent on Belden wealth as the last."

Bell flung up a hand in despair that he still rode this old argument. "Honestly, I don't know why I bother confiding in you. Money is the root of all evil, not the answer to prayers. Wealth exists to help people lead better lives, and yes, I'll certainly see that my siblings have a happier one than I did. Go away. I'll find a tutor on my own."

She opened the study door and rudely gestured for him to depart.

He didn't move but continued sipping the brandy and eyeing her with interest. Bell was too furious with him to preen. She'd been walking on pins and needles all day, frantically trying to deal with the immediate while fretting about the future. She had hoped for a little support. She really should have known Quent would strike at her weakness.

"I'll have three tutors on your doorstep by day after next," he said, as if promising a walk in the park. "I trust you have the documents proving the boy's legitimacy and will file them in a timely manner. I don't expect anyone to be foolish enough to fight his claim, but his future should be assured at the earliest possible instant."

Well, yes, there *were* those stupid enough to fight Kit's claim, if they thought they could do so without too much trouble. That was beside the point.

Bell sighed in exasperation at his interference. "I am not a simpleton. My father had his affairs fully documented." And those damned documents were the source of her current distress, but she would go to the courts as soon as her solicitor arranged it. "I merely need help with a tutor, not my affairs."

"Summerby is handling them?" he inquired. "He's a good fellow. I'll check in on him to be certain everything is filed appropriately."

That was the absolute *last* thing she wanted him to do. "I will thank you for the tutors, should they arrive, but I will not thank you for interfering in my business." She tapped her foot impatiently. "I'm quite capable of dealing with my solicitor on my own, and I do not appreciate you assuming otherwise."

Just once, *once,* she would like for a man to recognize her intelligence and capability. Why on earth she expected respect from this domineering horse's arse made her doubt her own intellect. Just because Quent was bigger than everyone he knew didn't mean he was smarter.

"It's unusual for a woman to be appointed guardian, that's all I'm saying," Quent said with a dismissive gesture of his snifter. "As legal representative for the family's wellbeing, I'm simply trying to look after your interests."

Bell swallowed her panic to respond tartly. "No, you're worrying that I won't have time for Sally and Margaret next season. I can assure you, I am perfectly capable of setting up my sisters and shepherding yours at the same time. It is only male pursuits that cause me consternation. Kit needs men in his life, and I have not had a gentleman's education or experience to know which tutors are best."

"Or the example of a good father, understood," he said, no longer looking amused. "You scaled the precarious ladder of society at the delicate age of eighteen and now command the top with the highest sticklers. Since Edward's death, you have had to learn how to manage his investments and households on your own, and you have done so superbly. I only wish to relieve you of unnecessary burdens. It will be a pleasure to make your family's acquaintance. I'll see myself out." He set down the empty glass and bowed.

She could smell his rich shaving soap and the clove he must have chewed after dinner. His muscled arm nearly brushed her breast as he passed her in the narrow doorway. She had to fight not to inhale sharply at the electric tingle created by his proximity.

Quent recognized how hard she'd worked to reach respectable security? She wasn't certain that Edward had *ever* noticed or appreciated her efforts to become the perfect marchioness.

Lord Quentin was the only man she knew who could unsettle her just by his existence. She resented that with all her heart and soul. If she were still the passionate sort, she'd smash the lovely crystal glass over his head—or fling her arms around his competent shoulders and weep.

She was not that lost child any longer, and she never would be again.

Three

THE SOLICITOR'S STUFFY city office reeked of cigars and old books. Documents in hand, Quent crossed his boot over his knee, aware of his surroundings and ignoring Summerby's nervousness. The solicitor's desk had once been rich polished mahogany but bore the damage of decades of boot heels propped upon it—or perhaps angry clients hammering it with their walking sticks. Shelves jammed with ancient leather-bound volumes and folios of musty paper created a confining environment, and Quent rolled his shoulders inside his tight jacket.

The stiff leather chair on its wooden legs provided no comfort as Quent scowled and perused the will in his hands a second time.

"As legal representative and son of the current marquess, you have a right to know," Summerby said anxiously. "But Lady Isabell is prepared to go to court to keep the guardianship in her hands. Her late husband and your father were distant relations and not on speaking terms. It is more than evident that Wexford meant for his children to be returned to their sister and her husband and not to a man they don't know. Your father has no family relationship to her sisters. It would be better if we found a compromise."

Quent massaged the bridge of his nose and wished he'd never asked to see Wexford's will, but he would have heard of it in a matter of time anyway. "She'll lose. No court will override a proper will and assign guardianship of an earl to an unmarried female. She might argue guardianship of her sisters, I suppose."

"But the court won't wish to make an exception. They'll rule on the codicil as one act and one alone. *Unmarried Descendants under twenty-five*, that's all they need. Your father, as the current marquess, has acquired the guardianship of all four children, even the widow and her child, since she's still under age and with no other male family. They will not consider a female as a responsible party." Summerby looked as uncomfortable as Quent felt.

"My father needs four more responsibilities like he needs another hole in the castle roof," Quent said gloomily. "Had the earl left an estate to support them, that would be one thing, but I assume he died as bankrupt as he lived."

"Yes." Summerby sighed and polished his wire-framed glasses.

"From what I gather, the church collected funds to send them back to England. The young widow was left a small account after her husband's death, but that was exhausted by the time the earl departed this mortal coil. I'm uncertain why they chose not to send word to the marquess when the earl passed away. Perhaps they feared he'd refuse the guardianship. It's all very sad, and if I could tell you otherwise, I would. The children would benefit from staying with the lady," Summerby added with a glimmer of hope.

"Possibly." Quent pondered all the angles of this new situation, looking for the one to his best advantage, but seeing only more unpleasant complications. "But guardians must meet certain requirements, and my father won't shirk his duty. The boy needs a tutor, not a nanny. An all-female household can't harbor a bachelor."

"Lady Bell will put up a fight. From what I know of the family, her sisters won't abandon their little brother. I do not desire an adversarial relationship with the marquess, but my duty is to the lady," Summerby said stiffly.

"As my father's man of affairs, my duty is to my father. I will apprise him of the developments and let you know how he means us to go on." Quent rose and returned the will to the desk.

Summerby dragged his portly frame to his feet. "Should Lady Bell marry, the court could be swayed to change the guardianship to her husband, especially if the marquess agrees."

That was Quent's thinking, but he seldom revealed his hand—especially when he wasn't certain he wished to play it. He nodded, slapped his tall hat on his head, and proceeded out of the aging edifice that had probably sat on this narrow medieval street since London last caught fire.

One did not go up against the unyielding majesty of centuries of English law without a great deal of ammunition. Bell had wealth on her side. Quent had his own wealth, his father's title, the earl's will, and his gender. The grimy stone buildings around him had been built on centuries of law that favored men, titles, and wealth. She would lose.

He would lose any chance of winning her bed if he fought her.

He damned well didn't want to recommend she marry anyone else.

He'd sacrificed his youth for his family. How much more of his hard-won freedom was he willing to sacrifice for Bell's relations?

He feared he was about to learn how a condemned man felt.

~~~

THE MODISTE had strewn the Aubusson carpet of Bell's newly-refurbished upper salon with bolts of silks, muslins, buttons, bows, and sample books. The delicately curved blue-and-gold sofa Bell had so carefully chosen last spring was buried under boxes of feathers, lace, and ribbons. The girls had jigged around excitedly with the bounty until the once-serenely elegant chamber now resembled an explosion of colorful plumage in an exotic zoo.

Bell allowed their delight to assuage her frayed nerves. She'd heard nothing from Quent or her solicitor. She was about to come apart at the seams with worry. Perhaps Quent really had gone hunting tutors instead of interfering where he shouldn't.

Even if Quent had behaved himself, Summerby would still be obligated to notify the marquess in Scotland. That gave her a little time to prepare, she hoped.

"Really, Bell?" Tess asked in wonder, stroking an elaborately woven fine cotton. "This is what you call muslin? Ours is so much coarser! And ladies wear fabric like this in public? It is almost... unseemly."

Since Bell was sitting there in the lightest muslin in her wardrobe in respect for the August heat, she spread the skirt over her palm to display it. "One wears petticoats, naturally, but muslin is all the rage. And Syd really cannot appear in anything else. If innocent young girls may wear white muslin, then widows certainly can."

Tess glanced sadly at her dark skirts. "Shouldn't we all be wearing black? It's only been six months since Father died."

Bell frowned. She had mourned the loss of her father a decade ago, when he'd still been alive but not to her. "It is very hard to think of him dead," she admitted. "I have been picturing him happily riding broader fields. Do you miss him terribly?"

Both girls looked more uncomfortable than distressed. Tess finally spoke with a sigh. "We were living in the boarding house that Jeremy's parents owned. We did not see Da much these past years since our step-mama died."

There was the earl Belle knew. She might paint pretty pictures of her handsome, laughing Irish father, but they were just that—the wishful images of a child who missed her home and family. She was certain he'd loved his family as best as he was able, but he'd spent more time with his drinking cronies than with his children. That was what he'd been brought up to do.

And judging from their work-roughened hands, her sisters had paid their own way—as Wexford women were taught to do to survive.

"I must write and express my gratitude and sympathy to your husband's family," Bell decided, already planning a substantial donation to them and their church. "I suppose you might wear lavender or gray out of respect, if you wish, but it's not wholly necessary. And white is also perfectly respectable mourning wear, plus absolutely necessary for an ingénue."

"If I must wear white, then I want the dotted one," Syd said with a defiant tone, holding up the fabric to her face and glaring at it. "With lavender ribbons all over."

"Syd!" Tess scolded. "Ribbons are far too expensive. You will not be going anywhere to be seen."

"Why can I not be seen?" Syd asked. "You were seeing Jeremy when you were my age."

"There is no one in Town to see you," Bell said, diverting the impending argument. "But there is no reason you can't have ribbons and sashes. We haven't been to the milliner's yet, so you may want to wait and choose your colors after that."

Grasping the opportunity, the modiste produced a rich white satin. "For the young lady's presentation, yes? With the lace and pearls..."

Both girls fell speechless as the modiste's assistant held up examples of how the gown would be adorned in seed pearls amid the lace.

Bell had adored dressing her protégées and Quent's sisters, but they had all been pragmatic young women, experienced in pinching their coins. Tess and Syd, however, had no concept of what materials could be had, much less their cost. Bell understood she should be careful not to over-indulge, but she loved shocking them. They deserved a little pampering after years of desperation.

"First, morning and walking gowns," Bell corrected the modiste, wielding her fashion authority. "Once they are dressed for the shops, we can explore and see what colors and fashions appeal most. They need a little town bronze before choosing more expensive garments."

"Very wise, milady," the modiste acknowledged, setting aside the luxurious fabric and returning to sturdier broadcloth. "Will the ladies need habits?"

"Naturally. Boyles are born on horseback. That forest green..." Bell realized her sisters hadn't resumed chattering, an unusual state if she'd ever heard one. She glanced at them questioningly.

"We lived in town and didn't have a horse," Tess murmured apologetically. "Daddy sold the mares he took with him."

The mares that had been Bell's life and soul for her first eighteen years. At the time, the pain of their loss had been as great, if not greater, than losing her family. "Even Little Dream?" she asked, trying to hide her horror. He father had *promised* to take care of her mare...

"No, we learned Dream was with foal before we left. He left her with Uncle Jim in payment of debts he owed," Tess acknowledged, lovingly folding a piece of lace over her hand, not recognizing the blow she'd just dealt. "Might I have some of this for a new gown for Beebee?"

Bell nodded, unable to speak through her despair. Dream, the mare she'd raised from birth, in Uncle Jim's ignorant care? How had she not *known* this? She'd been told their father had been allowed to keep his horses to set her sisters up in the new world. For all his faults, her father was an excellent horseman and would never let harm come to his animals. She'd thought Dream would be in good hands. She'd wept and pleaded to keep her mare, but Edward had refused, saying the valuable horse had been part of the bargain.

So she'd consoled herself thinking Dream would provide an excellent dowry for her sisters, and then she'd shut the memory and the pain out of her heart. She had turned her mind to learning to be the best wife and marchioness in existence, and done her best never to think of her horses again.

And now to learn that her Dream could still be alive...

She suffered the despair of an adolescent all over again, only this time with a mature woman's sense of responsibility... a deadly combination.

She wanted to rip off heads, and these days, she had the power to do so.

She'd have Summerby send a groom to Ireland—immediately.

Still stunned, Bell tried to imagine a world where her father did *not* proudly sit one of his Thoroughbreds. He'd sold them *all*? Tess had been a daredevil on horseback before the age of eight. Syd had already known how to groom her pony and ride like the wind when she'd been younger than Kit. The true awfulness of their circumstances finally sank in.

"Kit?" Bell asked in dismay. "An earl of Wexford who cannot ride?"

Looking a little surprised that Bell stuck to the topic, Tess bit her lip and nodded. She clung to the soft white muslin and lace she'd chosen for Beebee. "Horses are expensive to keep," she explained. "We had no land and no stable."

At the age of six, Kit couldn't even ride a pony? That would not do at all. Bell didn't know how she would rectify the omission, however. She hadn't touched a horse since she'd left Ireland. She didn't *want* to touch a horse, she reminded herself. The wound had healed. She refused to reopen it. But she knew her duty.

"That must be corrected at once," Bell said, hoping she hid her frown. Just because she would never ride again did not mean the children shouldn't. Turning back to the modiste, she gestured at the broadcloth. "Habits for both of them. Can you recommend a good tailor for boys?"

She jotted down the names but knew she must consult with Quent or his friends about suitable clothing for a young boy. She had no familiarity with male accoutrement. Fashionable Nick Atherton would have been an ideal adviser. He wouldn't harbor ulterior motives like Quent. And with four sisters, he was accustomed to shopping. But he and Nora were still on their wedding journey aboard Nick's ship.

She would think of *someone* besides Quent to ask.

When Jocelyn Montague sent up her card a little while later, Bell smiled in relief at the solution. Blake Montague, her husband, worked with the Duke of Fortham. He knew everyone. "Bring her up at once and fetch some tea, please," she told the maid. "Syd, clear some room on the sofa, will you? If you are to take town by storm, you will need sponsors, and Mrs. Montague is one of the best."

Moments later, statuesque Jocelyn Montague swept into the sitting room in all her golden glory. Bell watched in amusement as her sisters gaped. Jo flung off her gold-embroidered pelisse to reveal a stunning blue Grecian gown that flattered her generous figure. The lady sailed her feathered hat to a table, set her hands on her curvaceous hips, and studied Bell's guests.

"All these years and you've been holding out on me, my lady! I should turn around and stomp back out in utter outrage at the insult. You have sisters! Why did you never say so?"

Amused at this performance, Bell gestured for her stunned sisters to rise. "Mrs. Blake Montague, may I present Mrs. Jeremy Dawson and Lady Sydony Boyle, daughters of the late earl of Wexford. Girls, Mrs. Montague is the wife of a rising politician and related to Viscount Carrington."

Both girls bobbed polite curtsies. Jocelyn tapped a gloved finger to her cheek, nodded approvingly, and took the seat cleared for her. "Raise them like peas in a pod in Ireland, do you? They'll be as stunning as you, once you have them coiffed and gowned. Where have you been hiding them?"

Bell hid a smile at Jo's bluntness. Her former protégée might be young, but she wore authority with the ease of a duchess born and bred.

"It's a long story," Bell said with a tilt of her head, indicating the hovering modiste. "We'll explain later. Madam Evangeline, if you'll leave the samples and start on the walking dresses, we'll call on you again to complete the order."

Dismissed, the modiste and her assistant hastily gathered their supplies. Pretending to pick up around Bell's chair, Syd whispered, "Lady Sydony? I am a lady?"

"Of course you are, silly. As is Tess. But I assumed she preferred her husband's title. It is her choice. Women wield so little power, we must take advantage where we can."

"Women are the power behind the throne," Jo said solemnly, stripping off her gloves. "Blake and I will be holding a small dinner party in a few days, just a few of his boring officials and their wives. If the three of you would be so kind as to attend, you'll liven the dull summer, and we'll gain an advantage over the biddies for being the first to provide grist for the gossip mill. The whispers are already rampant."

"A private dinner party would be an excellent introduction," Bell agreed. "Perhaps just Tess, though. Syd would be bored faint."

"No, I wouldn't, honestly," Syd said in eagerness. "I love parties!"

"You have not suffered through a political dinner," Bell said firmly. "I assure you, you would slide under the table. We should contain gossip and direct it to anticipation of society meeting you."

Jo grinned. "Devious, milady. I bow to your better strategy." She turned to Syd. "We will think of a more interesting affair for your introduction, something that includes more young people. Will you be attending finishing school in the fall?"

Syd looked appalled.

"We've not had time to discuss anything but infants and clothes," Bell said apologetically. "And just now, horses. It has come to my attention that the earl of Wexford cannot ride. I have been debating inflicting the lot of them on Fitz and Abby or repairing to Belden Hall in Essex and buying my own stable."

The latter made her faint heart quail, but for her siblings, she would provide Paris, France, if required.

"Fitz and Abby, definitely." Jocelyn poured her own tea and helped herself to a biscuit. "Fitz can help you choose a stable should you decide to improve that distressing manse in Essex."

"You are right, of course," Bell agreed with a sigh. "I just hate imposing on their good natures."

She really needed to enlist Jocelyn's well-connected husband in her cause, but she had yet to tell the girls that their "guardian" was actually a crotchety old Scot who never left his northern hills.

Fortunately, a maid arrived with a message from the nursery, and Tess excused herself. Belle waved Syd after her. "Go. We'll just gossip about people you don't know."

Bell mentally commended the girls' Irish nanny stepmother when both performed correct curtsies and farewells before departing.

"They'll do splendidly once we polish their accents," Jo said in approval. "I take it they weren't entirely raised by wild Indians as rumor has it."

Bell gave an unladylike snort. "Not entirely, although I suspect the Indians may be more civilized than my father was. I have Summerby investigating the girls' circumstances. They claim Kit's mother was a nanny, but I suspect she was a governess. She seems to have taught them more than I knew at that age."

Jo sipped her tea and raised knowing eyebrows. "So, then, tell me what is troubling you and how can I help?"

Belle didn't hesitate. "You can ask your husband to speak with the duke to see if he will support me when I sue for guardianship."

Four

"I TALKED TO A DUKE," Tess was still exclaiming the morning after Jocelyn's dinner party. "And a viscount... That's less than a duke, isn't it? But he was so charming!"

Syd hung on to every word, crumbling her toast over the breakfast table. "Were any of them young? Handsome? What did they talk about?"

Tess wrinkled her nose. "Mr. Montague was handsome, but he was the youngest, and he must be in his thirties. And they talked politics and said terrible things about the American government."

Bell reached over and patted her hand. "I hope you do not have holes in your tongue this morning. You did an excellent job of smiling prettily and stabbing them with your eyes. I am very proud of you."

She was bursting with pride. Even Jocelyn had agreed that Tess would do well once she'd learned enough about society to actually converse instead of just giving speaking glares. At least, Bell hoped Tess would learn to speak up. Right now, her sister spent most of her time assessing the situation—probably as a result of their unfortunate upbringing.

"Do you ever have real parties with dancing and people my age?" Syd asked wistfully.

"We will." Bell didn't know how or when, but she would make it happen. Syd was much too young and unpolished to be introduced to the sophisticated society functions that Bell attended, but young people must gather somewhere. She added one more thing to her growing list to do.

She loved challenges and it was wonderful to have her family back. This might turn out to be the most exciting summer she'd ever had. Conquering society had been terrifying, but now that she'd done it, she was confident she could push her sisters to the highest peaks.

A footman arrived carrying a visitor's card. Bell glanced at the card and pushed back her chair. "Have Mr. Summerby taken to the study, please. I will be right with him." She picked up the papers she'd been trying to peruse while her sisters chattered. "We should be ready to take the shops by storm this morning. Wear your new gloves and forget those dreadful Methodist bonnets. Try the hats you picked from my wardrobe, and we'll be on our way in an hour."

That stopped any further demands for parties or arguments over politics. Shopping was a fabulous distraction, for now. Bell didn't know what she'd do once they realized all her friends were married and too caught up in their own lives to include the younger set. Bell might be content with a night at the opera or a card game with an elderly acquaintance. Her sisters wouldn't be. She couldn't rely on Jocelyn to keep them entertained—political dinner parties were really not the thing for young girls.

But neither was Scotland.

Mr. Summerby rose from the wing chair when she entered. Bespectacled, with receding gray hair, and a definite paunch beneath his unadorned waistcoat, he looked every part a fastidious solicitor. Bell had no idea of his age, but his face bore wrinkle lines only about his eyes. She'd hired him upon a friend's advice after Edward's death, when Edward's solicitor had insisted that she needed a man to look after her investments—and that man should be him.

Summerby, on the other hand, had agreeably accepted her orders, even when she'd been giving away fortunes to her protégées. If he made suggestions, he didn't argue if she rejected them. That didn't happen often. His recommendations had always been superb.

"Butler brought you tea?" Bell inquired. "Most excellent." Edward had always called his butler by the name of Butler until no one remembered the servant's real name. Bell had tried asking once, but the staid retainer had appeared horrified at the idea of change. "I thank you for coming out, sir. This is a delicate matter, and I didn't know how to phrase it in a letter."

"For you, my lady, I would sail the Thames," Summerby said with a twinkle behind his glasses. "Your projects always keep me on my toes."

"Yes, well, suing a marquess for guardianship ought to have you ballet dancing. I hope I will not be adding one too many challenges to your repertoire." Bell took the seat behind the desk and produced a paper of notes.

The solicitor returned to his chair and opened the portfolio he'd brought with him. "Your generous fees allow me to hire more assistants. I am at your disposal. I have notified the marquess of your father's will, as is required. I've not heard back from him. Your brother's credentials have been filed with the courts. Unless there is some complaint, there should be no difficulty with his claim to the title."

"My father might have been an inveterate gambler, but he knew all about English courts," Bell said dryly. "I'm sure he was more than happy to cough up whatever sum it took to ensure that his heir claimed his worthless title rather than allow the crown to have it. That may be a problem."

Mr. Summerby looked at her over his spectacles and politely waited for explanation.

Bell tapped her fingers on the paper, looking for a way to state the matter so as not to sound like an hysterical female. "The marquess may not be the only one we must take to court. My father had a younger brother. Uncle Jim was raised with my father and treated by my grandfather as one of the family. My grandmother was deceased, but Jim's mother never lived with us. I had assumed he was illegitimate, but I could be wrong. If he has been acting in my father's place, it's to be expected that everyone will assume my father looked on him as his heir. Knowing my father, he may even have even encouraged that belief, since he had only daughters when he left. I doubt that proof one way or another can be found."

Summerby clasped his hands over his paunch and waited.

Satisfied that he understood the first part of her difficulty, she continued. "Jim is not educated but he knows how to grab advantages, even if they may be illegal. He will not willingly release any control of the estate that he's achieved. One of the many reasons I adored Edward when I married him was that he legally bound and gagged Jim so thoroughly that he's not once come after me for money. I found this document in Edward's files after his death." She shoved a piece of paper across the desk.

Summerby scanned it. "Edward was a brilliant businessman, no doubt about it. So part of your settlement was that this uncle was granted a life estate in the earl's land as long as he made no demands on you or yours."

"Which is why I've never inquired into my father's affairs. The lands were not part of my dowry, and I had no wish to ever speak with Uncle Jim. The man is a lazy bully with a nasty temper. I was happy to be rid of him."

"But now… you have a little brother who will inherit those lands, and when he comes of age, he will have some say in their management. And this personage may even attempt to disqualify the boy's legitimacy."

Bell took a deep breath and tried not to cry. "Not only that. There is plenty of time to worry over land management, and I don't doubt our eventual ability to establish Kit's claim. My concern is more immediate. I have just learned that..." How did she say it without sounding a fool? "I had a mare, a powerful Thoroughbred I raised and nurtured after her dam died when I was only fifteen. Little Dream won every race I ever entered except that last one." When the mare had stepped into a mud hole and thrown Bell over her head, thus losing the match, the farm, and her freedom, but that was neither here nor there.

Summerby frowned and polished his glasses. Courteously, he waited.

"When Edward agreed that my father could take all his animals with him, he told me that Little Dream was part of the bargain, and that I could not keep her."

The mare had been the mother and confidante Bell had never had, the freedom and independence that had saved her sanity, the proof that she was more than an uneducated worthless female. Losing the horse had been akin to losing herself.

She'd tried to understand her father's decision at the time. Little Dream had been extremely valuable. Her family needed the money her horse could earn. She'd bit back her tears, surrendered a little piece of her soul, and grown up quickly.

Taking a deep breath and letting her eyes dry, she continued with determination. "I have just learned that the mare was with foal and couldn't be taken, so my father left her with Uncle Jim. I want her back. I want her and her *offspring* back. And I will not take no for an answer. Jim is a brute who beats animals. He has no doubt ruined my mare, but I will not let her die at his hands if it can be prevented."

Summerby nodded and began taking notes.

WITH THE LETTER from his father scorching a hole in his coat pocket, Quent strode stiffly toward the Belden townhouse. He clenched his walking stick so hard, he had to loosen his grip so as not to break the expensive piece.

He despised having his hand forced. He'd requested that his father be reasonable and give him time to find a compromise. But no, the old man had seen the glint of potential gold, and his resentment toward the late marquess raised its ugly head. Quent growled and a mangy dog dashed out of his way.

Send the wenches and the new earl of Wexford here, the letter had commanded. Quent could practically hear the glee in his father's voice. *We'll marry the girls off to your brothers and betroth the earl to your niece. The dowager can afford to dower them handsomely.*

If her hand were forced, Bell would no doubt tie any dower funds up in a trust so tight that his father couldn't lay hands on it. Not that his father cared as long as more of his liabilities were bartered off and provided for, whether they liked it or not.

The marquess thought in terms of assets and liabilities when it came to family members. Bell would tear the old man limb from limb if she knew.

In resentment that his request for compromise had been ignored, Quent had dashed off his own demand: *Give Bell the guardianship or the manor won't be seeing a new roof.* He could almost hear the old man weighing the coins on either side of that argument. Their battles always ended in a counting of coins. Quent almost preferred swords.

A drunk in disheveled tail coat returning home from an evening's revels staggered into Quent's path, then righted himself and nearly fell onto an elderly lady. With a snarl, Quent grabbed the fellow by his wilted linen and yanked him upright, daring him to take offense.

The drunk obliged and swung his fist. Quent caught it, twisted his opponent's arm behind his back, and shoved him on his way. The drunk yelled. The lady cooed. The altercation didn't provide satisfaction. He stalked on.

Belle had not called on his aid once in the past week—an ominous sign on top of the disaster in his pocket. Reaching her door, he rapped with his walking stick, harder than entirely necessary. Behind him, the drunk still staggered and shouted aimlessly.

Quent had a need to beat someone, but even he must admit that complete strangers might not be the best target. Bell's drunken father would be his preference, but digging up a moldering corpse might be considered a bit odd.

And he understood his own father's desperation too well to consider taking a stout stick to the old man.

Wondering what was taking Bell's servants so long to answer, Quent stretched his shoulders in his close-fitting jacket in a futile effort to relax.

He twirled his stick and promised himself that in a moment he would be holding a snifter of the late marquess's best brandy. The servants knew his preference, and he could settle into the handsome study with the latest newssheets until Bell deigned to acknowledge him. The late marquess might have been a pathetic old miser, but Quent respected his penchant for fine furniture and valuable books.

Still, no one answered his knock. Quent twisted his neckcloth in the heat. The whole household could not have taken a day off. He rapped again, more sharply. This time, a harassed looking footman answered, gazed at Quent in dismay, and offered entrance. The Chippendale tables in the foyer lacked the luster they'd possessed last week. The tall clock didn't seem to have been wound.

Howls of fury and outrage echoed from the normally tranquil upper stories. The footman raced off to the nether parts of the house.

Before Quent could find his own way to the study, a savage war whoop erupted on the stairs above him, accompanied by a clatter of boots. Unprepared to be assaulted in Belle's normally serene haven, Quent held his stick at readiness and braced himself for whatever descended.

He set the stick down again when his four-foot high attacker appeared on the landing clothed only in knee-length shirt and riding boots. Smears of red adorned his chubby cheeks, a bedraggled peacock feather hung from a braided lock, and he wielded what appeared to be a wooden kitchen mallet.

The brigand leapt from the last few stairs squalling war cries. With the benefit of experience, Quent grabbed him by his shirt back before he could cause harm, then dangled the imp above the floor. More whoops and shouts ensued but Quent's arm was longer than the wild Indian's legs, so he averted any damage.

Shaking his head at having his peace marred so precipitously, Quent marched the brat into the study and looked around. Spying the seven-foot-tall mahogany breakfront, he lodged the lad on top of it where he couldn't leap down. Howling, the boy kicked his boot heels into the delicate inlaid wood, but that was Bell's problem.

Quent turned and glared at the startled, bespectacled young man sitting in Edward's sumptuous desk chair—a chair Quent had coveted but not dared to usurp. Worse yet, the intruder was reading one of the rare Shakespearean folios from the locked cabinet, folios Quent had longed to peruse but felt he hadn't earned the right to ask for.

"Which one are you?" Quent bellowed as the young man awkwardly struggled to put the folio together, push back the overlarge chair, and rise.

"Uh, Albert Thomas," the man said. "His lordship's tutor." He glanced up at the boy swinging the wooden mallet as if it were a hatchet and winced as his lordship whooped, undeterred by his lofty position.

"I was told you were an *experienced* tutor," Quent yelled. He never yelled. He'd developed the patience of seven saints over the years of dealing with his large family. But he had an explosive letter in his pocket and the burden of nearly half a dozen lives—that weren't *his* family or responsibility—on his shoulders, and he was eminently Unhappy.

"I am experienced, sir," Thomas said, removing his spectacles and studying the rambunctious earl's perch worriedly. "But my former student Lord Heathmont was…"

Quent threw up his hands. "A cripple, right. No savage war whoops or running amuck for Heathmont. He made it into Oxford and is doing well, is he?"

"Yes, sir, milord, uh…"

Quent snatched the mallet from the boy when it became obvious the tutor wouldn't. When the half-dressed earl protested, Quent pointed the mallet at him. "I will leave you up there for the rest of the day if you don't quiet down immediately."

The six-year-old earl of Wexford pouted his bottom lip, crossed his arms belligerently, and glared.

Satisfied, Quent donned his civilized demeanor again and held out his hand to the tutor. "Hoyt, friend of the family." He wasn't in the habit of using the honorific *lord* that he'd acquired with his father's recent ascension to the marquisate.

The tutor's handshake was firm enough. "Lord Quentin, the gentleman who referred me? It's an honor, sir."

A man needed more than a handshake to deal with a ruffian. Quent continued, "If you feel you are not capable of dealing with a healthy young lad, then we'll give you one week's notice to find another position."

"Uh, yes, sir. Lady Isabell said…" He swallowed hard at Quent's glare. "Yes, sir. I'm certain I can learn to manage. Perhaps I should take him to the park more often so he might work off some energy."

"Yes, perhaps you might. Has he been given a valet yet? Or are the nursemaids still dressing him?"

"Umm, he just acquired a valet, sir. His wardrobe is not quite complete, but I'm fairly certain…" He glanced at the boy's strange attire. "I'm fairly certain he owns breeches."

The study door slammed open and a disheveled Bell flew in.

Quent had never seen the dignified marchioness less than composed. She always dressed in immaculate, fashionable gowns unmarred by the city's filth and held herself with the calm authority and grace of her title. She never appeared in public unless her shining chestnut tresses were elaborately coiffed in the latest style.

The furious termagant propping her fists on her hips and glaring at the miscreant on the cabinet was not the gracious lady he knew.

Silken curls had lost their pins and hung in lopsided disarray. Her shapeless morning gown—at three in the afternoon—was dusted with a fine powder of unknown origin. When she crossed the carpet and stood on her toes to grab her brother's leg and yank off his boot, Quentin noticed that she was barefoot.

Barefoot. He stared in fascination.

"I should leave you up there until bedtime and feed you only bread and water," she scolded. "You have ruined my paints and your sister's gown. You are much too old to act the part of a toddler who doesn't know how to behave."

"I want my pony!" the lad retorted. "You promised me a pony!"

"And you think you will acquire it faster if you act the part of infant?" she shouted back at him.

The marchioness had facets that Quent hadn't known existed. The pink in her cheeks looked natural. Her eyes flashed green fires. And those lovely slender toes... Quent raised his eyes heavenward. He would be pondering ankles and calves next, and then he would have to leave until he was decent.

"Perhaps if Mr. Thomas takes him to the park and makes him memorize the name of every tree, he might be allowed a better seat when he returns, although bread and water sounds suitable if he doesn't behave in the park," Quent suggested.

Bell turned and glared at him. "And where the devil have you been? You send me a tutor who can't teach and a valet who can't keep breeches on him and you disappear off the face of the earth."

Quent raised his eyebrows. "I wasn't aware that my presence was required. I had rather thought you'd be happily entertaining your sisters."

"Get me down, get me down!" the boy chanted from his perch.

"Umm, I'll take him to the park, if uh..." The tutor glanced uncertainly at the tall breakfront.

Mr. Thomas wasn't any taller than Bell. With a growl of disgust, Quent yanked off the boy's other boot. Then he lifted the wary earl down and handed him to the tutor, who staggered under the boy's rather hefty size and set him down.

"Put a leash on him if you must," Quent suggested.

Bell smacked his arm, grabbed her brother's shoulder, and marched him from the study, leaving the two men to stare at each other blankly.

Contemplating fleeing, Quent swung his walking stick and prayed to the almighty for guidance. He had never wanted more family. He'd fled to London a decade ago to escape the extremely large, stubborn, argumentative one he had. Wives and children had *never* been part of his horizon.

Despite all that, he had come here determined to do the proper thing—but bare toes had reduced his mind to rubble that had nothing to do with propriety.

"The boy knows his letters, does he?" he finally asked, wondering how soon he should send a servant to remind Bell that he was here.

"And his numbers. He has a quick mind," the tutor cautiously agreed. "It's just... The ladies have pampered him a bit, rightfully so, I suspect, under the circumstances."

"We can't allow him to behave like a heathen. The Boyles, in particular, need a firm hand. They're all headstrong. Again, if you do not feel yourself capable..."

Mr. Thomas ran his hand through his hair. "I can teach him. But the ladies are not likely to allow me to discipline him."

Bell marched back in in time to hear this last. Quent tilted his chin up to prevent looking to see if her toes were still bare. There had been little time to do more than hand the boy to a maid, so he suspected they were. It was hard not to keep glancing down.

"He will not be beaten just for being a boy," she said firmly.

"A good whack on his bottom will get his attention," Quent argued. "But there are better methods to bring him in line. Thomas, since it apparently takes two to dress the lad, go see that your charge is appropriately garbed and let loose in the park with some educational project."

The man hurried out wearing an expression of relief as Bell geared up to fire again.

"Don't," Quent warned, holding up his hand. "I am in no humor for it. You know perfectly well that the boy needs a man in the house, and you and your sisters shouldn't be dealing with tutors and valets. This house isn't large enough, for one thing. And it's improper, for another. I sent them for you to interview. I didn't expect you to hire them on the spot."

"Why shouldn't I? I'm an aging widow. Who's to question who I hire?"

"Aging widow!" Quent rolled his eyes. "You are scarcely older than your sisters! All of you need chaperones. Are you prepared to house them too?"

She glared. "I have written Edward's Aunt Griselda and asked her to attend us. She can help me polish the girls. I appreciate your help, Quent, but I don't need your interference. Did you have a purpose in coming here besides scolding me?"

She had powder on her upturned nose and a smear of black on her bodice, just above her left breast. If they married, he would have the right to kiss that pert nose and caress that breast.

His prick rose immediately to the occasion.

To cool his ardor, he reminded himself that if they married, his life would descend to a living hell.

But having Bell in his bed would be preferable to suffering that same hell without her. That was the conclusion he'd reached while studying his father's orders. If he was to suffer, so must she.

He produced the letter in his pocket. "You did not really believe my father would respond otherwise once Summerby presented him with the will?"

Bell glared at the vellum but refused to take it. "My father meant to send my family to *me*. You cannot tell me otherwise. Your father should be happy that I'm willing to take them in."

"My father believes in the letter of the law. He could be sued should he fail in his legal responsibility. As you're well aware, he doesn't have the wherewithal to spend years in court. As guardian, he has asked me to send Lord Wexford and Lady Sydony to the schools the family has always attended in Edinburgh. I can assure you, they are excellent schools. You may ask my sisters, who are products of the one Lady Sydony will attend. I and my brothers attended the other, and I have reason to believe we are well educated."

"Kit is a little boy!" she cried. "He cannot be shipped off with strangers just after losing his father. No, I won't have it. And Syd needs me and the family she knows. There are excellent finishing schools in London so she may come home whenever she wishes. She needs to meet London society, not Edinburgh's! You have seen how your sisters have struggled to fit in here."

She swirled to walk away. Quent blocked her path. "My father is opening a room for Mrs. Dawson and her daughter in our home. My sisters and cousins are eager to welcome her. She will be near Lady Sydony and her brother."

Bell stamped her... bare... foot.

Quent closed his eyes and prayed for salvation.

"No. Tell your father thank you," she said, her tone turning icy, "but if the children are to go to school, it will be only if they and I agree on the lessons and faculty and location. And there is absolutely no question of Tess going to Scotland. She is staying here with me so I may present her to society so she may have choices beyond your collection of impoverished relations."

"That is what I was afraid you would say." Quent knew what he had to do now, and he returned to seeking her toes for incentive. "My father will not accept your choices, and he has the law on his side. I have come to offer an alternative." He held his breath, wishing for better circumstances, or at least, some interest on Bell's part.

Although, somehow, seeing the sophisticated marchioness with a ringlet hanging over her nose, the moment seemed easier. When she merely tapped her tempting toe, Quent signed and just spoke plainly. "If you marry me, we can solve the problem. My father will allow the children to stay with me, and you will be there to make the decisions."

"Marry you?" She sounded as appalled as she looked. "Whyever would you even consider I might accept such a solution? We would never suit. You merely want to gain control of Edward's funds. No, no, a thousand times no! The children are my family, and I will spend every cent to keep them, if necessary."

She tried to push past him. Quent thought perhaps he could have done this better, but he was a businessman, not a seducer. He didn't move out of her way. "Bell, the funds are not in question. We can negotiate settlements and trusts. Be reasonable and at least let us discuss this sensibly."

She turned and glared at him. "Marriage is not an acquisition contract, my lord," she said heatedly. "I am a human being, not a ship or a load of silk, no more than my family is a piece of paper to be passed through courts. There is nothing reasonable about your proposal. I'll not hear another word."

She padded out on bare feet, leaving Quent in a state of furious arousal.

Her rejection shouldn't hurt this badly when all he'd done was offer her a better choice than going to court—where she would most certainly lose. He'd always admired Bell's independence, but now he wanted to shake her until she saw reason.

By Jove, why should he care? He shoved his father's letter in his pocket and stalked out.

Five

BELL HELD HERSELF together long enough to reach her room. There, she sank into the vanity chair, glanced in the mirror, and buried her face in her hands.

"I will call for some tea," her maid said worriedly, yanking a bell pull that would ring the kitchen. "Perhaps an egg-white masque and a short nap," she continued when Bell did not respond.

"No, an afternoon gown, please." Bell dug in to her reserves of strength, lifted her chin, and glared at the mirror which revealed her disheveled state.

Quent had *proposed*. She couldn't decide whether to be insulted, furious, pleased, or simply laugh hysterically. He had seen her at her absolute worst—well, not worst, that had been a decade ago—and he'd *dared* propose marriage.

There had been many lonely hours when she had considered inviting him into her bed. He was the only man she'd ever met who had intrigued her enough to even consider such indiscretion. But the knowledge that he and his family coveted her fortune had been too... demeaning. Divisive. She feared a connection would raise hopes when there was none.

Marriage was simply out of the question.

Taking deep breaths to calm her shattered nerves, she began removing the pins from her hair, shuddering at the unkempt horror of her reflection. A week with her family, and the household was already in a shambles, the servants were threatening to give notice, and she was in tatters.

And his solution was to send Kit and Syd to school! He had no understanding of what he asked. She would not have her siblings shipped off like so much unwanted furniture. Besides, Boyles never stayed where they were placed. They were bound to run away.

Ultimately, should she and Quent be forced into marriage, he would move back to Scotland rather than deal with the chaos of Boyle tempestuousness. She'd be an abandoned wife, since she would refuse to leave this home she'd created for herself. No, a thousand times, no. Now that she'd found a man she could almost respect, despite his annoying self-righteousness, she wanted his friendship. From painful experience, she knew marriage would make them enemies.

She shuddered remembering how she had adored Edward those first few years. She could easily have loved him had he given her any opportunity. In the end, her dreams had been so badly eroded with his neglect that she'd come to despise him. She knew other women could endure that sort of life. She had learned that she could not.

Negotiate! He wanted to *negotiate* a marriage.

She knew better than anyone the death of the soul that accompanied a marriage without love between both parties.

"Send up enough tea for my sisters," she told the maid who arrived. "And tell them to meet me in the parlor at the quarter hour."

Syd and Tess had to be told. She would not treat them like pawns on a chessboard as she had been. If she focused on her sisters, she would not have to think about Quent and his absurd proposal.

Tess arrived promptly just as the last pin was applied to Bell's curls.

"Whoever was that gorgeous man who sent Mr. Thomas and Kit packing?" Tess asked in awe. "I thought he'd come to arrest us all and throw us into the street. I heard his bellows all the way up the stairs."

"That's what happens when a man assumes too much authority at an early age," Bell said disparagingly, gesturing toward the sitting room. "He believes he is God, but he is merely the marquess of Belden's fourth son and his legal representative in London. Where is Syd?" she asked before Tess could devour her with questions.

"She is cutting her hair to look like the fashion plates. I told her to ask you first, but she is determined."

Bell muttered an oath under her breath, abandoned her soothing tea, and sailed down the hall to her sister's room. Reminding herself that she was too old to have a tantrum, she opened the door without knocking.

The bottom half of her sister's beautiful hair already lay on the floor. Syd's maid looked up guiltily, scissors still in hand. Without an ounce of remorse, Syd swung around on her bench and ran her fingers through her half-shorn hair. "Isn't it marvelous, Bell? I feel so much lighter already! Agnes said I shouldn't take it all off until I know if I'll like it, but I know I will!"

Bell wanted her sisters to love her, not think of her as some ogre who denied them their wishes. But she knew so much more than they did...

She sighed and tried not to scold like a harpy. "It's not done, Syd," she said sadly. "Young ladies cannot set the fashions until they've been out a season or two. That's for the fast set, the ones who have no care for their reputation."

Syd's expression grew stormy. "It's not as if society gives a fig about me. Why should I care about a bunch of old biddies?"

"Don't be so short-sighted," Bell snapped. "Until you know what you want for your future, you must not ruin your options. Agnes, pin up her hair, and do not cut more without my permission. Syd, if you wish to be treated as an adult, then you must behave as one. I requested your company for a very important reason. You will attend me immediately."

She swept out rather than argue. Tranquility had departed the household the instant her family had traipsed in.

"Syd doesn't like to be told what to do," Tess said apologetically as they settled at the tea table. "She's always been headstrong. When Charity tried to correct her, Syd would run to Daddy, who would tell her she could have anything she liked."

"Which is why we remember him with such fondness," Bell conceded. "Your poor stepmother. She must have been a saint to endure him."

Tess shrugged. "They had horrible arguments. She threw things at his head. Once, she turned over a kettle of soup he'd told her was too salty. You are a model of patience in comparison."

"Give me another week," Bell said wryly. "I will be ready to surrender all rights to the marquess and send the lot of you off to Scotland, except I'm afraid he'll toss you all into the streets for corrupting his very proper daughters."

Tess looked gratifyingly horrified.

Syd stomped in, scowling. Bits of hair still clung to her muslin, but she wore her dark mane pinned up to hide its lack of length. "I *hate* my hair," she announced.

"Yes, we all hate our hair, or our teeth, or our noses or legs and our parents and teachers and the sun that doesn't rise when it should. Now sit down and be quiet and use your head instead of your temper." Bell pointed at a seat near the table.

Syd flung herself into the chair with the grace of an angry bear and snatched a raspberry tart from the tray. Blessedly, she held her tongue and waited.

"Daddy's will left all of you as wards to the marquess of Belden," Bell said, gathering her thoughts to present her case. "He could not leave you to me because women are not recognized by courts of law, but I'm certain he meant for you to live with me."

The girls nodded agreement. Tess added, "He often spoke of how you lived in a grand house and would always take us in, but he could never save the funds to send us."

Because he knew Edward would pitch a fit, call in the earl's markers, and have him thrown in prison, but Bell wouldn't spoil their fond memories. "That's all behind us. The present has its own complications. Daddy thought my husband was still alive. Unfortunately, he isn't, and the title has gone to his heir. Because the will specifies that you are wards of the marquess, the current one has the right to direct your futures until such time as you turn twenty-five, or you marry, and your husband becomes your legal representative."

Tess raised her eyebrows and her teacup. Syd remained mercifully silent, helping herself to another tart.

"The current marquess has..." Bell wanted to say *ordered* but she was trying very hard to be objective in case she lost this fight. She didn't want her sisters to hate their benefactor. "He has requested that Tess and Beebee meet his family and live with him. He has several unmarried sons and nephews, I believe, and he knows I'll dower you handsomely, so he is no doubt hoping that you will become part of his family. They are quite respectable but poor."

Tess looked mildly interested. "If they all look like the gentleman who collared Kit, that might be interesting. He was a bit old, though. Are there younger sons?"

Bell bit her tongue and continued to be as fair as she knew how. "Lord Quentin is thirty-five. The youngest might be thirty. I don't know the nephews. They live in Scotland and never come to London. They farm."

Tess frowned. "We haven't lived in the country since we left Ireland. Is there a town like Boston nearby?"

"I fear not. As I understand it, their home is in the hills and quite isolated. Scotland does not have the green pastures of Ireland but cold rocks and gorse. You won't be able to raise horses. Sheep and cattle, perhaps." Swallowing, Bell hurried to finish. "The marquess wants Syd to attend school. It would be good for her, I'll agree, but—"

"I don't need any more school," Syd argued, interrupting. "I'm old enough for parties and beaux."

"You're an ignorant colonial bumpkin to these people," Tess said bluntly. "You need polish."

"You need friends," Bell corrected. "Getting about in society is all about who you know. I can't introduce you to the young ladies who will come out at the same time as you do. They're all still at home and not yet out for me to meet. But I can find out what schools they attend. Except, the marquess wishes you to attend the same school as his daughters in Edinburgh, and I fear they've become blue stockings because of it."

"Edinburgh?" Syd asked warily.

"Several very uncomfortable days' journey from here, in Scotland. You would have to spend the holidays with the marquess. It's not a journey young girls should undertake regularly."

Now both Syd and Tess looked horrified.

"We couldn't stay with you at all?" Tess asked.

"I could come visit occasionally, I suppose. You really don't know me much better than the Hoyts. It might all work out." She couldn't sound cheerful, but she strived not to sound skeptical. The Hoyts were pragmatic, educated, and managing sorts. Boyles... were the exact opposite, with charismatic, colorful, and tempestuous thrown in for good measure. Bell had learned a great deal of human nature and Hoyts in particular, since Edward had been one.

"What about Kit?" Tess demanded.

Bell sighed. "That's more of a problem. The marquess wants Kit to attend boarding school. It is the custom to send boys elsewhere for instruction and to let them meet their peers. And it is not quite proper for unmarried females to raise him with tutors and valets and such in the house. And again, all the marquess's sons attended school in Scotland."

"That will never work," both girls exclaimed in unison.

Given what little she already knew of her brother, Bell wholeheartedly concurred.

QUENT PACED his blasted, narrow study.

Holding papers to be signed, Penrose waited for him to sit down. "Do I need to polish a gun?" he asked cautiously.

"The option to challenge women to a duel would make life easier," Quent snarled.

"Shorter, but easier," Penrose agreed, not concealing his amusement. "Perhaps dueling hairpins at sunset? Why don't you take some time to sail your yacht or visit friends in the country and work off some of your energy. You never take time for pleasure."

"Work is my pleasure," Quent growled. "Find someone interested in building boats in Cornwall, and I'll happily sail him around."

"The carriage has returned from Scotland. Take it out to visit Blake. He and the duke are bound to have information that will create new business somewhere. You are about to walk through walls."

A good long gallop out to the edges of town... Would accomplish nothing.

He needed to treat Bell and this situation as he would any other investment that required planning and negotiation. "Quit distracting me. I found a perfectly sensible solution to Bell's problems, and she tells me no, under utterly no circumstances. What the hell does the woman want? And here I'd thought she was one of the sensible ones."

"Lady Bell?" Penrose asked in surprise. "She's the ultimate mysterious female. Surely there's someone easier if it's a woman you want."

"Easy women aren't very interesting," Quent pointed out, but the thought of other women had his mind leaping to a new direction. Sometimes, negotiating required looking disinterested. "I'm thinking my father might accept my taking charge of Lady Bell's sisters if I were married." He mulled the possibilities, looking for the advantages.

"Why would you want Lady Bell's sisters if you marry someone else?" Penrose asked, reasonably enough. "You have more than enough of your own."

"Pick one, and I'll give her to you," Quent said morosely. He *didn't* want any other woman he knew. Penrose was right. Marrying to inherit more females didn't make sense even to him. He simply refused to accept rejection without the kind of fight he knew how to wage—and Bell didn't.

"Lady Bell is planning on taking her sisters to visit Fitz," Penrose said helpfully.

"She's running away in hopes her solicitor can find a solution before my father starts enforcing his demands." Quent understood the fool woman to that extent, at least. It's the same thing he would have done had he been in her shoes.

But he was not in her shoes. He was a man of authority who didn't run away from his responsibilities. And besides, he'd seen a side of the lady that intrigued him and almost convinced him that marriage wasn't a complete sacrifice. "I'll follow her down and write my father that we're introducing her family to friends. He can sit up there on his throne and spin webs on his own for a while."

"Web spinning being a family trait and all," Penrose acknowledged, nodding wisely.

"Quit chuckling up your English sleeves and tell my valet to start packing. Then help me create a list of eligible females I might marry. Fitz is undoubtedly the first person I should discuss this with."

"Oh certainly," Penrose mocked, "because all the world knows he chose so wisely by marrying a poor farmer's daughter with a herd of young siblings."

"He's a gambler. I'm not. Betting on love is the worst sort of foolishness, although Fitz manages to win even in that. I prefer to make an informed choice." He knew Bell better than any woman in London. He was more than informed. He'd seen her toes.

Six

"KIT, IF YOU DON'T sit still and quit kicking my seat, I'll have the driver tie you on back with the trunks." Bell hid her exasperation as her brother ignored her warning and continued kicking with the new boots he'd insisted on wearing.

"Why can't I ride on the horses?" he whined.

"Because they are carriage horses. I have told you we are going to look at ponies, but if you don't behave, I'll assume you don't want one. Read one of the books we brought."

"We could tie his feet," Syd suggested helpfully. "How much longer before we arrive? I'm perishing of thirst."

"Me, too," Kit shouted, bouncing in his seat.

"You need a baggage wagon to put him in," Tess said, digging through their lunch basket for the last of the cider.

Bell hadn't wanted to ask Quent if she might borrow his carriage to transport tutor, maids, and wiggly six-year olds. He'd accuse her of absconding with his father's wards. Bell preferred to think of it as strategic retreat until she heard from Blake Montague, or better yet, Blake's mentor, the Duke of Fortham, about her chances of winning guardianship.

She had heard nothing from Summerby about Little Dream. She told herself that no news was good news.

Disturbed by Tess's movement, Beebee woke from her slumber and began to whimper. Bell lifted her chubby niece into her lap and hummed a lullaby. At least the babe was easily pleased. She leaned against Bell, sucked her thumb, and drooled down Bell's spencer. Bell twisted the babe's fair curls around her finger. She had no idea what she was doing, and her doubts were piling higher than the sky.

"Isn't that the large gentleman who visited the other day?" Tess asked, glancing out the window after putting away the empty jug. "The handsome one who shouted at Kit?"

Bell thought a foul word and dipped her head to look out the far window. Muscled legs and narrow hips in tight breeches might be anyone, but the stunning black Friesian gelding was all Quent's. A smaller bay bearing a more slender man rode along side of him.

Bell gestured at the driver's door and Syd. "Tell the driver to halt, please."

She transferred Beebee back to Tess and unsuccessfully tried to wipe the drool from her spencer.

"Exchange seats with me," she demanded, indicating that Tess scoot over as the carriage pulled to a halt.

The horses obligingly stopped with the carriage. Bell lowered the window glass. She was far more comfortable flirting than scolding like a fishwife, but she would learn to shout if that was what it took to reach through a man's thick head.

Quent lifted his hat in greeting. "Good morning, my lady. Warm day for a drive."

"Equally warm for riding, I should think. I do not remember asking for an escort." There, that seemed respectable and polite without a fishwife in sight.

"I have business with Fitz and heard you were heading that way also. We thought it might be pleasant to keep you company." Quent's dark eyes danced with mischief.

"Certainly, my lord, most pleasant. I do not believe you have formally met my sisters." Once Quent had dismounted and opened the carriage door, Bell made the introductions, leaving Kit for last.

He was kicking the seat as hard as he could, chanting "pony, pony, pony." Bell grabbed him beneath the arms and shoved him out the door in Quent's general direction. "Here. Wexford would like a horse ride. I'm sure that will make the journey more pleasant for all concerned. Have a good gallop."

Startled, Quent grabbed the young earl. She almost laughed at his stunned expression.

Relieved of her burden, Bell found a grip on the door and yanked it shut, then signaled for the driver to resume their journey.

Sitting back in her seat, she couldn't see Quent's reaction, but she imagined it with great satisfaction.

"Lord Quentin is quite handsome," Tess said warily. "Does he court you?"

"He courts my money, and I will not have him. Men take away all our rights and treat us as porcelain figurines for their sideboards. They despise it when a woman has a mind of her own and power to go with it." Bell crossed her arms and glared at the gelding side-stepping nervously outside the window. Kit was probably kicking the unfortunate animal.

"Is he poor?" Syd asked with interest, dipping her head to watch the struggle between man and boy.

"No, he's wealthy in his own right, but he supports his father's large family. Big houses and big families are a constant drain. They all need to marry well."

"But Tess and I are poor," Syd pointed out. "Why would any of the men in his family be interested in us?"

"You're not poor. You're my sisters. They know I would provide you with a handsome settlement." As she had her other protégées. She would never let her friends or her sisters do without—which meant their husbands benefitted. "Perhaps I shall have Quent tell his greedy father that I will not settle anything on you if you marry into his family."

"That would start a very unpleasant fight with the family with whom we might have to live," Tess said reasonably.

So it would. Of course, suing them would have the same effect.

In less than a fortnight, her tranquil life had descended into turmoil and conflict. She might as well have never left Ireland.

JOHN FITZHUGH WYCKERLY, seventh earl of Danecroft, and Abigail, his countess, lived in the run-down family estate in Berkshire. The huge towers and ponderous, sprawling silhouette of Wyckersham impressed new arrivals, until they were close enough to notice boarded-up windows, unmown lawns, and deteriorated gardens.

Considerable improvements had been made in the time since Fitz had taken possession of the family manor, but even the king would lack the fortune necessary to correct generations of neglect.

Quent decided it was just the sort of medieval atmosphere for pondering his father's latest irascible demands. The marquess now threatened to send Syd and Kit to school as charity students if Bell didn't pay their tuition.

Lachlann Hoyt did not understand women who chose to disobey his orders, and his temper was not ameliorated by his son's refusal to jump instantly to his command. Quent lived in fear of a carriage-load of Hoyts arriving on his doorstep, demanding the truants and freeloading off his hospitality until he produced them.

He held his mount and the sleeping earl steady as the carriage pulled up to a halt at Wyckersham's front stairs. He needed to see Bell again to reassure himself that he was doing the right thing in defying his father's orders for a woman who had just rejected his suit. At the moment, escaping on his yacht sounded preferable, but he wasn't a coward.

Before Bell's footman could pull out the carriage steps, the front doors of the house exploded open, and children, servants, and the countess spilled down to greet them.

"I am so glad you have come! Here, let me have Beebee. What a precious doll! Look at your new bib!" Lady Danecroft cooed at the toddler. At the same time, she directed servants to relieve Quent of his sleeping burden and sent children scampering back up the stairs with bags and parcels.

Quent admired her efficiency. "Wellington should hire you, my lady," he said, dismounting to aid the ladies from the carriage. "Your troops respond instantly to command."

"The trick to children is keeping them interested and busy. They're all agog at having visitors." Lady Danecroft returned to oohing and ahhing over new travel costumes as the girls emerged from the carriage.

Bell glared as Quent helped her out—possibly because he glanced down to catch a glimpse of her trim ankle. He was developing an unhealthy obsession with the lady's limbs.

"Perhaps the trick to children is hiring tutors to keep them interested and busy," Bell said sweetly.

Well, maybe her glare was for other reasons. Quent shrugged off the barb. "You're the one who left without tutors and maids. Fortunately, you won't need to buy another carriage to transport them. My father can handle that. He's quite adept at dealing with rambunctious boys."

That remark earned him an even blacker glare, and he bit back a smile. He'd badgered, negotiated with, and twisted the arms of far wilier businessmen than Bell. He knew how to achieve what he wanted, and his spirits rose in anticipation of the challenge.

He just needed to be more certain of what he wanted. He'd *wanted* Bell for ten years. He'd never wanted marriage. Or children. He'd moved to London at first opportunity to escape his chaotic, noisy family and enjoy the ordered serenity of a bachelor life. It would behoove him to study the lady's preferences—did she *want* the chaos of family disrupting her well-organized household? He couldn't fathom it.

Assuming her stiffly dignified marchioness posture with nose in the air, Bell swept after the countess and the children without a second look back.

"She's not the chatty sort, at least," Penrose said, following Quent's gaze. "A bit like you, actually, subtle and clever."

"Doesn't mean we can't discover her weak spots. Let's find Fitz." He strode after the stable lads leading his Friesian, knowing Danecroft was far more likely to be working with the horses than his account books at this hour. John Fitzhugh Wyckerly had been *Fitz* for so long, and the title so unlikely to be his, that his friends had difficulty recalling his recent acquisition of the earl of Danecroft title.

"Shouldn't you tell the lady that your carriage will be arriving tomorrow? She could send for the rest of her servants." Penrose limped to keep up with him.

"I'm thinking about it. Is it better to let her learn how family oversets everything so she might finally surrender and send them to my father? Or will she be more grateful for my aid and give me what I ask if I solve all her problems?"

"If you're asking me, she's most likely to take a dirk to your gullet if she learns you're pulling her strings as if she were a puppet in a Punch and Judy show, but I'm just a soldier, not a lady's man."

"We're both bachelors. We need the advice of a married man. And there's one now." Quent hailed the slender earl.

Fitz Wyckerly only bore a slight resemblance to the refined man-about-town who'd once gambled at the best tables wearing silk and lace. Today, his riding coat sported worn elbows, his linen had mysterious spots, and his once-polished boots appeared ready to part from their soles.

But beneath his cow-licked mop of light brown hair, he still wore the unmistakable grin that had charmed his way into London's parlors. "Quent! Acton! You're sights for sore eyes. I thought I was about to be inundated with petticoats. What brings you here? Not my wine cellar, I'm certain."

"We have come for a professional consultation. And to see the horses, of course," Quent said. "I've heard you've expanded the stables."

"Horse acquisitions are a question of balance. Come along, I'll show you." The earl loped back toward the horse barn. "Since this building is the only decent thing my father left, it's served me well."

Quent remembered the enormous edifice with high oak ceilings and polished stalls that stretched nearly as far as the eye could see. The late earl had been a spendthrift, a gambler, and a drunkard. Fitz was probably still paying the debts on the construction of this monument to selfishness. But Quent admired his friend's eye for good horseflesh, so at least the expense was now being put to good use.

"The balance?" Penrose asked when Quent didn't. He'd gone to school with Fitz.

"The craze for perfectly matched Cleveland Bays as carriage horses has been replaced with a need for speed now that London has seen Prinney's Yorkshire Coach horses. I already have a Thoroughbred stud and rights to half a share of another over in Newmarket. I bought a couple of excellent Cleveland Bays at bargain prices when we first began the stable, so I bred them last year to the Thoroughbreds. I already have a start on a stable of speedy carriage horses." He gestured at a couple of stalls with bay foals.

Quent admired their sturdy flanks. "Even I can see the beauty of these. And they will be speedier than my Bays?"

"On good road, they will practically fly. My mares have bred two colts and a filly and I'm looking for more. Those are my future profit. The balance comes in not putting all my coins in one basket. For now..." He led the way down the aisle. "I have current profit on my Welsh ponies and Irish hunters, basic breeds everyone wants. If I were richer, I'd start developing another Thoroughbred stud, but they cost the earth."

"Lady Bell is in need of several good mounts and a pony. She can afford any price you name, so start planning your next generation," Quent advised.

Fitz laughed. "I don't bite the hand that feeds me. She sends me most of my buyers. And she only sends good ones, not the ones who damage their cattle. I am learning the value of loyal patrons."

"The lady knows everyone worth knowing and is a good judge of character, admittedly. I hadn't realized she kept up with the horse market, though. She's had those same carriage horses for as long as I can remember." Quent strolled through the stable, marking the horses most likely to suit her sisters.

"The marquess bought them," Fitz said with a shrug. "Lady Bell has never bought an animal of her own. Since she seldom leaves town, she doesn't really need a mount. Perhaps that will change now that she has her sisters." Fitz studied his own inventory with interest, evidently sizing them up for the lady's needs.

"I believe she mentioned that Boyles lived on horseback, but I've never seen her on a horse. Did the marquess keep her from owning her own?" Quent wondered aloud.

"That wouldn't stop her. Perhaps you misheard. Or she is one of the Boyles who don't ride. It happens every generation or so," Fitz said cheerfully. "I never had the funds to appreciate animals before, but I'm caught up in them now."

"I couldn't afford to join the cavalry, but I know the men cherish their Irish hunters. Sturdy and reliable the times I've ridden them," Penrose said, almost wistfully.

"Marry a wealthy lady and own your own stable," Fitz said. "I recommend marriage to all my friends now. Gives one a new perspective."

"Because bachelorhood is so tedious?" Quent asked with sarcasm. "But we have come for your advice as a married man. I need a brandy before I'm ready to discuss the matter, though."

"There might be a bottle reserved just for you." Fitz slapped him on the back and shoved him toward the door. "Anytime you're willing to discuss marriage is a good time for a drink."

That was Quent's opinion, too. A drink... or three. He shuddered, remembering the last woman he'd proposed to marry—before he'd learned the folly of confusing lust for loyalty and love. The experience had scarred him for life.

Seven

"WHY HAS LORD Quentin arrived with you?" Abby whispered after they'd left the children in their rooms and strolled the corridor to Bell's chamber. "I thought your intent was to remove your family from his notice."

"He spies," Bell complained morosely. "He knew I was coming here, probably even before I did. I have no idea why he decided to follow. He doesn't have much interest in country life."

"Well, I suppose business is slow now that the season is over and everyone has retreated from the city." Abby puckered her forehead in a frown and opened the door to a chamber on the far end of the corridor. "But he has never visited just for the pleasure of it. Will this room suit? It's not the tower. You didn't give me time to clean that out."

Bell glanced at the lovely airy chamber with freshly starched muslin bed curtains, ancient blue velvet draperies, and a newly waxed wood floor sans whatever moth-eaten carpet had left the large light square in the middle of the floor. This was so far above the ruins of her origins, she could not begin to quibble.

"This is charming, and you know it," Bell said honestly. "You have an excellent eye for creating warmth. I am sorry to have barged in upon you like this, but I needed time to think, and Quent isn't leaving me alone to do so."

"That's almost promising," Abby said with a twinkle in her eye. "Has he finally realized what a gem you are and decided to pursue you?"

Bell dropped wearily onto the soft mattress. "He asked me to marry him. He says he can talk his father into letting him keep the children so I might have them instead of sending them to Scotland. But we both know he's just using this as an excuse to lay his hands on my purse strings."

"Not necessarily," the countess contradicted. "He's been sniffing around you for years, and you cannot be so blind as to not know it. Perhaps he's decided it's time to settle down. He's never seemed fond of housing family, so proposing marriage is quite a condescension for him."

"It's pure arrogance," Bell retorted. "I have been married once for convenience. I will not do so ever again. I will go to Scotland with the children should it come to that."

"Wasn't he the one carrying Kit when you arrived?" Abby asked in puzzlement. "That doesn't sound like a man who doesn't like children."

"He likes getting his own way. Kit is simply a means to an end. No, we shall choose horses for the girls and a pony for Kit, and then retire to the house in Essex, where Quent will not be welcome," Bell said decisively. "The children will be too tired this evening, but in the morning, perhaps, we can see what Fitz has. Then we may disappear in a cloud of dust."

"Do not hurry off!" Abby protested. "You must take your time, let the children come to know each other. And if Fitz doesn't have precisely what you need, he'll be happy to go to Tattersall's. He's beyond thrilled to have this opportunity to help you, after you've helped us so much."

Bell almost grew teary at the kind words when she was feeling so beleaguered. "I have done nothing that shouldn't have been done years ago, had Edward not been such a miserable misogynist who thought of all women as no more than useless ornaments, at best. He and Quent are much of a kind, a family trait, I fear."

"I don't think Quent *hates* women," Abby argued. "He's simply too busy to look beyond his nose."

Bell shrugged wearily. "Not much difference. Women have no power or wealth, so they're beneath his notice. I'm the only challenge of the fairer sex that he's met. Should I ever give in to his whims, I'll be reduced to the same level as all other women. He's just being stubborn because I've bested him for so long."

"I hate to see two good friends at loggerheads. Perhaps we can find a solution if we all talk these next few days. It will do Quent good to take some time out of the city to enjoy life. Rest a bit, and I'll send a maid to help you dress for dinner."

Abby bustled off to keep her nest pleasant by performing other missions of mercy. Bell wished she could be more like her friend, able to find love in adversity and be happy under any circumstances.

She had thought she was happy living alone, but now that she had her family again... It was chaos. She had to admit that she was miserably incompetent at childcare. Still, she felt as if some long-lost part of her was returning to life. And she knew she was up to the challenge of learning to deal with her siblings—if given enough time.

Real families *loved* each other, wanted the best for each other, and stuck together through thick and thin. She would not abandon her siblings the way she had been cast aside.

SYD EAGERLY threw back the moldering draperies of their bedchamber window. "Have you ever seen anything like this, Tess? It's a castle! Look, the village is way down there in the valley. That's where the common folk live."

"Common folk, as in people like us?" Tess asked in amusement. They'd been given a chamber to share, but a nursemaid had carried off Beebee and Kit, so she was free to indulge in silliness for a few minutes.

"That's just it," Syd said excitedly. "Here, we're special! We're the daughters of an earl. No one cared about that back in Boston."

"That's because we were living with dirt poor Methodists who despised aristocrats and no one told them who we are. It's hard to be special when you're working for food. And you will notice that the windows in this castle are cracked, the bed posts are older than any existing forest, and we have no carpet on the floor. I'm betting the sheets are threadbare, too. This is no palace, Syd, just a mountain of old rocks, larger but not so different from home."

Despite her words, Tess didn't mind any of that. She lay back on her mattress and admired the grand space. Once upon a time, the plaster ceiling over her head must have been molded with cherubs and garlands and probably gaily painted. Now, the crumbling plaster cherubs had patched flat places where their noses and wings had been, and the paint had paled to specks of pastels.

It was still more charming than any place they'd ever stayed, including her moldy room in Ireland. She remembered that pile of rocks for its greenery—even growing inside on the walls. As a child, she used to bring snails into her room to see if they'd live on the moss on her windowsill.

"I wonder if Lord Quentin's home in Scotland is grander?" Syd asked idly, examining the wardrobe where the maid had hung their still meager attire.

Syd never asked anything idly. Syd was young, but she'd always been a schemer and a reckless doer. Tess was the one who pondered for a long time before acting. But she didn't have to think too deeply to understand Syd's concern.

"Even if his Scots home is a castle, would you want to live there?"

she asked. "What would we do all day in someone else's home? I'm sick and tired of being a poor dependent. I want a home of my own."

"Lord Quentin is a wealthy man," Syd said slyly. "If Bell really doesn't want such a lovely man…"

Tess sighed. Even her mind had traveled that road. "Do you really think he's in search of any wife, or is it just Bell he seeks?"

"You look much like Bell, so where's the difference? If you were his wife, it would be most excellent, in my opinion," Syd said loyally. "I don't mind being a dependent until I've had a grand ball and been squired about by dozens of handsome suitors!"

Syd was right. If Bell didn't want to marry the gentleman, Tess had no such compunction. She could have a home and stability for a change, plus have her family around her.

Tess had married the love of her life and lost him. She didn't expect to ever love again. She could marry an older, wealthier man for the sake of her family—just as Bell once had. Really, it was almost her duty to do so.

"I THINK you're inviting disaster," Fitz warned his guest as they sat about the dining table, drinking their brandy, after the women withdrew. "My gambler's instinct says this is entirely the wrong way to go about pursuing a woman."

"That's not your gambling instinct, that's your innate honesty. Whereas Quent has the morals of a cheap pettifogger," Penrose corrected with the bluntness of a man who had been a friend longer than an employee.

Quent laughed. "I don't come *cheaply* these days. And Bell isn't any woman. She doesn't want to be courted, especially by me. I need to catch her attention first."

He *needed* to be the one in charge, but his friends understood that. They might not understand why, but they accepted his leadership as a given. He was older, wealthier, and in many ways, wiser. Life had pounded experience into him—with a cudgel—at an early age.

Unfortunately, Bell really was like him in that measure, although he supposed her experiences had scarred her in different ways. Finding a path around her defenses was akin to finding one around his own. He twitched his shoulders in discomfort, fingered the list in his pocket, and set his empty glass back on the table. Time to leap into the fray. Nothing ventured, nothing gained, and all that.

The sooner he settled this marriage/guardianship problem, the faster he could pry his father off his back and return to generating cash for the family roof. Making money, he understood. Dealing with warring family—he avoided.

He accepted that Bell would insist on tying her funds up in a trust for her sisters and herself. He wouldn't argue with her over the marriage provisions, and he would never ask her for money—even for the roof. He was confident that his family's fortune would be repaired on what he earned. Money was not the question in his suit—although his sanity might be.

At least, this time he was entering into courtship with eyes wide open. Lust and a need for commitment were more sensible than weak affectations like *love*.

The women were scattered about the parlor when the men joined them. Quent knew all the ladies to be pretty, but his gaze just naturally gravitated to Bell. She'd always had the ability to draw his eye, even when he'd been young and perishing of a stupidly broken heart and had vowed to never let another woman into his life. For Bell, he was now ready to make a reluctant exception.

He knew she couldn't play the pianoforte, but she'd draped herself elegantly on the bench, idly punching the keys and matching the notes to a musical score she was trying to read. A sconce above her head emphasized the red threads in her dark hair. A curl adorned her bare nape. Her gold silk dinner gown draped seductively over a curvaceous figure that had developed from a child's skinniness to that of a full-grown woman over the years he'd known her.

And her position revealed one dainty shoe and stockinged ankle. Quent reluctantly dragged his gaze away and bowed to the amused countess. Fitz's wife could be an annoying know-it-all, but she was generally demure and kept her thoughts to herself—

—Unlike Bell's sisters. They leapt from their chairs to usher the men in, chattering about a game of charades. Penrose seemed particularly stricken when the younger chit grabbed his arm and led him toward a chair near the pianoforte.

The older one—Tess, he thought Bell called her—took Quent's arm and steered him toward a loveseat beside her. "We thought we could have a challenge in the evenings, gentlemen versus the ladies. We are well matched, aren't we? Four ladies against three gentlemen?"

Bell arched an eyebrow in apparent surprise at her sister's eagerness, but she shrugged in reply to Quent's questioning expression. He resisted being placed and strode to the cold fireplace instead.

"I am not much at games, but I'll be happy to judge, if you like." He leaned against the mantel, wondering how to steer the conversation in the direction he had in mind. He'd only been thinking in terms of shocking Bell, not her young sisters. Should he wait? Or would they all go upstairs together?

"Oh, but it will be fun," the younger girl cried. "You don't want to spoil the fun for everyone."

"Hush, Syd, I'll sit out the game with Mr. Hoyt, and the rest of you can play," Tess suggested.

That did not sound as if they were planning on retiring soon. His own sisters could stay up later than he had any inclination for, particularly if he was in their chatty company.

Fitz took a seat beside his wife, who was adding trim to a child's attire. Very practical woman was the countess. Abby leaned over and kissed her husband's cheek but didn't object to the game.

Penrose actually looked interested. The ex-soldier hadn't had the time or funds to play in society's drawing rooms. And now he had the attention of two attractive single ladies. Quent knew his friend would cut his own throat before disagreeing with the women. Penrose took the empty seat beside Mrs. Dawson.

Quent refrained from rolling his eyes. While the younger ones chattered about the best topic for a charade, he removed the list from his pocket and handed it to the countess. "I am calling on your expertise, my lady. Fitz agrees these ladies are all suitable for courtship, but he has more insight into their wealth than their personalities. May I have your opinion?"

Abby looked surprised. To Quent's gratification, even Bell sat up straight and sent him a suspicious look. He rather liked the quickness of her mind.

"You are looking for a wife, Lord Quentin?" Mrs. Dawson asked with interest, dropping her charade of playing charades.

"I am considering it, yes," he said stiffly, figuring he sounded pompous but not knowing how else to start this inane discussion. "I cannot continue relying on Lady Bell to bring out my sisters and cousins. I need a respectable female to shepherd them about."

"I've told you I can still herd them," Bell said irritably, rising from the pianoforte to take the list from Abby's hands.

"I fear I don't go about much in society," the countess acknowledged. "The names are familiar, but I wouldn't pretend to know any of them well enough to judge their suitability. Bell would know more."

Which was entirely what Quent had anticipated. Subterfuge was the only tactic they'd ever used between them, and he didn't mind employing it now.

Bell was shaking her head and tapping her pretty slipper as she scanned the list. "Fitz, you know better than to include the Wellingham chit. She has her cap set for a title, preferably one who takes his seat in the Lords so she can steer his career."

"That doesn't make her ineligible," Fitz argued. "She's smart, pretty, and capable, right up to Quent's mark. She might make an exception for him."

"Even if she is intelligent enough to see Quent's worth, her parents aren't. They come from a long, aristocratic lineage. The Scots are far beneath their dignity."

"And one in trade, further still?" Quent asked silkily. He'd already assessed the list and had come to the same conclusion.

"I didn't say that, you did," she retorted. "One cannot account for the prejudices of society. They just are. For a little reverse prejudice, you cannot consider the Smith child. She has no lineage at all. Her father is a smarmy village merchant who gambled himself into a fortune. Yes, she's pretty, but as vapid as they come, without a single thought of her own."

"And she and her family would be thrilled at Quent's suit," Fitz argued.

Quent had done business with Smith and had barely been aware that he had a daughter until Fitz had added her to the list. "The main concern is that she can hold the advantage over my high-handed sisters, isn't it?"

"She's not eighteen. Not a chance," Bell said firmly. "You need a widow already wise in the social arena. Perhaps Lady Charlotte," she said with less certainty, studying the names.

"Who has the face of a horse and two left feet, I'm here to attest." Quent verified her doubt. "There is no one perfect woman. I must settle for the one who can chaperone my sisters— and possibly your sisters, if my father has his way."

Belle slapped him with the paper and returned to the pianoforte.

She was quick to catch on to his ploy, but he'd made his point. *She* was the only one suitable for his wife.

Eight

BELL SEETHED. *There was no one perfect woman,* indeed! She was perfect for Quent's purposes... except she demanded love, and he didn't know emotion existed. So, strike her off the list, too.

She'd go back to Ireland and take her family with her before she let any of those *less than perfect* women introduce her sisters to society.

Why on earth had the bull-headed man suddenly decided he needed a wife to deal with his sisters? She would ponder that, but she was too angry. She could not imagine why men and women were on the same planet except for the basic necessity of procreation.

Since she had never provided Edward with children in their years of marriage, she obviously didn't need men.

Once, the lack of children had broken her heart, but she didn't believe in looking back. There was no shortage of children in the world, as her family proved.

Across the room, Tess boldly took Quent's arm and asked him to walk her around the parlor, presumably to discuss his requisites for wife, if Bell knew anything at all. Her sister was safe practicing her limited wiles on a skilled bachelor like Quent, so she let them go.

She would truly dislike seeing another woman holding his arm and attention. That realization only heightened her anger. She had grown complacent in believing she could rely on him as family friend. She must stop that, at once. He must follow his own course.

While Bell pecked at the pianoforte keys, Syd engaged Acton Penrose in an enthusiastic conversation about Spain. Her sister would gain a reputation as a bluestocking with that kind of talk, except no one who saw her excited gestures and heard her laughter could ever call Syd a bluestocking. No, she'd be an Original if Bell had her way—if Syd wasn't whisked off to a cold corner of Edinburgh and buried in books for the next few years. Bell had no objection to education, but she knew from experience that it must be well-rounded with social instruction as well.

She'd forgotten how family added to worries. She would simply have to learn to handle their problems again, as she had while still a child—a child who had carried the weight of the world on her shoulders. She was in a far better position to aid her siblings now.

Fretting over her family's future was a small price to pay to have her sisters back, and it certainly relieved the enormous fear of wondering if they were still alive.

Of course, now she had to fret about the mare who had been the only loving companionship she'd really known, but she hoped Summerby had that in hand. She should ask Fitz if she could house the mare here. She didn't want to grow attached again, but Dream deserved rich green pastures.

"Do you know what type of mounts you and your sisters will require?" Fitz asked, pulling Bell from her reverie.

"The girls haven't been on horseback since they left Ireland. Let's start with some of your gentler mares. Most of their riding will be in the city for now, so they don't need endurance, just a patient temperament." Bell knew precisely the mare she would have chosen from her father's stable, but she wasn't familiar with Fitz's stock.

"I have several that will suit, although one is older, steadier, but not as pretty."

Bell thought she heard amusement in the earl's voice. Fitz had a warped humor. He was comparing his mares to the list he'd drawn for Quent.

"Syd doesn't have to marry her horse," Bell said tartly. "Reliable is the best trait for her until she's acclimated to horse and city."

"How about a pretty one for you, then?" the earl suggested. "I have a spirited Irish hunter almost the same color as your hair. You'll look magnificent together."

Bell waved off the suggestion. "I won't ride. I'll hire grooms to follow them about. But Kit will need a steady pony." To prevent further questioning, she buried her refusal under Kit's requirements. "I don't think he cares if it matches his hair, but I'd suggest one that will endure constant kicking."

She had no desire to explain why she'd vowed never to become attached to another animal. Once she'd lost Little Dream, she had learned to limit the amount of misery to be invited into her life. She wouldn't summon more pain by doing more than providing her old friend with a happy retirement. From experience, she knew her family was likely to provide enough heartache.

"I have a Welsh that will nip his lordship every time he kicks," Fitz suggested with a laugh. "But I suppose that won't teach him the proper way to ride."

"It might teach him consequences, but it might also cause him to fear horses. Tempting as that sounds, that's probably the wrong direction." Bell thought of the gentle ponies her sisters had learned to ride on. If only...

She closed off that thought. The past was past.

"I have more agreeable ponies," Fitz said smoothly. "Jennie learned to ride on the Welsh, so our twins probably can, too."

"Knowing my sister, she probably encouraged the poor thing to bite," Abby said with a laugh. "It would keep everyone else away. She's possessive."

Bell smiled, remembering her childhood self doing much the same with a different mare. She hadn't wanted her stepmother riding Little Dream's dam. She wished she'd been kinder to the poor woman who had died birthing Syd. The painful memories she'd buried years ago kept crowding back with all this talk of horses.

She stood and brushed out her skirts. "I think I'll go up and check on Kit and Beebee, make certain they're sleeping, and then I'll retire. Thank you for the lovely dinner, Abby. You're a marvelous hostess."

Ignoring protests, she glanced at Tess, who tilted her head as if to catch every precious word that Quent uttered. Bell scowled. "Syd, Tess, it's been a long day. Say your good-nights."

"I'll be up in a little while," Tess said with a dismissive wave.

Quent sent Bell a questioning look that she couldn't quite translate, but at least he recognized her authority. She really didn't want to be at constant odds with him.

"Do I have to?" Syd didn't rise from the love seat, although the ex-soldier had stood up the moment Bell had. "Mr. Penrose is explaining how the Portuguese make wine."

She wasn't their mother, Bell reminded herself. Abby was a perfectly eligible chaperone. Just because Bell was irritable didn't mean she had to ruin everyone else's evening.

"Lady Danecroft may wish to retire soon," Bell reminded them. "You cannot remain down here with the gentlemen. It's not done. Abigail, the instant you're ready to turn in, send these chits upstairs, please."

"Actually, I need to check on the nursery, too. Let us all go up together." The countess set aside her sewing.

"Why can we not stay and talk with the gentlemen?" Syd asked peevishly, flouncing from her seat. "Tess and I aren't children."

"Yes, you are, if you don't see the impropriety. Besides, the men want to drink and play billiards and discuss inappropriate topics without you about. The world does not revolve on your whims." Bell ushered both her sisters in front of her, then turned to glance at the men they were leaving behind.

Fitz and Penrose were already engaged in a lively discussion of horses. Only Quent was watching them depart. He arched one eyebrow and saluted her, as if she were the officer in charge.

Oddly, that pleased her, which only served to irritate her more—which was just too ridiculous for words.

QUENT TRIED to ignore a tug of abandonment as he watched Bell shepherd her sisters from the salon. Now that he'd set his mind on the course of marriage, he hungered for the feel of her mouth on his. He was a man accustomed to going after what he wanted. Denying himself was no doubt his problem. Once he had a marriage settlement, life would return to normal. Almost normal. After the sisters were out of the house.

"Don't think your list worked, old boy," Fitz said cheerfully after the ladies had departed. "Bell sounded just a wee bit peeved, not the smoothest way to courtship."

"If I sent her flowers, she'd dump them over my head," Quent said unrepentantly. "She's not your pleasant-natured Abby."

"So, let her dump them over your head. At least you will have indicated you're still interested," Penrose argued.

"You're just interested in the sisters and want me to give you better access to them," Quent countered. His aide's blush confirmed his guess. "What was that about Bell not wanting her own mount?"

"Nothing. She simply said she didn't need one and that her grooms would be riding with her sisters." Fitz shrugged. "She has a carriage. She doesn't need a mount for showing off in the park."

That wasn't quite right. Quent had been watching Bell's expression, and there had been something there... But she wasn't apt to tell him if he questioned. Damned hard trying to court a woman who didn't want to be courted. Harder still when he didn't entirely understand his own motivation.

"The remark about there not being a perfect woman was an error," Penrose informed him. "A proper suitor would have said there was only one perfect woman and let her wonder."

"Bell has spent these last years hearing all the pretty phrases. She won't believe flattery," Quent scoffed. "If I'm to go forward with this, I have to be frank and not pretend I'm the kind of man she knows I'm not."

"She rejected the man she thinks you are," Fitz said with a laugh at Quent's expense. "Did you ever consider that you might have to change a lot if you give up the bachelor state?"

He had. And he didn't like it—except for the part about having Bell in his bed. He growled irascibly and looked for the decanter. "Perhaps we could keep separate households. We're both set in our ways."

"Then you want a mistress, not a wife. It's a good thing both of you will be together here for a few days. You'll discover whether you can tolerate each other's company in the long hours where you aren't being entertained by business or parties. Anyone for billiards?" Fitz asked, rising. "If not, I'm off to join Abby."

Quent declined a game and took his glass up to his chambers. He could hear feminine chatter around the corner but knew better than to join them.

He'd brought work with him. He wouldn't be bored.

Although... His step picked up as he considered an even better, time-honored, and traditional method of relieving house party boredom.

"I'M BORED."

After opening her chamber door, Bell stepped away in startlement. Her visitor took advantage by crossing his arms and leaning against the jamb in all his glorious dishabille, preventing her from slamming the panel in his face.

Quent divested of neckcloth and coat, with his waistcoat open to reveal the breadth of his manly... she took a deep breath... his shirt, was a sight to behold. His thick dark hair had fallen over his forehead as if he'd been running his fingers through it. The open neck of his shirt, even in this dim light, revealed a few crisp curls.

She had never mistaken him for a weak clerk type despite his business pursuits, but she had never fully comprehended the extent of his raw masculinity. She kept her gaze firmly on his... shirt... which was embarrassing enough without looking lower. Without a coat to distract from his tight trousers, she would have far too much to view.

"You're bored and you came to me to complain because...?" She let her voice drift off with ennui to disguise how her pulse raced.

"Because you never bore me. Even though it's more concealing, I think I like your robe better than that pretty gown you wore this evening." He eyed her open neckline, although he had to see that she wore a high-necked shift beneath it.

A *summer* shift, one sewn from the finest muslin and nearly transparent because the room was hot. She had *not* expected male company.

"I am not part of the evening's entertainment," she retorted. "Please remove yourself so I might decently close the door. What would my sisters think if they saw you now?"

"That we are pursuing the age-old tradition of house parties? Although they might not be aware of our traditions." He came in and shut the door. "There, now the door is decently closed. I live to serve."

She backed further into her spacious chamber, heart improperly pounding. "I'm not certain what ideas you have created in your feeble mind, Hoyt, but I am not in the habit of entertaining men in my chambers. If you live to serve, then depart now."

"I'm fairly confident that you have not entertained other men, or I'd have heard them bragging. I simply think it's time you considered it. We have the perfect opportunity here, where there are no city streets between us, no London audience to observe. Your sisters are at the other end of the corridor. What better chance will we have to see if we might suit? I promise not to tell."

He stalked her, as a lion hunts prey. Bell was fairly certain she'd read that a cat was more likely to chase prey that ran, so it was better to hold still, but instinct was difficult to fight. She crossed her arms over her robe and clutched her elbows.

"It does not matter if we suit. I will not marry you, so there is no point in pursuing me." She had learned from experience not to be easily intimidated, but she'd not learned how to combat her own desires.

Lord Quentin Hoyt was a very desirable man. She'd dreamed of him for years—in a lascivious way, of course. She wasn't quite dead yet. But romance simply wasn't in the cards or stars or any other part of her life.

He traced a finger down her jaw, and she tried not to shiver at the gentle contact. It had been a long time since she'd been touched with tenderness. Edward's disappointment in not producing an heir had made him bitter and cold those last years.

"Don't tell me you aren't a woman, Bell," Quent said, "because I won't believe it. Tell me I turn your stomach with disgust, and I won't believe that either. We know each other too well, and we've deliberately avoided exploring our needs. But life changes. It's time to take this one step further."

He lifted her chin with the side of his hand and placed his firm lips against hers. And she let him.

Lord help her, she let him kiss her. The sensation spiraled straight from the brush of his masculine mouth into the pit of her soul. And lower. Very much lower. To parts much less innocuous than a feeble soul. She wanted to grab his arms and pull him closer, to rub against him and feel all that glorious masculinity, to part her lips...

She shoved away before she could descend into the depths of hell. Her heart pounded, her blood raced, and desire pooled in places she'd thought long dead. Her breasts ached with need—for a man who was little more than a money-making machine, like Edward.

"I cannot do this, Quent. I cannot. If you don't wish to kill me, leave." Frozen, she couldn't even run. She simply trusted him to do as she asked.

He brushed his finger down her jaw again. She flinched at how much she needed him to keep touching her.

"I'll leave for now," he reluctantly agreed, "but I think we both know what we could have would be very, very good. I haven't rushed you before, but I'm about to start pushing. Life is too short to deny our very natures."

He kissed her cheek and slipped out.

A tear slid down that same cheek. She had spent ten years denying her impetuous nature. Could she spend ten more years denying herself—and all the years left after that?

Nine

BELL SCARCELY slept all night after the encounter with Quent. She tossed and turned and... *burned.*

By morning, she was even more irritable than she had been the night before, but she donned her best smile for the sake of the company and descended the stairs wearing a riding habit, even if she had no intention of riding.

She knew the tailored green spencer with the black braiding flattered her complexion, but her intent was to stay cool in the sleeveless chemisette beneath while keeping her more delicate muslins from being ruined in the dust.

It was also her best travel costume. If she must, she could order her carriage and be gone by afternoon.

Her sisters clattered down in their new boots, delightedly swinging their long trains and flashing their ankles as they did so. Of course, their ankles were encased in boots, but Acton Penrose was an appreciative audience. Bell thought it lovely that serious Tess had been relieved from her burdens enough to tease him a little.

Bell looked for Quent, but he wasn't there to escort them into breakfast. Or to escort them to the stable afterward. She refused to inquire after him. She didn't have to. Her sisters did.

"He's taken his gelding out for a gallop, said the animal needs a holiday, although I think it's Quent who needs to let off steam," Penrose said, readily offering both arms to escort the girls to the stable, leaving Bell to rein in Kit. "Fitz has a neighbor with a Thoroughbred, so he's probably visiting there."

Keeping an eye on the next earl of Wexford so he didn't break his little neck kept Bell well occupied, so she needn't become too involved with Fitz's beautiful animals. She trusted Fitz to choose suitable mares for the girls. She concentrated on the ponies for Kit.

"Wanta ride that one!" he cried excitedly as his sisters' mares were led out. "Want that one!" he shouted even louder when Quent rode in on his enormous Friesian.

"When you are as large as Lord Quentin, you may have that one," Bell told him. "But first, you must learn to handle one your size." She pointed out a dappled gray contentedly munching hay in his stall. A groom ran to fetch a saddle.

Back outside, Kit tried to climb the fence. She held the back of his coat so he couldn't go over. She didn't remember her sisters being so rambunctious at this age. Of course, they had been taught to mind their manners. Kit obviously hadn't. The nanny stepmother must have died when he was young. Bell mourned a woman she didn't even know.

"Oh, Lord Quentin, come help us decide!" she heard Tess coo. Looking tousled and manly and good enough for breakfast, Quent had emerged from the stable and lingered between the two enclosures that separated the pony from the larger mounts.

Bell gritted her teeth but didn't turn around to watch. She didn't want to lose her sisters to Quent's large family, but if it happened, her sisters needed to be familiar with at least some of the Hoyts. Quent was a safe start.

Edward had taught her that his pragmatism was far more effective than her irrational outbursts. She would not yell at her sisters for being themselves.

Kit had unbuttoned his jacket while her mind wandered. Before she could react, he slid out of it, leaving Bell clutching empty wool as he leaped over the top of the fence.

Never let it be said that Boyles were dumb—just insanely reckless. Kit ran straight toward the unsaddled ponies.

Paralyzed, Bell didn't know which way to turn. She wasn't afraid of harmless ponies, but she hadn't been near a horse or a child in a decade. Her mind was a blur of panic.

The groom had gone inside to saddle the pony she'd chosen for Kit. She couldn't climb a fence in her damned long skirts. The animals were calm and well-behaved. *Kit* was not.

Before she could react, Quent sprinted to the fence and leaped over the bar as if he performed that acrobatic feat every day. Bell hadn't realized she'd stopped breathing until she expelled a sigh of relief.

Kit was grabbing a long mane and attempting to pull himself up— no doubt a maneuver he'd seen his damned father execute. The late earl of Wexford could have performed at Astley's Circus had he been so inclined.

Quent merely used his long arm and greater muscle to snatch the boy before the pony had time to take a chomp out of Kit's sleeve. Fitz was running wide-eyed with horror across the stable yard. The slender earl stumbled to a halt beside Bell when it became apparent that Quent had Kit in hand.

"He's not civilized," Bell said tranquilly, although she felt anything but.

"Who, Quent or your brother?" Fitz asked dryly as Quent tucked the kicking, shouting boy under his arm and strolled toward the gate with him.

Excellent question. There was a reason the Scots had been deemed savage by the English. They'd run about half naked in blizzards not so long ago. She'd always thought of Quent as eminently civilized, but after last night...

Quent deposited the boy on a tall feed bin and pointed an accusing finger at him as Kit attempted to scramble down. Bell couldn't hear his admonitions from this distance, but they were sufficient to force Kit to stick out his bottom lip, start kicking the bin, and sit still.

Maybe she *ought* to let the Hoyts have him. Her heart hurt at the thought—all the more reason she ought to give him up, she supposed, but her wretched head and her heart were at war. She turned to check on her sisters.

Syd was attempting to balance on a side saddle in the other enclosure. Both of her sisters had learned to ride astride when they were little, as Bell had. Instead of mounting her horse, Tess was worriedly watching Kit to see if she should run to his rescue.

"Go see to the girls," Bell told Fitz. "They're mostly civilized. If I'm the one who will inherit the responsibility of raising the next earl, then I must learn to deal with him."

"I can recommend a lion-tamer," Fitz said, "But Quent apparently has experience. I'll leave you to him."

She couldn't do this alone, she realized with a pang of regret. She would have to call for the tutor and maids and valet if they stayed here any longer. And judging from her sisters' inexpertise on their mounts, it looked as if they might have to impose on the Wyckerlys for a while. She had always been competent. These last years had given her new strengths and independence. It was horribly humbling to recognize that she needed help.

The groom led the saddled pony from the stable. Bell reluctantly joined Quent and Kit. She truly had no experience at dealing with little boys. How did one make them behave?

"Shall I tell the groom to take the pony back, that his lordship is too ill- mannered to deserve a good animal?" she asked, eyeing her brother with disapproval. "Or do we just let the pony bite him next time?"

She was excruciatingly aware of Quent's masculine proximity. She had never seen him in less than perfection in London. Now, he smelled of male musk and horse. He had made her indecently aware of how his broad shoulders narrowed to a flat waist and muscled thighs, so unlike most of the pot-bellied gentlemen of her acquaintance. Perhaps she ought to consider his indecent offer—if only so she'd quit having such thoughts around children.

"I'd recommend a week in his room with bread and water, but I suspect that would bother everyone else more than it would him." Without even looking down at her, Quent adjusted her hat so it didn't tilt so rakishly.

Rebelliously, Bell tilted it again and glared at her brother. "You nearly had a chunk of your arm removed, Christopher James. You are an undisciplined heathen not fit for a gentleman's saddle. Until you show yourself capable of behaving with the proper respect toward others, including the ponies, I think you need to be demoted to lead ropes. Like a baby."

She gestured at the groom, who obediently returned to the stable to find the appropriate tackle.

Kit, of course, had no idea what she was talking about, until she reached the last part. He kicked his heels harder and hollered, "I'm not a baby."

"That behavior is precisely like a baby's," Quent intoned solemnly. "And if you continue behaving as you are, I will take you to the nursery with little Georgie. You can eat porridge and roll balls with him."

Georgie was Fitz's toddler son, just learning to walk. He and Beebee had been having a fine time when Bell had checked on them last.

Kit wailed louder. Quent lifted him from his perch, stuck him under his big arm, and marched back toward the house.

Kit shut up.

Quentin halted and lifted a questioning eyebrow at Bell.

"I want a pony!" Kit cried piteously. "I'll behave. I promise."

Finally established in her saddle, Tess sidled her mare in their direction. "I can take him up, Lord Quentin. I've had charge of him since he was little."

Bell hid a smile at Quent's exasperated expression. The man was human after all. She hastened to intervene before he bit his tongue in two. If Tess had been in charge of the brat, she'd been far too lenient, but she'd only been a young girl with no experience.

"Tess, you need to stay with Syd. She hasn't your skill. I think the two of us can deal with Kit a while longer."

Tess looked dubious, but Quent set the young earl on his feet, pointed his finger, and the boy obediently stayed where he was put.

Fitz rode up on a restive gelding, effortlessly keeping it under control. "I want to take the girls around the yard first, see how they handle the reins. Do you want to wait until we're back before putting his lordship in the saddle?"

The groom was leading the dappled gray pony into the now-empty paddock. Bell could practically feel her brother's longing to run and climb over the fence. She handed Kit back his coat and watched him pour his energy into struggling into the tight arms.

"I think between us and the groom, we should be able to handle him," she said dryly.

"Famous last words," Fitz warned with a grin, reining his horse around.

"Quite possibly," Bell muttered. "I truly dislike being incompetent at caring for a child. I need a teacher."

"You are already doing a better job than Tess," Quent told her, shrugging. "I have watched you learn everything you need to know over the last years, and then go on to use your knowledge to exceed the pinnacles. You'll catch on to the nuances of child-rearing quickly."

Bell stared at him surprise. A man who actually respected what she'd accomplished? Or was he being facetious?

Fitz laughed and kicked his mount toward the other paddock. "Come on, girls, we can watch the circus from afar."

Bell didn't have time to be envious of their escape. Still stunned by Quent's praise, she didn't object when he gripped Kit's shoulder. He marched the boy toward the pen—or more like, kept him from running full tilt at the gate. She appreciated the aid, but she knew what would happen as soon as her brother was placed on the saddle. She might not know child care, but she had experience in Boyle behavior.

She remained outside the paddock as Quent handed Kit to the groom to be hoisted up. Kit's fingers were fisted, as if to keep from grabbing the pony as he'd tried earlier. He sat patiently while the stirrups were adjusted. He was large for his age. He wouldn't be on a pony for more than another year. The guide rope really was an insult, but it had to be done.

As soon as he was released and in the saddle alone, Kit whooped, grabbed the pony's mane, and kicked. Bell shook her head. Male

Boyles were simply too predictable.

The pony obediently followed the groom's tug on the rope and didn't budge.

Quent made a quiet threat. Kit settled down and pouted again.

Bell was nearly as ready as Kit to tear her hair out at the pony's slow pace around the paddock under the groom's guidance. Quent came to stand beside her, placing a proprietary hand at the small of her back. Bell started to move away, but he ran his finger under her jacket, discreetly caressing her spine through the thin chemisette. A river of need flowed through her. Knowing the others were too far away to notice, she couldn't tear away.

It took half an excruciating hour before the boy could be forced to sit quietly in the saddle. Bell feared her brother would burst into tears of frustration at any minute. She sympathized, but it was like taming a yearling. Kit would be good to no one if he was left unrestrained.

As if possessed of second sight, Quent removed his hand just before the girls trotted back. She missed the caress, damn the man. But her sisters were shouting excitedly over their triumphs and deserved her attention.

Kit saw them riding in without guidance and finally gave in to tears, wailing his heartbroken protests.

Tess immediately dismounted with a wide-eyed look of concern. Bell blocked her path. "He's fine. He's just angry because he's being punished for his earlier behavior."

"But he's just a little boy! He so wanted his own pony. Can't you let him go now?" Tess skirted around Bell, hurrying toward the fence.

Seeing her, Kit cried louder.

Quent stepped in, sweeping the boy off the pony, plopping him on the ground, and marching him toward the gate, quietly scolding.

Kit wept and tried to run back to the pony. Quent lifted him and swung him over the fence, where Tess crouched down to hug him and give everyone black looks.

"Thank you," Bell whispered to Quent. "You are about to be called all sorts of dreadful names, but I am grateful for the way you handled him."

"How grateful?" he asked, lifting a leering eyebrow.

That look caused her to shiver with unwelcome desire. She pinched his arm through his coat sleeve. And Tess launched into her furious tirade about the poor little boy and his pony. Quent took it all in stride, reaching up to help Syd down when she rode over to see what the commotion was about.

"Excellent seat, Lady Sydony. Less pressure on the mare's mouth next time. The groom keeps apples inside, if you want to take your mount back to be brushed down." Quent pointed at the open door.

And blessedly, Syd did as told.

The wretched man was not only turning her into a puddle of wax, he was making himself useful, Bell realized. Did he do so on purpose? Of course. Quent never did anything without a purpose.

Fitz swung down. "Want to try Wexford on another pony? It's hard to test them out on leading ropes."

"No, I think this one is fine. He has excellent conformation and best of all, patience. I'll take Kit back to the nursery, if you'll show the girls what else might suit. I'll be back shortly to look them over. I do appreciate this, Fitz. I wouldn't trust their horses to anyone else."

"Not even me?" Quent asked, falling into step with her as she half-dragged a rebellious Kit toward the house. He stooped down and picked the boy up, placing him on his broad shoulders. "I'm a pretty good judge of horses."

"But not of women riders," she retorted. "Or of my sisters. Or Boyles in general. Fitz pays attention to what they want, not what *he* wants."

"Which is why he'll never be a successful businessman," Quent pointed out. "But he's happy and he'll fare middling well, even though he has a couple of mares in there that would command a much higher price than the ones you're looking at."

"I saw them," Bell said, irritated that he kept inflicting his presence on her but relieved she didn't have to wrestle Kit. "They're too high strung for riders who haven't been in a saddle in a while, and far too high strung for the crowds and noises of the park. I respect him more for not showing them to my sisters. Fitz will have clients lining up at his door because of his honesty."

"As I said, he'll earn a middling income that way. He'll get by," Quent agreed with a shrug. "I need to *more* than get by. I didn't have his title or name or acres of land when I started out. A middling income wouldn't have fed my family."

"I can't help it if Edward was a miser!" Bell shouted, finally aggravated beyond all reason over this ancient argument. "It wasn't as if I recklessly spent his wealth. He wouldn't even let me have the windows re-glazed. He's dead, it's over, you're rich. You don't need to prove yourself any longer, and I don't need to marry you to make your fortune. Why have you decided to harass me now?"

"Because you need me," he said decisively, with what sounded like surprise. "You've never needed me before."

Bell shut up and glumly faced that unpleasant fact the rest of the way back to the house.

Ten

"I'M NOT SURE LORD Quentin even knows I'm alive," Tess whispered to Syd as the company gathered in the family parlor prior to the evening meal. She nodded toward the formidable gentleman, who was leaning against the mantel, talking to a much more approachable Mr. Penrose.

"That's just the English way," Syd insisted. "They're very reserved, if you haven't noticed. Even Bell isn't the same anymore. I remember her as being quite fun, but she's more strait-laced than the countess!"

"She's a marchioness now," Tess said doubtfully. "I'm sure that means she must be dour and authoritative. She must have much on her mind if her husband's holdings were large."

"All the more reason for you to snare Lord Quentin," Syd insisted. "We'll be one less burden for her."

"How does one attach a man who pretends we don't exist?" Tess asked in puzzlement.

A footman arrived in the doorway, distracting Syd from any inappropriate suggestions. Always eager to learn her new surroundings, Tess watched the countess nod for the footman to approach. He handed over a note on a platter.

"Do they expect a reply, Wrigley?" the countess asked, glancing over the contents and raising her eyebrows.

"I've sent the messenger around to the kitchen for a bite to eat in case you wished to send an answer, my lady."

"Well, tell them of course they're welcome, if they don't mind joining our small house party." The countess waited for the footman to leave before addressing Bell.

"That was from Lady Anne Montfort. Her father's estate is a short ride from here. She says she's acquiring more horses and would like to come over for a few days with a friend of hers. She's never so much as visited us before."

"Jocelyn mentioned that the duke is entertaining the widow of a distant cousin," Bell said. "I like Anne, but I haven't met her guest."

So many names to learn! Tess didn't think she'd ever master society. Jocelyn Montague had been the grand lady who had given the political dinner party, but how did a *duke* fit into the conversation about their visitors? Was this the same old duke that Mr. Montague assisted?

Lord Danecroft entered just then, and Tess noted that Lord Quentin was now listening to the general conversation. She pinched Syd to make her pay attention, then strolled in Lord Quentin's direction.

"We're to have company, dear," the countess said, waving the note at her husband as he came toward her. "Perhaps you'll need to start buying new stock if we stay this busy."

"Lady Anne has been useful," the earl said, glancing at the note. "But I don't know this Diana, countess of—"

Tess didn't hear the rest of the name. With her gaze focused on Lord Quentin, she was only aware that he froze like a panicked deer.

BELL NOTICED the same. She'd seldom seen Quent express any emotion other than supreme confidence. Now, he looked as if he wanted to bolt.

The moment was brief. He took a sip of his drink and returned to speaking with Penrose. Fitz's wobbling old butler arrived to announce dinner. Bell remained seated until Quent came over to offer his hand, frustrating Tess's apparent attempt to reach him first. Penrose stepped in to escort Tess.

"I thought I knew everyone in society," Bell whispered. "Who is the countess of Renfrew-Fife? That sounds Scots to me."

"Widow," Quent said curtly. "Youngest daughter of the Duke of Graham. No reason to know the family. Like my father, they never leave Scotland."

"Well, it seems she has left Scotland if she's visiting Lady Anne. Do you know her? Is she likely to scorn my sisters?" Bell watched his expression as he held out a seat at the table for her. The man knew how to be as impassive as a butler.

"I haven't seen the lady in a very long time. I cannot say."

She detected a definite hint of bitterness in his tone. Bell bit her lip and spread her napkin on her lap and let him be. There was history there, she was sure of it, but Quent wasn't any of her concern.

After dinner, Quent didn't join the ladies in the parlor, much to her sisters' disappointment. They had to practice their wiles on poor Penrose, who practically glowed with delight. He was a decent young man, of good family, Bell knew. He just didn't have a feather to fly with.

Bell excused herself to check on Kit. The boy needed constant attention, it was apparent. Abby's young siblings were a help, but she thought it best to keep her hand in so that he would be accustomed to her authority when they returned to London. Without other children in the city, he would need amusement. How would she arrange that?

After verifying that he was sharing a room with the other boys, ostensibly settling down to sleep, Bell slipped down a side corridor and outside into the still-warm summer night.

She didn't know what drew her. She wasn't a country sort of person any longer. She didn't know one English weed from another. Fitz's shrubbery was too overgrown to be called a pleasant garden. She lied to herself for a while and pretended she didn't want Quent finding her in her chamber again.

She gave up that pretense when she found him standing by a dry fountain. She didn't turn around and go the other direction.

"It's hard to drown one's self in granite," she reflected aloud, warning him she was present. "Although I suppose one could flip a coin into the cracked basin and wish for a bubbling spring."

In the shadows of dusk and shrubbery, his expression was hidden. "When I was young, I wanted to race yachts. I thought there could be nothing more splendid than sailing the high seas and seeing exotic sights. What happens to those dreams?"

"I wanted to be recognized for my ability to race horses," she admitted. "When I disguised myself and rode my father's stallion, I could beat every man in the county. When it became apparent that I *had* to win purses to put food on the table, and that men would never appreciate my ability if they knew I was female, I learned the dark side of dreams."

"Is that why you don't ride now?" he asked, lifting his head to study her through the darkness.

"Not any more than you don't race yachts. You still own one, don't you?" She gracefully dodged the subject.

She really didn't know why she was out here in the still night air, breathing the summer scent of mown grass, and the sensuous aroma of bergamot toilet water. The blasted man had shaved before dinner and smelled good enough to nibble. For her own well-being, she ought to leave, but she waited for his reply.

"I use my yacht for business and to transport my family from Scotland," he said stiffly. "Faster and safer than riding the northern road."

"But that's not why you're out here now, pondering youthful

dreams. I gather you and Lady Anne's guest have a history?" Bell generally preferred the subtle approach with this man, trying not to show her curiosity for fear he'd take it as interest. But she'd never seen him so discomposed. He'd helped her today. She wanted to offer what little she could in return.

"Ancient history," he said with a shrug. "It's her present history that concerns me. I believe the lady produced only daughters, and her husband's estate fell to a younger brother. If she's applying to old school friends for entrance to society the moment she's out of mourning, she's in financial straits. Her father must have had an apoplexy when she left Scotland. He despises England."

"And this concerns you how?" she asked, fascinated despite herself. Quent seldom told her anything.

"Because of ancient history," he said with a shrug.

Without warning, he caught her waist with a powerful arm and dragged her up against his hard torso. This time, his kiss wasn't so polite as the night before. He poured real need into it, a hunger that fired her own banked desires.

Bell clutched his coat and surrendered to the consuming heat, knowing the danger, craving it anyway. His mouth was hot and demanding, as if he'd been saving up all his explosive emotions for this moment.

She'd never truly recognized the passion concealed by his civilized composure. If this passionate man was the real Quentin, he terrified her—and made her crave more of what she'd never had. She parted her lips and allowed him a brief moment of triumph, but the moment her hands started sliding to his shoulder, she used them to shove away.

"No, no, no, I am not going down this road again," she muttered, backing away. "I need you more as a friend than a lover."

"One does not preclude the other," he said irritably, tugging his coat back in place.

"Yes, it does, really," Bell said with sadness, turning back toward the house. "I can't take a lover without marriage. It would present the wrong appearance to my sisters, not that I'm inclined to take lovers anyway. And marriage is a different sort of trap. Once you have me where you want me, I'm no longer a challenge. I'll just become a nag who wants to do things that annoy you. You'll set up an office in the city. And then you'll set up a mistress so you don't have to come home. I've watched it happen too often."

"You are talking to a man who has had his sisters cluttering his house during the Season for two years. If that's not enough to drive me out, I doubt I'll be dislodged by you." Quent took her arm, pressing unnervingly close as they traversed the gravel walkway. "Just let me show you what you've been missing by denying yourself for so long. You're too young and beautiful to become a nun. You're a widow. Take advantage of that freedom for a bit. I fear my father's escalating demands about the guardianship will soon generate lawyers, but at least give me a chance to win you over."

"Such sweet words to turn a girl's head," she murmured.

"I didn't think you wanted flattery." He drew her to a halt just outside the side door. "You saw that list of eligible females and you know perfectly well you're the only one who would suit me. Shall I make a list of eligible males so you can decide if another would suit you better?"

"Why can't you see that I don't *want* another man in my life? The ones I had simply made me miserable. I *like* my life the way it is." Bell tried not to shout. "Is it so very difficult to understand that men are not indispensable?"

"Once women discover that, civilization as we know it will disintegrate," he said wryly. "So think of it as more a joining of forces, a rather pleasant joining, if only you'd allow me to demonstrate."

"I need to go pummel a pillow," she grumbled, yanking from his grasp. "Go away. Court anyone you like. Just don't mix me up in it."

She practically raced up the stairs in her need to escape his persuasive logic.

QUENT RESISTED following Bell. He didn't possess the seductive skills to persuade a woman to do what she didn't want to do. He wasn't certain that he wanted to win her in such a manner.

But he was increasingly convinced that Bell was in over her head if she thought tutors and servants would be sufficient to deal with her sudden new family. Her siblings hadn't been raised with decades of proper training. They thought for themselves and acted on their own and they were Boyles—willing to take dangerous risks.

It must be something in the blood, Quent decided the next day, finding Syd timing Kit's slide down the banister with a watch she must have stolen from Bell. The ancient rail creaked threateningly as the boy flew past him on the stairs, shouting in glee. Boyles were meant to be devil-may-care soldiers.

At sight of him, Syd fled into the upper story shadows, leaving her brother to Quent's wrath.

Quent was about to grab Kit by the back of his coat and march him back upstairs when a footman opened the front door and their visitors spilled in. *Damnation.*

"Go back up and tell Bell the guests have arrived," he told Kit, capturing him as he tumbled off at the newel post. "And if I ever catch you on the banister again, I'll glue you to a chair. The rail is old. It breaks. So will you."

"Bell will stick me with my stupid tutor," Kit said, pouting.

Quent's carriage had arrived that morning bearing his luggage and Bell's servants. He was definitely questioning the efficacy of the boy's new tutor if he'd let his student escape already.

"Tutor now, pony later," Quent promised.

"No ropes," the boy countered.

"Ropes until you quit kicking the animal." Quent was used to bargaining. Kit didn't stand a chance.

Kit glared. Quent blocked his escape to the lower floors. Kit gave up and stomped back up. Quent followed him, but Syd was long gone. She definitely needed a finishing school. He only hoped she was warning her sister about the guests because he didn't intend to search Bell out while her siblings watched.

The tutor emerged on the upper landing just in time to grab Kit and scold him back toward the schoolroom. Taking the back stairs down to the stable, Quent avoided the clatter of servants carrying luggage and preparing rooms.

Mostly, he was avoiding Camilla. Unless she'd changed, she wasn't here by happenstance. She had a purpose, and Quent was quite confident that impoverished Fitz wasn't her goal. The lady had expensive tastes. Quent hadn't maintained his bachelor status all these years without learning a few fast maneuvers.

Penrose and Tess were just leading their mounts from the stable when Quent arrived.

"Lord Quentin," Tess cried. "Join us, please. The rain has stopped, and I do believe we may even see some sun."

Quent kept his snort to himself at his aide's unhappy expression at this invitation. "I promised your brother a ride, sorry. Take a groom with you. Penrose, behave yourself or I'll rip your good arm from its socket."

His aide gave a wry salute and waited while Quent told a groom to saddle up and follow the pair. Where the devil was Bell and why wasn't she keeping an eye on her troublesome siblings?

He glanced toward the carriage spilling its contents on the front lawn and groaned. Of course! Bell would be right in the midst of the new arrivals, pumping Camilla and Lady Anne for information in the guise of aiding her society-shy hostess. If he had any secrets, they wouldn't be secret for long. Wellington could use a good spy like the lady—and there was the Boyle in Bell. She might no longer ride into battle, but she possessed a formidable mind and instinct for infiltrating the enemy's defenses, so she might bring him down from within. It was how she had survived and conquered a society that had originally scorned her.

Quent gazed longingly at the stable and wondered how it would look if he just rode back to London without farewells.

Eleven

THE EARL AND countess of Danecroft were not inclined to waste their limited funds on stylish clothing. In their company, Bell had happily accepted the freedom of wearing her more comfortable summer gowns and little jewelry in the interest of staying cool. Her sisters didn't own a variety of fine evening gowns as yet, so they fit their rural surroundings as well.

Camilla Abernathy, Countess of Renfrew-Fife, apparently had different notions, Bell noted sourly as Abby's guest entered the great hall that evening. Even the duke's daughter, Lady Anne, had not garbed herself in silk and jewels—although Lady Anne seldom drew notice to herself as her relation apparently did.

No longer burdened by mourning, the countess wore a splendid gold silk gown to complement her red-gold hair, and a topaz-and-diamond parure that glittered on her ears and wrists and accented her ample bosom. Large diamonds gleamed on her fingers.

Only a woman on the prowl glittered that much.

"I'm contemplating a new occupation as jewelry thief," Fitz murmured irrepressibly in Bell's ear. "One of those rings would buy me three Thoroughbreds."

"Learn to tell gems from paste first," Bell recommended. "If those are real, I'll help you advance in your new criminal livelihood."

Fitz chuckled, then strolled over to address their guests. Bell noticed that in the process, he hugged his intimidated wife reassuringly and treated her as if she were a princess more grand than the widowed countess. In his presence, Abby regained her confidence sufficiently to lead her bejeweled company around the hall, introducing the newcomer to anyone she had yet to meet.

They'd been using the smaller family parlor these past nights. Apparently for the benefit of their grandiose visitors, the servants had set up tea and drink trays in the towering medieval great hall with its massive wooden beams, wall-sized fireplace, and echoing spaces. Wyckersham was rather devoid of furniture since Abby had pragmatically used all the pieces that had rotted beyond redemption as firewood. A few good sofas and settles remained scattered about an enormous—much repaired—carpet. Conversation was limited to shouting across the emptiness or running down elusive prey to speak one-on-one.

Standing by the broad stone hearth, Bell sipped her sherry and watched Abby introduce the countess to Quent—or not introduce, as the case seemed to be. Over by the leaded windows, Quent bowed stiffly. Lady Camilla rested her gloved hand on his immaculate coat in a gesture far too familiar for propriety. She stood on her toes and whispered in Quent's ear, leaving her hostess to flail awkwardly on her own.

"I do not think I like Lady Camilla," Bell murmured to Tess, who was also observing the scene. "But I would like to know more of how she knows Lord Quentin."

"He doesn't seem happy to see her, if that's any consolation," Tess said. "I don't remember the modiste showing us any gowns in quite that style. Is it the fashion?"

The widow's bodice revealed that after bearing two children, she possessed a pair of well-developed udders, Bell noticed spitefully. She'd have to ask for the name of the lady's corsetiere. Such ampleness did not hold itself up magically, especially when the silk bodice appeared ready to slip off.

"Is it the fashion to look like a courtesan?" Bell mused. Then remembering her sister needed insights into society, she continued, "No, decidedly not the style, especially for young girls. It's a design that says *I'm available and desperate.*"

Tess giggled but replied sensibly. "Men like it, though. If a gown catches their attention, hasn't it served its purpose?"

Bell thought this an excellent moment to begin teaching her sister what she'd learned over the years. "You'll see more gowns like that once the Season is in play again. Just notice who is wearing them, and you'll see what I mean. Men don't mind the display, but they prefer to do the hunting. Once they've sampled what she has to offer, they'll move on to other ladies more suitable for wives they can trust not to roam."

"I'm thinking he's already sampled what she has to offer," Tess replied. "I don't think human nature is any different between England and America."

"You are quite possibly right. They're of an age. The lady is older than I am. But that's none of our concern. Let's help poor Abby. She's quite out of her depth when it comes to such rudeness." Bell started across the room, picking up Lady Anne as she did so.

Quent was now wearing his frozen gargoyle expression. Abby glanced helplessly about and smiled in relief at Bell's approach. Lady

Camilla had hooked her hand possessively around Quent's elbow and was whispering in his ear.

"Where did you find this personage?" Bell whispered to Lady Anne as they crossed the carpet.

"She more or less found us," Anne said with what sounded like exasperation. "Father wants her brother to vote for some bill and one thing led to another, and here she is. She's been a decent guest, but I suppose she doesn't know our ways well."

"I don't think ignoring one's hostess is well done anywhere," Bell said dryly. She donned a beaming smile as they reached Abby. "I love this hall. Do you decorate it in winter with evergreen branches and a Yule log? You must have us down, if so. London is much too boringly sophisticated on the holidays."

Without waiting for a reply, Bell turned to Quent. "Fitz and Lady Anne need your opinion about some horse or another." She gestured dismissively in the direction of the earl, who was pouring himself a drink and speaking with Penrose and Syd.

Lady Anne took her cue and Quent's free arm. He looked grim. Bell didn't think he seemed relieved, but at least he wasn't casting daggers at her.

"If you'll excuse me, my ladies," he bowed and walked away, forcing the newcomer to drop her possessive grip or be dragged with him.

"Well, that was rude," Lady Camilla said brightly, her smile as flashing as her diamonds. And probably as false. Bell couldn't quite tell. "Quent and I haven't seen each other in ages. I don't remember him being quite such a high stickler."

"Oh, yes," Bell purred, squeezing Abby's arm so she unfroze and joined in the joke. "As a tradesman, he must be all that's proper to hold his place in society. A Scots title is so meaningless in London, and a courtesy one at that... well, you know how it is." She shrugged.

"Lord Quentin is all that's proper," Abby agreed faintly, not quite grasping the social pitfalls she straddled.

Bell loved her former protégée for her virtuous inability to think badly of others. Abby deserved rescuing from any cat fight that Bell instigated. "I think Syd is about to consume all the lovely delicacies your cook has prepared to entice us. Why don't you let me entertain Lady Camilla while you wave your wand and perform the magic that keeps this enormous place running?"

"Cook has heard of the French custom of serving small bits prior to the meal and has been dying to try it. I wonder if I should tell him to fix fewer, so our guests don't ruin their appetites. Dinner should almost be ready. Lady Camilla, a pleasure to meet you." Abby bobbed a brief curtsy and hurried away.

"The country sort, I suppose," Camilla said dismissively of the countess. Apparently assuming Bell's position in society worthy of her attention, she drawled, "I am so very tired of dowdy and practical. Is the rest of society in Bath this time of year?"

"Bath is quite déclassé these days," Bell said, donning her most imposing dowager marchioness expression. She waved her fan languidly and studied the magnificent hall with false ennui. "If Prinney is at Brighton, then there might be a few parties there. It's less than a day's drive, but I'm quite tired of society for now. Our small family gathering suits me."

"Quent is part of your family?" the countess asked with suspicion.

"Of course," Bell said in feigned surprise. "I am a Hoyt, after all," she added with a dollop of hauteur. "He's been no end of help to me since Edward died. Really, I am quite astonished that he has never mentioned you. You say you are an old family friend?"

The lady's brilliant smile developed an edge. "Oh yes, we practically grew up together. Our family estates were close. So were Quent and I at one time. But his family was poor and rural, and my family preferred the city, and we drifted apart, I suppose. You know how it is."

Yes, Bell feared she did. Poor Quent, if he had fallen victim to this avaricious witch. "He has quite a few extremely handsome brothers. It must have been hard to choose between them back then, before they were married."

"That was long ago," Lady Camilla said with a dismissive gesture. "Back then, they had no hopes of inheriting the title or estate, except for the brief period after the late marquess lost his first wife. Once he re-married, even that hope was dashed. I assume you're the one everyone expected to produce the heir to the marquisate."

Bell heard the shrew's disdain of her childless state but didn't react to it. Edward had taken his chances and lost. Her failure had been personally painful, but it was no longer of relevance. What mattered was the implication behind the shrew's comment. Apparently, once Camilla had realized Quent's family might no longer be in the line of succession, she had turned elsewhere.

Bell fanned herself and discreetly watched Quent over the top of the boned silk. He had his back to them, but she read the stiffness in his shoulders. "Since Quentin never had a chance of taking the title, then you are saying there was never really anything between the two of you."

"I didn't say that," the lady purred. "He was the Hoyt closest to my age. As I said, we were very young."

You were young, Bell thought spitefully. Quent would have been some years older—and ready to make a wife of any woman he took to bed, as Camilla seemed to imply. No wonder the man had never married. Once burned, twice shy.

"And now you're not. Such a shame, really. He'll need heirs for his fortune," Bell said sweetly, fanning herself and lying through her teeth. "He is looking at younger women who can give him children. He seems quite taken with my sister."

Tess had gravitated toward the group discussing horses. Quent chose that moment to glance down at her and say something with a smile. It almost made Bell's teeth grit, had she not known that was just Quent's brotherly interest. But the lady next to her swelled with possessive wrath.

"A chit like that won't interest him. I believe that doddering old man has come to call us for dinner. Let's join the others." Lady Camilla sailed off, leaving Bell behind.

You're in my society now, Bell thought with determination. *You'll not hurt me or mine, if I have anything to say about it.*

Of course, did this fierce protectiveness toward him mean that Quent was hers?

Camilla nabbed him to escort her into dinner. Bell went in with Syd and Tess, leaving Lady Anne to Penrose.

"Our numbers are uneven," Bell said as they took their seats. "Quentin, you need more bachelor friends to call on. Surely there are one or two who haven't married my protégées yet."

Quent didn't acknowledge her jab about their ongoing wagers over Edward's unmarried female relations and his group of impoverished younger sons. He merely shrugged and sipped his wine.

"Too many of us have gone to war," Penrose explained in his employer's place. "Our only other choices are vicarages or marriage. There are few available bachelors left in our set."

"*All* Lord Quentin's friends are younger sons?" Camilla asked after sampling the soup and pushing it away with an expression of disdain. "I should think cultivating men in power would be more practical."

"One has no choice with whom one does business," Quent finally replied in a curt tone. "Real friends are those who care for you, not those who wish to do business with you."

Huzzah, Quentin! Bell mentally cheered. She knew she liked him for a reason.

"Well, some of us do both," Fitz said cheerfully, stomping through the undercurrents. "If it's even numbers you'd like, I still have a few bachelor acquaintances. But you must promise to take them with you when you go, or they'll never leave. They eat like locusts."

Bell laughed, and her sisters followed suit. It wasn't the world's most comfortable dinner, but with genial Fitz taking the lead, they kept the conversation flowing. Lady Anne was never talkative, although she seemed to enjoy hearing about the horses Tess and Syd were acquiring. Lady Camilla, sitting across from Quent, did her best to fix his attention, but he stoically ate his meal and responded only when addressed directly.

Bell could already see him making his excuses and fleeing back to London. She ought to be glad to see the back of him. But she was just the tiniest bit afraid of dealing with her instant family in this unfamiliar setting without his aid. She might have to return to London, too, where she was on firm ground.

She hated to retreat in the face of difficulty, though. She'd prefer cutting off a few heads and staying the course. She pondered her options over the exquisite trout.

Her brother's shouts rang down the corridor. Silverware dropped all around the table. Tess hastily scooted back her chair. Alarm surging through her, Bell did the same.

The boy burst past a footman unsuccessfully guarding the doorway. "Beebee's sick. She's crying. She needs you," he cried—flinging himself into Tess's arms.

Tess paled, pried Kit loose, and hurried from the room. Bell caught the boy's shoulder to prevent him from running after her.

"What an ill-behaved child!" Camilla commented. "Surely there are servants who might have passed the message more discreetly."

Rather than scratch the witch's eyes out, Bell gestured at Syd to stay seated while she led her little brother after Tess. Beebee and Kit came before cutting off heads.

Kit was red-eyed and trying not to weep in fear. Bell understood that he'd seen far too much of death in his short life. He needed reassurance, not correction.

Their hostess followed close on their heels.

"You don't need to abandon your guests," Bell protested as they hurried up the stairs. "I'm sure it is nothing. Tess can handle it."

"I'd rather be with the children," Abby admitted. "I'll take Lord Wexford back to his bed, if you wish, and you can go back and deal with that horrible woman."

Bell managed a small smile. "I would spit and roast her in the fireplace, so I'm probably not the best choice."

Abby sent her a grateful glance. "I'm glad I'm not the only one who dislikes her."

"For all I know, she gave her wealth to charity and her family adores her," Bell said, "But she must have been raised in a pigsty. I am trying to be generous."

"Yes, I can see that," Abby said with mock approval as they reached the nursery.

Beebee was, indeed, crying in pain. Tess held her over her shoulder, rubbing her back, while the babe screamed and kicked. Helplessly, Bell left them to deal with the two-year-old. Tense and worried, Kit needed to be tended as well.

She led him back to her bedchamber, sat in a rocking chair, and lifted his chunky body onto her lap. He sat stiffly at first, but relaxed a little as they rocked.

"She isn't going to die, is she?" he asked anxiously.

"She probably ate something she shouldn't. Babies cry a lot. I'm glad you told us, though. Beebee needs her mama to make her feel better. Everything must be very strange for her since she came here. How about you? Is it all very strange for you?"

He leaned against her and nodded. "But I like it here. I got a pony now, and Tess doesn't cry so much as she did before. Maybe we could get Beebee a pony."

If only horses would solve all life's problems. Bell smiled and stroked his hair. "When Beebee is old enough to run without falling over her feet, we'll think about it. I'm glad you're big enough to look after her. But next time, try to tell us without terrifying all the dinner guests, all right?"

He sniffed and nodded. "I *told* the nanny to fetch Tess, but she wouldn't listen."

Because the nanny had been trained not to disturb her employers with nursery problems. That wasn't going to work with her independently-raised family. And it wasn't a rule with which she was comfortable.

But once the season was in full swing again, what choice would they have? The nanny couldn't send for Tess if she was out dining or dancing.

Bell had known raising a family would be challenging, but she was just starting to grasp the full extent of the difficulties.

She'd left her chamber door open so she could hear when the nursery quieted. She hadn't expected Quent to abruptly fill the entrance.

"I'll be leaving in the morning," he announced, wearing a grim expression. "I can take Kit with me. He'll like school once he gets used to it."

Twelve

STOICALLY, Quent waited to see if Bell exploded or handed over the boy. By now, she should be tired of dealing with the brat's impetuous behavior. Most wealthy society women would have taken the boy straight to the nursery and sent the maids packing for allowing such a scandalous breach of polite conduct.

He tried not to place any importance to her rocking and soothing the young earl—instead of flinging things at Quent or sacking the nursemaid. Bell was smart. She'd soon realize he was doing her a favor by taking the boy in hand so she could return to her normal activities.

He'd been the one fooling himself to think a wealthy marchioness would have any interest in marrying a Scots merchant so she could keep her family together. Good thing Camilla had come along to remind him of his proper place—or lack of it.

"He's not ready for school," Bell told him coldly, her delicate features freezing into disdain. "Flee to London, if that's your preference, but he stays with me."

He wanted to be relieved that she defended her brother, but knowing Bell, he assumed she merely rebelled because she could.

"You know perfectly well that you cannot handle him, that he will be a danger to himself in the city—that your life and household don't have room for him." As long as she would hate him anyway, he might as well be blunt. "I'll make the arrangements with the school. He'll need to be ready by September. You should see by then that I'm right."

There, that should partially satisfy his father's demands, and it was the right thing to do. The boy needed more instruction than Bell—or a tutor—could provide.

He swung on his heel and marched back to his room to start packing. Quent was accustomed to dressing himself and traveling light. He had a valet to care for his clothes, but he preferred to leave the man in London. His life required freedom to move swiftly. Marriage would have been a burden. Damn Bell for being right again—although she still didn't grasp that it was her bed and company he craved, not her money.

~~~

TESS PERSUADED enough chamomile tea into Beebee to relieve her cramps, then put her back on her stomach in the cradle. She smiled gratefully at the plump countess who hovered with concern. "I wish I knew as much about babies as you do. No one ever told me how to cure her upset tummy."

Lady Danecroft rubbed the toddler's back. "The twins used to eat green apples every spring. I had to ask questions and learn or just strangle them to put them out of their misery. I fear our nursemaid is still inexperienced. I'm sorry Nanny Mary had to abandon us this week to see to her ill sister. When she returns, I'll ask if she knows anyone else as skilled as she is with little ones."

They had sent the young nursemaid back to bed once Beebee quieted. Tess lingered with the countess, rocking Beebee and the earl's heir in their cradles until they slumbered soundly.

"Would it be dreadfully impolite of me not to return to the company?" Tess asked. "I know your cook must be miffed to have his splendid meal so rudely overset."

The countess laughed. "We usually let the children dine with us. And Fitz runs to the stables in the middle of the meal if one of his mares is foaling. Our staff is rural and pragmatic and expect such interruptions. Shall I have a maid bring up your pudding so you don't miss out?"

"Send Syd up with it, perhaps. She shouldn't be left alone, unless Bell has returned downstairs." Tess hoped Bell had been able to settle Kit down. She hadn't heard any more wails from the schoolroom.

The countess sighed. "I dread going back down to that woman, but poor Lord Quentin shouldn't be left to her clutches. I'll keep an eye on your sister if she isn't quite ready to retire."

Lady Danecroft fluttered off, leaving Tess to the darkened nursery and the two sleeping infants.

It was obvious that Kit and Beebee would never fit into Bell's sophisticated household. Tess had only just begun to realize how much Bell had sacrificed by marrying the elderly marquess to save their father from debtor's prison. She'd always considered Bell happily married and been jealous of her easy life. Instead, Tess understood now that her sister had given up her youth, her love, and apparently the chance for children by marrying a man who had turned into a miserable old miser.

She simply couldn't let Bell sacrifice the lovely life she had earned the hard way.

When Syd arrived bearing a cream pudding studded with blackberries, Tess led her sister back to their shared chambers. Shutting the door, she set the pudding aside. "Does that witch have her claws in Lord Quentin yet?"

Syd grimaced. "He left early, saying he must pack and leave in the morning on business. I vow, if Lady Frosty-Frou knew where he was going, she would ride after him. You don't stand a chance against her."

"Not if I play by the rules," Tess agreed. "Anything Bell might grant me as dowry could not compare to the jewels she was dripping tonight. And it's obvious they knew each other quite well at one time."

"You always play by the rules," Syd said scornfully. "Lady Camilla does not. I overheard her telling Lady Anne that she should arrange to be caught in a compromising position with some gentleman Lady Anne fancies if she wants to catch him, that he'd *have* to marry her then. What if I do that to Lord Quentin? Then you could come running to my rescue and Bell would make him marry me."

"Don't be ridiculous. You don't want to marry yet, and Bell would most likely shoot Lord Quentin and lock you in a nunnery. Do they still have nunneries here?" Tess mused, while her thoughts ran rampant. Compromising position? She could do that.

"I don't think Anglicans have nunneries," Syd said dejectedly. "Bell is far more likely to send me to a school with ice baths than to a nunnery."

"But she can't send *me* to school," Tess said. "And if Lord Quentin's father will take me in, if Bell throws me out, I'm the most obvious candidate."

Syd looked at her in disbelief. "Candidate for what?"

"Being compromised," Tess replied, thinking quickly. "We'll never have a better opportunity. This is a time for doing, not plotting. Here, help me out of this gown."

EXPECTING PENROSE, Quent answered the knock on his bedchamber door without thinking.

Bell's widowed young sister swept past him wearing the barest wisp of a robe and gown. "Lord Danecroft failed to include the best candidate for your wife on his list, my lord," she announced as she entered. "He can be forgiven, I suppose, since he has not had time to know me."

Leaving the door open, Quent leaned against the jamb and folded his arms. "Did Bell set you up to this?"

"Bell?" She lifted her fine dark eyebrows in surprise. "Of course not. She thinks I'm a child. I'm not. I've come to prove that."

"Have you now? I'll still send Kit off to school no matter how you work your wiles. He needs discipline, and you can't provide it." Quent gestured toward the open doorway. "I think you'd best leave before you cause untold numbers of problems for all of us. We'll discuss Kit's schooling at a better time."

"We're not talking about Kit." She stamped her slipper.

Quent had no interest in Tess's feet. Had she been Bell, however... He stopped that thought before it hit the gutter. "We're not talking at all, not here, not now. You're leaving, if I have to pick you up and remove you. Perhaps Bell did not explain. I am not a gentleman."

"Of course you're a gentleman," she said with a casual wave. "But I am not a lady. Close the door and let me show you."

Quent rolled his eyes and crossed the room to catch Tess's elbow. "Out, now." One hand on her barely-clad arm, the other pushing at her spine, he shoved her impolitely in the direction of the door.

She wriggled and fought and cried out before Quent had the presence of mind to catch on.

By then, it was too late.

A horrified audience had gathered in the doorway.

AFTER PUTTING Kit back in the care of the servants, Bell dragged herself down the stairs to her bedchamber. The uncomplicated rural visit she had planned had degenerated into a nightmare. She wasn't certain how she would manage so many unfamiliar problems on her own—but sending Kit off to school was not a solution. Clobbering Quent over his arrogant head would provide satisfaction but wasn't the answer either.

Hearing feminine voices emerging from the gentlemen's wing, she frowned. Surely that was not Syd shouting in such an unladylike fashion? She truly did not need another outburst of unseemly behavior from her siblings this evening.

She peered around the corner and saw Lady Camilla—wearing a robe and little else—arguing with a furious Syd, who appeared to be blocking a doorway. A bemused Lady Anne looked on. Where was Tess?

Bell froze when she heard Quent's voice raised in anger. He never lost his temper. Was that *his* room the ladies had gathered around? What on earth...?

And was that Tess's high-pitched, nervous voice coming from inside his chamber?

None of the scenarios Bell's creative mind conjured were pretty. Experienced in house party shenanigans, she tested the latch in the nearest door. These old houses were like rabbit warrens with their interconnected rooms. The long corridor was a later addition, if she was lucky.

She held her candle up to the empty room she entered and found an interior door. It opened with a squeak, taking her into an antechamber. The door on the next wall led to a small bedchamber intended for a servant. Quent had brought none. She pressed her ear against the next door and heard Tess more clearly.

"Of course he wasn't forcing me," Tess cried in indignation. "Lord Quentin is a gentleman. We were having a quarrel, that is all."

Bell wanted to slap her sister, then shake her, but that would have to wait. As would explanations. Tess in Quent's room would be the gossip of all London, ruining her sister's chances of a good match—and Quent's reputation as well. He placed a great deal of pride in his honesty and integrity. Those were the qualities people of the highest sort respected. Being deemed a rakehell who ruined young women would cost him immense amounts of business.

Being a man sampling the wares of a bored widow would merely gain him approval.

And as a titled, wealthy widow with no intention of marrying again—Bell had little to lose in comparison to Tess, who had a child to think about.

Thinking quickly, Bell dropped her shawl over an old dresser and untied the ribbons of her bodice, letting the sleeve fall loosely off her shoulder. She'd kicked off her too-tight shoes earlier. Now, she stripped off her stockings. She couldn't reach her back fastenings, so that was the best she could do in haste.

Opening the interior door into Quent's masculine chamber, Bell covered her mouth in an exaggerated yawn and stepped into the weak candlelight to get her bearings. Tess was the only one visible. She startled, then had the grace to look guilty.

The massive tester bed draped in blue curtains blocked any sight of the doorway, but she could see the angry stiffness of Quent's shirt-clad back separating Tess from their audience.

Wickedly, Bell crawled up on the bed's velvet counterpane and peered through the draperies. "What on earth is the commotion, Quentin, dear? Is the house on fire?"

Quent swung around looking quite marvelously stunned. That instant of shock and discomposure from the eminently assured gentleman was almost worth whatever happened next. She'd forgotten how much fun it was to shock people. With a surge of laughter she hadn't experienced in much too long, she almost anticipated Camilla's dropped jaw.

Obviously, her life had been in danger of becoming too dull. With a seductive smile just for Quent, Bell swung her bare legs from the bed. Quent's gaze instantly dropped to her ankles, and she rewarded him by pulling her gown up a little before she slid off the bed and walked out where their audience could see her.

"Hello, dears. Did our family squabble disturb you?"

Oh, yes, that was just the dropped-jaw effect she'd hoped to see. Although Bell suspected Lady Anne was hiding a smile as she stepped back to enjoy the show.

"I'm so sorry if we woke you," Bell continued, narrowing her eyes to study the intruders. "Although, really, Lady Camilla, I cannot understand why you'd be interested. Is that dressing gown from Edinburgh? I've never seen anything quite so... practical."

The dowager countess pulled her velvet robe closed over her ample bosom with a huff. Her angry glare said she wasn't buying Bell's charade.

But whatever plans the lady had made for Quent had been permanently disabled. Bell barely hid her triumph.

Catching Tess's shoulder from behind, Bell gently shoved her sister toward the doorway. "Save your histrionics for when we're home, please. I'm aware we haven't discussed how Quent will fit into our little family, but surely we need not do so tonight. Say good evening and take Syd with you, please." She squeezed Tess's shoulder reassuringly, warning her not to protest.

Syd started to speak, but Quent had apparently dragged his mind back from Bell's ankle and to the matter at hand. "No more outbursts, Lady Sydony. Your sister and I delayed making the announcements because of your arrival. I see no further reason for delay. You're disturbing the other guests. Good-night." He pointed sternly at the door.

Bell didn't know whether to laugh, run after her stricken sisters, or smack Quentin for escalating her charade to the next level of *announcements*. "Really, life has been so unbearably tedious until now," she drawled, following her sisters and giving them hugs. "I anticipate circuses and operas hereafter. Off you go, now. You, too, Lady Camilla. So sorry to disappoint, but the show is over." Bell winked at Lady Anne. "Horses aren't as entertaining, are they?"

Lady Anne's lips quivered in amusement, but she simply shook her head and led her furious guest away. Aping Quent's gesture, Bell pointed at the corridor when her sisters turned with pleading glances. "In the morning," she commanded.

Before she could even shut the door, Quent circled her waist and dragged her backward.

"Since we are apparently affianced, my *dear*," he whispered mockingly, "shall we continue where we left off earlier?"

Thirteen

QUENT didn't know what the devil had just happened or why. He simply knew he finally had Bell where he wanted her. Why think further? He'd thank her sisters later.

He slammed the bolt home on the door, then wrapped his arms around the lady's supple waist and lifted her beautiful mouth to meet his. Her lily-of-the-valley perfume wrapped his head in spring. Her pliant figured molded to his. And her kiss... sapped all his brains from his skull.

Her lithe tongue tangled boldly with his. Nearly undone by this unanticipated surrender, he staggered backward until he had the sturdy bed to support his suddenly weak knees. She was Eve and Delilah and every wanton woman known to mankind, all wrapped in one intriguing package. And he wanted her... *now*.

Her smooth fingers slid beneath the open neck of his shirt, massaging his shoulders while her mouth dissolved his will. He'd known Bell hid a well of repressed passion. He hadn't anticipated the powerfully seductive result of liberating her inhibitions.

Quent dragged her down into the bed with him until they lay sprawled across the mattress, their legs entwined. He found the untied ribbons of her bodice and slid his fingers beneath the silk. "Do you have any idea how I felt when I saw you crawling out of my bed?" he murmured, moving his mouth to her ear and down her throat.

She gasped and wriggled, then ran her hand boldly over his shirt. "Cheated?" she asked teasingly.

"Not even half of it." He jerked her sleeve down so he could release her breast, but her chemise defeated him. Planting kisses anywhere he dared, he began untying ribbons. "You made me feel like one of my blue-painted ancestors. I wanted to slay dragons and drag you back to my lair and have my way with you. Repeated times."

Her chuckle was low and sexy and incited him more.

"Surely the mighty Lord Quentin has had his moments of passion. Is there a simmering cauldron behind your polite composure?" She nibbled his ear and tugged at his shirt, attempting to remove it from his trousers.

He unfastened buttons to ease the constraint of the cloth. "I assure you madam, I am a temperate man. You have simply driven me to madness."

"Fie, you lie. And we cannot do what you think we're doing, so you had best prove your temperance and let me up." Her hand lingered at his waist, tugging at his linen.

"Not a chance." With her bodice sufficiently unfastened, he released her breasts. Rosebud tips puckered temptingly, and he teased one with his tongue.

She nearly came up off the bed, and Quent smirked in satisfaction.

"Bad example for my sisters," she murmured. "Cannot do this."

"Your sisters are the bad example. It's no matter now. We'll marry and do this every night. And morning. And maybe at noon. It will make all the rest of the chaos worth it." Right now, with this amazing woman in his hands, he almost believed that sexual congress would make the world go away.

He suckled, and she moaned. He caught the curve of her hips and pulled her under him.

She arched to brush against his arousal. "*No*, nothing is settled. This is not how to do business."

He snorted inelegantly. "I should hope not." He tugged her skirt up until he could finally stroke bare flesh. "Business tomorrow. Tonight, I show you what I have to offer."

"It's been so long..." she murmured worriedly.

His heart raced at this hint of capitulation. "I assure you, you can do nothing wrong. Practice isn't necessary." He kissed her again, making it long and slow, soothing her with caresses so she grew accustomed to his touch.

She retaliated by sliding her hand between them and squeezing the bulge in his trouser placket. "I am not a yearling to be gentled to the bridle. Do not think there will be a repeat of this occasion because you will it so."

"You underestimate me, Bell." He turned on his side and finished opening his placket. "You'll want this as much as I do."

"Maybe I'll find others to scratch the itch, then," she taunted, tugging his shirt free and finally running her hands freely over his torso.

His gut clenched with fierce possessiveness. "If I thought that, I'd just tether you to the bed and never leave. Don't make light of what's between us because you're frightened. We'll make it work."

He hoped. And prayed. And removed their clothing so he could see all of her. If he was to have only one night, he wanted heaven.

~~~

THE DAMNED MAN knew her too well. Too much was happening too soon. Bell had only just discovered this part of her that had been lost. Lowering all her careful guards to rediscover what she'd so thoroughly buried...

Her reactions to his touch both excited and terrified her. No other man had created this uncontrollable need. She wanted to do things she'd never thought of doing with any other man, not even Edward. And blast Quent—he wasn't giving her time to recover.

Without modesty, Quent stripped off his linen and trousers and let her gaze with impunity on his awe-inspiring physique. The candlelight cast his arousal in shadow, but she could see enough to doubt their compatibility. She was slender and only of average size.

He was over six feet of brawn. Muscles rippled as he captured her beneath him. He was beautiful and formidable. She wanted to flee and kiss all those hard planes at the same time. The magic he created with his mouth and hands kept her fastened to the bed better than any velvet ties.

She was hollow inside, aching, hungry, craving. With his terrifying ability to understand her needs, Quent sucked her breasts until she cried out with desire. He slid his fingers between her thighs in answer to her cry. She had to stuff a pillow in her mouth to prevent screaming at this intimate invasion. She tangled her fingers in his gloriously thick black hair, trying to tug him away. She needed a moment to regain control, but he nipped at her breast and pressed his fingers deeper. Pressure mounted below her belly, and she couldn't find escape from the tension.

He grabbed the pillow away from her and slid it beneath her hips. Then he inserted a second finger and pressed where she ached the most.

All her restraint shattered. Bell surrendered to a glorious flood of sensation. She cried out in joy, then bit her tongue at the desperation of such an animal noise emerging from her own throat.

Unperturbed by her uncivilized behavior, Quent continued his rhythmic thrusts and exploratory kisses. She writhed as the tension built impossibly higher.

"Quent, please," she pleaded. She tried to reach for his arousal, to help him if he needed it, as Edward often had.

Quent kneeled over her, making it obvious he needed no help.

"Say you're mine, Bell," he ordered, his voice rasping from deep in his throat. "From this moment on, we forsake all others."

She didn't believe him, but she had no interest in other men if this one failed her. "You're mine," she repeated tauntingly, using his words and turning his request around.

He grunted in appreciation. "You always have to be right."

He parted her thighs. She raised her knees. He leaned over to kiss her—and buried all that long masculinity deep inside until she cried out in pain and ecstasy.

She was no longer empty, but oh, the joy! How could she ever have given this up?

QUENT LASTED until Bell shrieked and rocked again with release before he took his own pleasure, plunging without restraint, encouraged by her caresses, roaring with the explosion of desire. Not having to withdraw was a luxury and joy in itself—he'd finally found a woman he trusted with his seed. He needn't rush but could linger in her tight warmth, joining in the aftermath of the best lovemaking he'd ever known.

"Stay with me," he murmured, rolling over to remove his heavy weight but carrying her with him so she rested across his chest. "I can never have enough of you."

She kissed his shoulder, then eased away. "Nothing is settled," she warned. "I must talk to my sisters. They'll be at my door in the morning."

Quent wanted to tie her down, refuse to let her go, make her see sense, but his possessive nature would never work with an independent woman like Bell, which made him uneasy. Grudgingly, he released her. Cold air blew over his sweaty skin, leaving him chilled.

"Your sisters know where to find you," he reminded her, dragging the covers over them.

"And I'll pay for that in a thousand ways in the future. Give us time." She sat up, threw off the covers, and slid out of bed.

Knowing what he did of his own sisters, Quent groaned and granted her that. He didn't know how the devil he would deal with two families, but after this night, he wanted Bell enough to move the moon and stars. "We'll both talk with them in the morning," he promised.

She shimmied into her chemise and leaned over to kiss his cheek. "Don't count on it," she whispered.

Wrapping a sheet around his hips, Quent rose and helped her back into her gown. "I'm relentless," he warned. "I won't let you retreat into your hiding place again."

"Give me time to think," she whispered, pushing against his chest when he tried to hold her.

"Bad strategy." But he let her go, reluctantly sending her off through the route she'd used earlier.

QUENT SHOULD HAVE slept like a log after that. He didn't. He never did the night before closing a major deal. Complacence wasn't in his vocabulary. Until he had Bell exactly where he wanted her, he needed to keep an eye on her.

He'd already recognized that tying her to his bed wasn't reasonable. At least he wasn't that far gone yet. After last night's little drama, though, she didn't have a great deal of choice about agreeing to marriage.

If marriage was what it took to have her in his bed every night, he was now prepared to make the sacrifice. He had the uneasy notion that Bell could still slip back behind that dispassionate façade with which she'd learned to address society. He couldn't give her time to slip away.

He was dressed and in the breakfast room the next morning before the servants had set out the buffet. Grabbing coffee, he strolled toward the stable, wondering if he dared take a quick ride before the women arrived downstairs. Deciding he didn't want to appear disheveled and smelling of horse, he merely sipped his coffee and wandered toward the paddock.

"Help me up!" pleaded a childish voice on the other side of the hedge.

Quent halted.

"Spies don't need help," another, more familiar, voice whispered. "Hand us those apples. You can be our gunner."

"Hurry up," a third voice commanded. "They're almost here."

Quent wasn't entirely familiar with the Wyckersham nursery set, but he knew the countess had a couple of much younger half-brothers. And then there was that familiar American accent— no doubt instigating the mutiny.

Quent located the open entrance to the kitchen garden and found the culprits in the corner overlooking the stable yard. The youngest was oblivious to anything except gathering fallen green apples and placing them in a basket so that the *spies* in the tree could haul them up.

The thick leaves hid the other two well enough, except his little lordship hadn't donned his coat and the white of his shirt gleamed through the thicket. Out of curiosity, Quent peered over the hedge to discover their target.

Lady Anne was already mounted on her elegant Thoroughbred. She was a fine figure of a woman in her tailored coat and draping skirt. He'd learned his lesson about duke's daughters and would have given her wide berth even if she hadn't been the quiet, boring sort.

Closer to the hedge, however, stood flamboyant Camilla, haranguing a coach driver on the placement of her trunks. They were leaving already? Most excellent.

Quent didn't have to be six-years old again to understand the temptation of such a target. Camilla wore a rounded hat with a trailing feather and a brilliant red coat of a style that hadn't been seen in London since last century. No doubt it was high fashion in the hills of Scotland, and the brilliant color drew the attention the lady craved.

But to an American boy, the scarlet was that of the notorious British redcoats. And the pheasant-feathered hat... Even Quent itched to pick up an apple.

Shrugging, he let the boys get off their first volley, just to see how good they were. One of them hit the red coat square in the back. The other just missed the hat. The lady screamed anyway.

In a few quick steps, Quent was at the tree. He pointed the youngest at the walled herb garden. "Go," he ordered. Abby's wide-eyed sibling scampered. Then he reached into the tree and hauled down the white shirt on the lower branch.

Kit predictably squealed and kicked. Quent tucked him under his arm and peered up at the eldest boy. "Inside, before I tell your mother where you are," he commanded. More obedient than his lordship, the freckle-faced ginger hurriedly scrambled from his perch.

While Camilla ranted in the stable yard, Quent strolled back through the hedge and toward the house, carrying his captive. "I should tie you up in bows and present you to your sister," he told the miscreant. "You really don't want that pony, do you?"

"I want my pony!" Kit cried. "We're spies. We're supposed to stop the enemy! Put me down!"

"In this case, lad, we want the enemy to ride away. A good spy learns the lay of the land before attacking."

Kit quit kicking. "What does that mean?" he asked with suspicion.

"It means your sister already drove off the enemy. Attacking a retreating army will only cause them to turn around and strike back. Stupid move. And next time, make certain your target actually is an enemy. She could have been a spy disguised in a red coat. Always have complete knowledge of your target if you're to live to fight again."

Since he'd never been a soldier, Quent was making up the strategy as he went along. It wasn't that difficult from the business world. He'd accomplished what he set out to do, at least. The boy was paying attention.

"Who is the enemy then?" Kit inquired.

Quent set him down and marched him up the front steps. "I'll let you know when I find them. Until then, practice target shooting with trees. Who aimed for her hat?"

"Tommy did," Kit said in disgust. "He was showing off. Everyone knows to aim for the broadest part of the target to bring them down, then go for the head."

"Boyles are not only reckless idiots, but blood-thirsty as well?" Quent asked, rhetorically.

That should cause a quiver of trepidation. Bell was a Boyle, although she'd hidden it well all these years that he'd known her.

He and Kit arrived in the hall just as Tess and Syd swept down the stairs. Noses in the air, they marched past Quent as if he didn't exist. The cut direct, even if they hadn't a clue what that meant.

Kit escaped and ran after them, heading for the breakfast room.

Quent practically slavered, waiting for the last of the contingent to emerge. Bell didn't disappoint. She was wearing her travel gown. The deep green brought out the red highlights in her hair and gave her fair complexion an otherworldly glow. She would make a gorgeous forest sprite—except for the wary expression she wore.

"Going riding?" he asked hopefully.

"My sisters tried to seduce and *compromise* you," she said in resignation and disgust. "My family and I are going home... to Essex. I don't advise that you follow until we've all reached a better understanding."

Fourteen

"WE DIDN'T DO anything wrong," Syd insisted as the carriage rattled down the road toward town. "We only did what Lady Camilla intended to do, except we got there first."

Bell thought she might climb out of her skin and run away. She glanced out the window to be certain Kit hadn't set fire to the baggage carriage carrying the servants. She'd been amazed that Quent had still been willing to lend his equipment.

"Lady Camilla is *desperate*. I thought I made that clear. Proper ladies do not trap husbands. It's not only very bad *ton*, it's hare-brained. Men resent wives who force marriage on them. You are not desperate."

"Yes, we are!" Tess stood up for her sister. "We don't want to go to Scotland to some stranger or to a horrid school. We want to stay here, together. Lord Quentin said he might have our guardianship if he married, so why shouldn't he marry me?"

"We didn't know you were having an affair!" Syd cried. "How could we know? You act as if you dislike him."

"I do not," Bell answered crossly. "We are the oldest of friends. And we were not having an affair. I just wanted to protect him from your foolishness."

"Then marry him," Tess said in the same peevish tone. "Then we needn't worry about going to Scotland. We thought to save you from having to marry for our sakes, but if you're friends anyway, why not?"

Excellent question, one too difficult to answer. How could a woman of her years claim to be holding out for love? She was well past the age of romantic silliness.

"We have different interests," Bell answered, sounding petulant even to herself. "I spend money. He saves it. Marriage would destroy our friendship."

That settled the argument for the time being. Her sisters knew all about men who *spent* money. Men who didn't want to spend it were beyond their ken.

Which made Bell the reckless spendthrift like her father. Fine. So, she was the villain here. A villain valiantly attempting to do what was right for her family, she tried to tell herself.

But she had to admit that she was lying. She was running away from the way Quent caused her to lose control and indulge in the reckless, dangerous urges of her youth.

Running away was a coward's way out, and she really was too old and wise in the ways of the world to believe in love and romance. Requiring love was simply another means of running away, she supposed.

With a sigh, Bell mentally composed a business letter that would link her fortune with Quent's. The letter wasn't pretty. How could she turn the perfect night they'd shared into a negotiation? It went against the grain.

She'd have to have Summerby write it.

BACK IN LONDON a few days later, Quent crumpled Summerby's damned letter and paced his study. "Why am I doing this?" he asked. "I'm perfectly fine as I am. She's the one who needs *me*."

Penrose dropped a stack of documents on the desk and imitated Quent's inelegant snort. "Right you are. You pace like a testy stallion. You haven't gone after the steamboat deal since I presented it to you. You nearly snapped off your housekeeper's head when she merely asked if you wanted to call in a window cleaner. I think the lady has you by the bollocks."

Worse, the lady had hit him where it hurt—in his pride. He'd been so damned certain he could prove that she wouldn't want to leave his bed that he'd never given any other result a consideration.

He certainly wanted back in *her* bed again. Bell in the height of passion—was more glorious than racing yachts on the high seas. He wanted to paint her naked and hang the image over his bed, if only he could paint.

He couldn't believe she didn't feel the same. Pride goeth before a fall, indeed. He'd spent years imagining how he'd teach her the pleasures her old goat of a husband hadn't. He didn't see how he could be so wrong. Bell wasn't the cold conniver this letter said she was—unless he really was thinking with his cock and not with the brain that had conquered London. He glared at the legal letter and flung it at the painting of his yacht on the wall.

He should be out generating cash for the family fortress, not fretting over feckless females. Alliteration. Maybe he should take up poetry.

He was losing his mind. And his focus. He couldn't afford to lose his focus.

He picked up his father's last letter. *I'll buy my own roof,* the bold handwriting declared. *I already have two offers for Tess's hand—Angus*—one of Quent's nephews who was still in school—*and Mackie*—a widower cousin with half a dozen children to raise. *A dower of the same two thousand pounds a year the dowager gave her protégées should save a fortune once I have Mackie off my hands! I have someone looking into the boy's lands. Between them, that will buy the roof. Send them to me—now!*

Quent had a notion that the Boyles would shoot his father and cousin before they married either of them. How far would he have to run to avoid the war?

He'd originally thought of Bell as the perfect wife because she was independent and he needn't spend time worrying about her. Now the damned woman was flaunting her independence with this wretched settlement letter, and it was damned well interfering with his ability to negotiate with his infuriating father.

"Write a counter offer," Penrose suggested, jarring Quent from his reverie.

Quent didn't want to *negotiate* anymore. He wanted nothing short of complete capitulation. Immediately.

The study was suffocating. He loosened his neckcloth and continued pacing.

"My father will be hiring a new representative to enforce his guardianship if I don't act soon." Quent tried to make this strategy work in his head, but threats never worked with Bell.

"I'd start figuring out a counteroffer for that *marital duty only once a week* clause," Penrose said, not bothering to hide his amusement.

His aide had hit the sorest point of all. Quent picked up Summerby's crumpled settlement letter and flung it on the empty grate. "Send my father a reply telling him Bell will not dower her sisters if he won't surrender his guardianship, but she'll dower Sally and Elizabeth if I control the guardianship. And there will be no roof forthcoming until such time as the matter is settled."

"I can hear his roar now," Penrose said with a wince.

Quent grabbed his hat off the stand. "I'm taking the yacht to Essex. If you want to join us, take the Friesian and your mount by road."

He stalked out, leaving Penrose still protesting.

He damned well didn't need to be negotiating with both Bell *and* his father. This had to stop or he'd never earn another farthing.

Quent debated taking his own lawyer with him to hammer home *his* demands, but he didn't have the patience for arguing. Besides, marriage was between a man and a woman, not a couple of solicitors. He just needed to remind the lady of that.

Racing his sailboat down the Thames to the Channel returned his perspective. With the wind in his hair and the sun on his face, he was almost the boy he'd been long ago, in a faraway place. He hoped he was smarter than that boy had been, because he was about to make a rare fool of himself otherwise.

"BELL, BELL, there's a cart coming up the drive," Syd cried, racing down the corridor of the rambling manse.

Bell scowled at a bird's nest on top of the china cabinet in the butler's pantry. "I haven't ordered any deliveries. The footmen can handle it."

"The same strapping footmen who are afraid to remove that nest?" Syd asked cynically. "I think you should have left them in London."

Bell hated it when her sisters were right. "They know how to answer doors. As soon as I can hire a few country lads, we'll straighten this place out." She hadn't wanted to acknowledge that they'd be here long enough to hire more people.

She hadn't wanted to admit that she wouldn't be returning to her civilized city home any time soon.

Syd flitted around the enormous pantry, lifting silver platters and candelabra and ornaments even Bell couldn't name. "I love it here! I can only remember a little of our home in Wexford, but I imagined it just like this—with endless chambers and room to run and no one looking disapprovingly down their noses at me."

"I'll look disapprovingly down my nose if you run and break your silly neck. Make yourself useful and examine the linen closet. Anything with holes goes to the church. Tell me how many good linens are left."

"Not enough," Syd said cheerfully. "We used them all on our beds. But I'll fetch a basket to load the others in."

She danced off. Bell was thrilled to see her happy. She was less than thrilled to be returned to filth and decay. As a child, she'd practically lived in the stable and never tended the house. She had never dealt with bird and wasp nests, pumps that didn't pump, drains that didn't drain, and holes in the roof.

Since her marriage, she'd hired excellent servants to handle the city household. But Edward had let the entailed country manse deteriorate. He'd never visited here, so neither had she. After his death, she'd taken a look at the place, shuddered, and left it alone. It had seemed a waste of funds if she couldn't leave the estate to charity or her sisters' offspring.

Quent's family now owned the entailed land to Belden Hall. She possessed only a life estate. The house was their problem—unless she wanted to live here.

Until now, she hadn't been so inclined. She would rather invest her funds in people than things. But she would need green pastures for Little Dream. The pastures might as well be her own, since it was obvious she couldn't inflict her sisters on society, or vice versa, until they had a little more polish. She'd had Fitz deliver their horses here.

Bell hoped Edward's Aunt Griselda could help with polishing her sisters' behavior while lending propriety to the household, but Boyles would always be Boyles. Perhaps she should send them back to Wexford.

Not without wealthy husbands.

Kit's war whoop warned he'd escaped the classroom again. Tess arrived in the pantry wearing a worried expression, a certain sign that trouble loomed on the horizon.

"It's Lord Quentin," Tess whispered. "He arrived in a cart. I can't tell him to go away, can I?"

Oh, devil take it, why couldn't that interfering man let her *think*?

Remembering the letter that Summerby had sent him, Bell quailed and abandoned the pantry. "The footmen have forgotten how to answer the door?" she asked, striding briskly toward the foyer, trying to hide her nervousness. "And why a cart? We sent his carriage back to him."

Even as she said it, Bell knew—Quent had arrived on his yacht. Which meant he'd needed to race off his fury and arrive here faster than horseback. That wasn't promising.

In trepidation, Bell approached the front door. She had no elegant visitor's parlor to greet him in. Belden's medieval hall was worse than Fitz's rambling shambles.

"You weren't invited," she caustically told Quent when she reached the foyer to see him doffing his hat and handing his walking stick to her sturdy footman.

He looked marvelously windblown and sunburned, and her heart nearly tripped over itself in its eagerness to leap from her chest. What would it feel like to be clasped in his embrace, as if this were truly a homecoming?

She had to rid herself of these romantic notions. He was probably here to kill her.

"That's odd," he replied cheerfully, leaning over to peck her cheek as if he had that right. "I thought certain the letter from your solicitor was an open invitation. You are looking beautifully harassed, my dear."

Bell knew better than anyone how civilized behavior could hide a multitude of sins. At least he didn't throttle her in front of family. "I'm not your dear anything. We have no extra linen. The beds are full of mice. And my cook refused to leave town. She says she can only cook in a real kitchen, not a country hovel. You'll just have to turn around and go home."

"I'll have to take you to Scotland someday. We mend our threadbare linen and just spit and roast whatever died that day." He bowed to Tess. "How do you do, little sister? Are the grooms keeping you from racing your new mare?"

Tess glanced uncertainly from him to Bell, then dipped a quick curtsy. "We are still learning the land. It would be dangerous to race without knowing the course. I'll help Syd with the linen."

She hastened off, leaving Bell and Quent to stare at each other. Bell felt awkward. *He* seemed his usual over-confident self.

"Words to live by?" he asked with a quizzical lift of his eyebrow. "Should we learn the lay of the land before racing the course?"

"We know the lay of the land," Bell said irritably. "And if you have some notion of staying, then you'll have to work with the rest of us." She stalked back to the pantry.

"The apron is quite a domestic touch. I like it," he said, striding along beside her, reminding her of how much larger and broader he was.

Manly, masculine, physically capable—all those things she wasn't and the reason she'd hired strapping young footmen, who were apparently useless out of the city. "Don't let the apron fool you. I still wield a horsewhip better than a duster. But men have their uses."

She pointed at the broom she'd abandoned when she'd answered the door, then pointed out the bird's nest and cobwebs well above her reach.

He dragged a massive walnut chair from the dining room and

climbed up on it to swat the filth to the floor.

The chair leg snapped with a loud crack. Quent and bird nest toppled toward her. She shrieked and tried to break his fall with her hands. He rattled the contents of the dish cabinet by catching the corner in an attempt to slow his descent. Terrified they were all about to die, Bell hastily backed against the wall, away from the swaying cupboard.

Releasing his grip before he toppled anything else, Quent hit the floor, boots first. He staggered into Bell, pushing her up against the wall.

Too shaken by the freakish accident, Bell instinctively wrapped her arms around his waist. "You could have broken your fool neck," she muttered, burying her head against his shoulder, as if that would prevent him from falling again. She swore furiously while he grasped her shoulders and breathed a little harder than normal. She could hear his heart pound.

He held her tighter than necessary, but she wasn't inclined to shove away just yet. She'd had flashes of seeing him cracking his skull, and she hadn't quite caught her breath. She didn't wish to let him go. "The place is dangerous."

"Life is short. We should take advantage of every minute," he countered.

Before she could react, he lifted her chin and kissed her, a kiss that started at her lips and burned clear down to curl her toes. *She* was breathing heavily by the time she pushed away. But she no longer feared for his neck.

She took a deep breath and pushed away.

"This is ridiculous, spooning in the pantry like adolescents." She dusted herself off, glanced at the broken chair, and stalked back to the main dining room to glare at the sheet-covered furniture. "It's probably all got wood rot."

She spoke coolly, but her blood was racing so fast, she thought she might give in to the vapors. How could he *do* this to her?

"I could stand on each one and test it," Quent suggested with amusement, picking up another chair and bringing it down hard on the wood floor. The floor creaked. "But I want two kisses for the next one that breaks and three for the third. And a whole lot more than that if the floor caves in."

He was needling her over the contract she'd had Summerby send.

She swung on him and smacked his broad—hard—chest. "Stop it, stop it this instant. I have agreed to negotiate the possibility of marriage. That's as much as I have agreed. This is *not* a love affair. This isn't remotely romantic. We're two sensible people admitting marriage might be convenient."

"I admit no such thing. Marriage is a terrific inconvenience as far as I can see," he growled, glaring down at her. "I'll be stuck with two families demanding my time and attention, hosts of vaporish females running in and out, and a shrew of a wife who will want to spend every farthing I earn. The only pleasure I can hope to gain by marriage, you want to deny me. So let's start there."

He hoisted her from the floor and stomped back through the pantry toward the servants' stairs with Bell pounding his back and attempting to bite his ear off.

Fifteen

DAMN, BUT Bell was a raw handful of female. Her delicious bosom bounced against his shoulder as she twisted and attempted to either unman him or bite off his head—although her nibbles were more erotic than painful. He stumbled on a step when her tongue reached his ear.

He was fortunate she'd kept her shoes on or the sight of her bare toes might cripple him entirely. He'd be forced to take her right there on the servants' stairs. Just the notion that he might have that right raised Quent's spirits. He cupped her firm round bottom to hold her in place, and for the first time since childhood, he felt almost giddy with absurd joy.

He knew he was acting out of bruised pride, but Bell's kiss hadn't been forced. She'd reacted to his tumble with concern, embraced him with affection, and kissed him with passion. That's all he'd needed to bolster his confidence. She was wrong to deny what was between them. He was right to demand they push past whatever invisible hobgoblin existed in her ridiculous head.

Except Bell was never ridiculous. That recognition took some of the steam out of his fun. Then he reached the landing for the private floors, saw the long corridor of doors, and realized he had no idea which chamber was hers.

The American earl put an end to any further notions of intimate entertainment. Kit raced down at them from the next flight of stairs, whooping and hollering and brandishing... a rolling pin?

"Separate houses," he muttered, setting Bell down on the landing carpet. "One for us, one for them." He caught the brat on the second step up, before he could behead anyone.

"Where's your tutor?" he demanded, turning the whooping boy upside down and proceeding upward, abandoning a disheveled Bell. At least she wasn't shrieking at him.

He should probably be grateful to the lordling for preventing him from a rash action that would have ruined everything, but he wasn't feeling grateful. He was feeling deprived and set upon, like a boy who had just had his snowball fight interrupted by chores.

Bell pattered after them, ominously silent. Kit whooped with glee at his upside-down position and tried to swing from Quent's arm.

Quent almost grinned at the boy's incorrigible high spirits.

Stalking through the upper warren of doors and rooms while holding a wriggling six-year-old, he searched for anything resembling a schoolroom. Muffled cries emerged from behind a closed door in the center of the attic. Quent waited for Bell to reach him, set the boy down so she could wrangle him, then turned the ancient key in the lock—on the outside of the door. Maybe the Hoyts once locked mad aunts up here.

Inside, the tutor was half-tied to a chair, tangled in yards of frayed gold braid from the draperies. He was still pulling off the last tangle when they entered.

"I resign," Mr. Thomas said with as much dignity as he could muster, dropping the braid on the floor and rising from the chair. "There aren't enough demons in hell to control the boy. Without servants and under these primitive conditions, it's utterly impossible."

"Is he ready for school?" Quent demanded. Bell still said nothing but she was keeping a firm grip on Kit's shoulder.

The tutor blinked in disbelief from behind his wire glasses. "The question is, is there a school ready for *him*? I believe the answer is no. He will develop a reputation as difficult, and in a year or so, no good school will have him."

Quent grabbed the boy's chin and forced him to meet his eyes. "And what do you have to say for yourself, my lord?"

"Geography is boring. I don't like books. I wanna go riding." His glare was defiant and not the pout of a week ago.

"Tying your tutor to a chair doesn't look like geography. Would someone care to explain?" Bell asked in a faint voice.

Quent could have told her. He and his brothers had pulled this feat more than once. One more reason she needed his help. Women would never understand. He waited expectantly.

"I was using a history text to explain the differences in societies and cultures of different lands," Thomas said stiffly. "Combining subjects is a very effective learning technique."

Quent rolled his eyes at this explanation and translated. "He let the demon lord talk him into practicing sailor knots."

"It was apropos of discussing how sailors reached the Americas," Thomas asserted.

The boy giggled, not in the least ashamed or afraid. Quent squeezed Kit's small shoulder to catch his attention. "You're a worthless knot tier. You'll have to do better than that if you're to sail with me. Now get down on the floor and do twelve floor-dips."

The boy glared. "I don't know what they are."

"And I'm not dirtying my knees showing you. Get down on the floor and I'll tell you when you get it right."

Apparently intrigued by the opportunity to explore under the furniture, Kit obligingly dropped to the floor. Once the boy was on his knees, Quent returned his attention to the tutor. "Obviously, you were never a small boy. If you wish to resign, I'll send for the next man on the list. If you wish to learn how to actually teach, start by finding ways of keeping him occupied and thinking one step ahead of the brat. He's not stupid. He needs activity."

"I should show him how to do floor-dips?" Thomas asked dubiously, watching the boy sprawled under their feet.

Quent put his boot on Kit's back and forced him to lay still. "Push up on your arms," he ordered.

Bell murmured a puzzled protest, but already thoroughly frustrated, Quent swung his glare to silence her, before answering the tutor. "*Never* let him bring you down to his level. You are the authority in this room. Unless you descend to corporal punishment, which we won't allow, you have the right to demand obedience at all times. And the authority to enforce it. Use your wits, man. Think like a boy but don't behave like one. He can learn to lead after he's learned to obey."

The tutor shoved his glasses up his nose and watched as Quent let up his boot and Kit attempted to push up on his skinny arms. "He needs to be challenged physically as well as intellectually?"

"That's a start." Quent turned back to Bell. "Exactly how primitive are the conditions here?"

She gestured with despair. "The flues don't draw, the plumbing is inadequate, the rodent problem is horrendous. The schoolroom must have been abandoned in the middle ages, as was the kitchen. If you want to spit your cow, we have the equipment. A delicate cream sauce and a good yeast roll, however, are beyond our capacity. I am having difficulty hiring anyone decent willing to work in this ruin."

Narrowing his eyes, Quent turned back to the tutor. "Make a list of what the schoolroom needs to bring it up to standards. I'll not inflict society with any more drunken Irish earls if we can prevent it. He needs discipline and education. If you can't provide it, we will find someone else."

"Yes, my lord. I've already started a list. Shall I mention the flues and plumbing or if the lady is already aware of the problem..."

"Major improvements will take time," Quent said curtly, "but we're aware of the problems. Just tell us what books and so forth are needed. And keep his lordship occupied in the meantime." He hesitated and glanced at the cracked plaster ceiling. "We used to fill bags with barley and hang them from the rafters to pummel. That would probably bring down the roof here. Have the stable hands put something together in the barn. He can learn how to box."

Bell gasped, but Quent caught her elbow and dragged her from the room, pocketing the crude key while he was at it. It probably locked every door up here.

He hurried her toward the stairs, occasionally flinging open panels to see what hid behind them.

"You are being arrogant and obnoxious," she protested.

"Some of my better qualities," he admitted, finding nothing but moldering draperies and child-sized beds and servants' quarters. Nothing good enough for ravishing Bell. "Thinking on my feet is another one. Bringing the lad here was an excellent idea. Pity the place is a cesspool."

"This is *your* family's estate," she protested. "I am not responsible for its condition."

"Understood. My father despises all things English and won't waste an eye-blink on this place. He collects the rents and lets it rot. Edward did the same, mostly because he didn't grow up here and despised the country."

They reached the front stairs, and he tested the walls. "Sound structure, though. Just needs improvements."

"A fortune's worth," she said in exasperation. "I was hoping to keep my siblings reined in for a while, until I could civilize them a little. My townhouse is simply too busy and too small, as you said. But punching bags in a barn..." She apparently didn't have the words to express her horror.

"Better than tying up tutors. I was thinking Syd and Kit belonged in school instead of the city, but this way, we can bring school to them." The stairs were just wide enough for the two of them to walk side by side, so Quent continued to hold her arm.

He needed to feel her delicious curves next to him while he pondered the next step. Just smelling her enticing perfume encouraged him to stay the course. He required all the incentive she could provide to deal with the idea of setting up his own nursery with Bell's hellion brother in it.

"They'll still need school," she argued. "I simply wanted them to go in with a little experience first. I don't want them labeled as

American oddities and bullied. Not that I think anyone could bully Kit," she added with a sigh.

"No, I rather think your siblings would lead revolts and end up expelled, but I take your point. They need the knowledge to fit in, if they want, and right now, they don't, like my sisters when they're in London." Quent started opening doors on the next level down, until he heard the girls. He hurried Bell past that chamber.

"Your sisters are gems," she argued. "Any sensible gentleman should see their value. But yes, they are independent thinkers. I don't intend to change that!"

She stopped and held out her hand. "The key, please."

Knowing these ancient locks were easily picked, Quent surrendered the bit of metal with a questioning look.

She locked the door they stood beside, pocketed the key, and sailed off down the corridor toward the front stairs. "You haven't agreed to my terms yet. Until you do, you will have to sleep elsewhere."

Well, at least he now knew which chamber was hers. Quent grinned at the challenge. Apparently, he didn't want an *easy* woman.

LORD QUENTIN Damnable Hoyt left Bell in such irrational humor that she didn't know whether to fling the candlestick in her hand or polish it. She'd never done either. Well, perhaps she might have done when she was a child, except the candlestick would have been pewter, at very best.

He'd meant to carry her off and ravish her!

And then, he hadn't.

She rubbed the rag over the silver in frustration and tried to decide if she was disappointed or not but couldn't. She'd never been so unreasonable in her life. She'd always known just exactly what she wanted and gone after it.

She'd never had the tables turned and been relentlessly pursued, though, unless one counted the absurd duel a couple of penniless bachelors had fought over her after she'd first been widowed. She'd quit flirting after that. Like all the others, the duelists had had more interest in Edward's wealth than her. Quent, on the other hand... was a complex man with complex goals.

Quent was a man who knew how to handle Kit.

Her ridiculous, absurd, irrational heart wanted that man, a man who cared enough about children to see they were taught well and raised properly. As a child, she'd longed for an adult to step up and take charge and ease some of the responsibility from her small shoulders. No man ever had—unless there was something in it for him.

That's where her reasoning bogged down. Even her father's family…

She shook off that unpleasant memory. Uncle Jim and his family had nagged at the back of her mind ever since the children's return. She could only hope they'd continue to leave her alone, but Summerby still hadn't reported back on the horses. She'd thought she'd succeeded in suffocating the dreamy adolescent inside her—but the child still longed for her horse. Dratted tears lined her eyes at all the years she'd unwittingly left Dream to her lazy uncle's neglect.

She shook off what couldn't be changed. Experience had taught her that everyone wanted to take. Very few wanted to give—not even when all she asked was a little love or kindness or simple understanding.

She slapped the gleaming candlestick on the table. Her protégées had appreciated what she'd done for them, even when she'd hidden the source of their financial good fortune under the pretense that miserly Edward had actually remembered them in his will. They'd enjoyed her hospitality and her introduction to society. So she wasn't a total failure or totally unlikable. She had friends. She didn't need more.

Yes, she did. She wanted love, like some moon calf adolescent.

Unwanted tears returned to her eyes, and she hurried down to the kitchen to avoid thinking about lonely nights and empty days. She had her family now. Really, she didn't need more—unless the marquess won and took them away.

Reaching the cold stone floor of the cellar kitchen, she nearly tripped over a man-sized mountain. She blinked in disbelief at Quent's long frame sprawled across the stones while he examined the kitchen chimney. Even the old country cook she'd hired had protested the poor draft in this horrid hall. Bell had sent out word for a sweep, but she worried the chimney would crumble once centuries of soot was removed.

"More birds' nests," Quent called from his position on the filthy hearth.

"Add them to the soup we were having for supper," she said acidly, kicking his boot sole. "The kitchen staff are standing about, waiting to prepare our meal. What are you still doing here?"

"Taking charge." He scooted out of the fireplace, leaving a trail of ash. His face and traveling clothes were blackened, with the whites of his eyes and teeth a striking contrast to his begrimed face. "Someone needs to."

She kicked his boot again. "I've hired as many good people as I can find. It's not as if I can turn the place around in a few days. And you're enjoying yourself entirely too much." She added that last because his grin didn't diminish. He really *was* enjoying himself— fastidious, dignified Quentin Hoyt liked playing in dirt.

The staff very properly looked appalled as he dusted himself off. Quent made no apology. He merely pointed at one of the young boys standing around. "Take a broom up there. No more fires until the nests are cleaned out. We'll have to have a cold supper."

Bell glared and pointed at the back door. "Leave that way and wash. I'll have someone bring you clean clothes. Then be on your way." She turned to the cook. "Have the staff use the old linens that Lady Sydony gathered to cover everything thoroughly before anyone attempts to clean nests."

The cook looked relieved and sent a scullery maid running to find the housekeeper.

Quent shrugged. "I can fix things. I didn't say I'd keep them clean." He trailed a cloud of dust out the back door.

She couldn't fix things *or* keep them clean. But she knew how to tell others to do it.

Twenty-eight years on earth, and all she was good for was ordering people about.

She couldn't order Quent about. She didn't know how she felt about that.

Sixteen

THE GROOM IN the stable eyed Quent askance when he appeared in all his sooty glory, but the stoic man pointed out the well and pump and the barrel the stable boys used for a cold shower. Quent admired their ingenuity as the water sluiced over him. Even though the skies had clouded over and started to mist, the August heat was still oppressive. Besides, the shower was just the thing to cool off his ardor.

He needed to strip Bell down to her bare self as she had done to him, he decided. But he had to do it in a way she enjoyed. He whistled happily as he scrubbed his face.

He ought to feel guilty for not raising the cash for his father's roof. His family shouldn't suffer for his father's sins. But if Quent was forced to choose sides, he would choose Bell, he had to admit. He hoped it wouldn't come to that, but for now, he ignored the castle roof.

Besides, the Hall needed work too. He could feel the coins trickling from his pockets—and he still whistled. Chasing after Bell was even more interesting than steam engines, although considerably less profitable.

A footman—thoughtfully provided by Bell, he assumed—carried his valise into the stable. Once dressed, Quent refilled the water barrel so the men could enjoy it at the end of a weary day.

Undeterred by Bell's admonition that he remove himself from the house, he talked to the groom, examined the new horses Bell had bought for her siblings, and determined that this part of the estate was almost in decent order. Stables were simple in comparison to houses. Feed could be bought, hands could be hired. The roof could be repaired, but a little rain wouldn't harm a dirt floor in the meantime.

Wickedly, he gave permission for the head groom to hire a roofer and buy canvas to protect the feed. He'd been slow to realize the leverage he could employ if Bell truly wanted to redeem the family manse. The estate belonged to his family. He had a *responsibility* to aid with the repairs. He added another negotiating point to his side of the ledger.

His pursuit of Bell damned well surpassed his father's demands. Choosing his own path instead of his family's for a change felt good, as if a small planet had been lifted from his shoulders. He could almost taste freedom.

He'd never realized he'd felt like a beast of burden until he'd shaken off part of the load. Rebellion had its positive sides. What could his father do—cut off his non-existent inheritance?

Well, the old man could take him to court over the guardianship, but a lot could happen in years of fighting. He'd take his chances. He'd made his fortune by taking calculated risks.

Knowing the servants wouldn't lock the doors until dark, Quent entered the side door of the house without knocking. Now that he knew where Bell's chamber was, he could find his own. He slung the hand with his valise over his shoulder and began exploring.

The house had two enormous wings off the main medieval hall. Bell had apparently chosen the east one for her family. He remembered from a brief visit last spring that there had been several decent chambers along this corridor. Apparently his ancestors had updated this wing at a later period than Fitz's, because the warren of rooms on this floor didn't interconnect so usefully. He couldn't find a side entrance into Bell's chamber.

Syd materialized while Quent was examining a large tester bed in a chamber next to Bell's.

"Are you moving in?" she asked with adolescent curiosity.

"No, Bell tossed me out. Says she's not ready for company yet." He deliberately confused her. He hadn't quite forgiven either of the two conniving females for tricking him into that embarrassing incident at Wyckersham.

"Is it proper for people who are only betrothed to live together?" she asked.

Well, hell, now he had to give lessons in etiquette and morality. He could see Bell's difficulty. "Generally not, no."

He'd had to arrange with the duke of Fortham to send Camilla away before her tart tongue cut a swath through London. Quent was fairly confident that Bell's respectability would win over Camilla's crassness, but he saw no reason for gossip to tarnish his intended.

Of course, marriage to an untitled tradesman would reduce her status. She hadn't used that as a negotiating point, so he assumed that didn't cause her concern—another reason why Bell was perfect for him.

"But Bell is a wealthy widow and well established in society and she has you and your aunt for chaperones," he continued. "She doesn't have the same limitations as a young girl. And someone should look after her," he added righteously.

"Bell has always taken care of herself," Syd protested, not falling for his argument. "And now she has us to take care of her. Why did she throw you out?"

He had sisters. He knew how their minds worked. Mostly, he ignored them, or he'd never get anything done. But the only goal he wanted to accomplish right now was Bell's hand in marriage. Toward that end, it was probably best to enlist her sisters.

"Bell thinks I'm after her money. She thinks I'll interfere in how she wishes to spend it. So we're currently a little at odds." And not just over money, but the girls didn't need details. He distracted her with a question of his own. "Do you know why she doesn't ride anymore?"

Syd shrugged. "She used to ride astride like a man and race Daddy's horses. I don't know why she won't even go out with us any longer. Maybe we're too boring."

Quent kept his passive face on, but this nugget jolted him. He'd known she'd had a hard life in Ireland, but he'd never really looked into the extent of her poverty. He'd merely ascertained that her father had a title and an estate, and her mother's family came from a distinguished line of Irish titles, even if most of them were Catholic, poor, and powerless.

Why would an earl's daughter—a lady who appeared to be grace personified—race horses like a hoyden? The thought appalled and intrigued him.

Had she been that rebellious—or had she needed to win the prize?

"Perhaps she was thrown once," Quent said, to divert any suspicion.

"Maybe," Syd said doubtfully. "Are you staying for dinner?"

"If Bell doesn't heave anything at me. Tell her you want to learn sailing, and I'll offer my yacht. Perhaps that will persuade her to let me stay."

Predictably, Syd lit up like a sunbeam. "Oh, that would be prodigious fun! I'll tell Tess."

She ran off in excitement. Quent hoped he damned well knew what he was doing because he didn't want to make an enemy of the woman he wanted for wife. Just because there were a hundred practical reasons they should marry didn't mean he didn't need her just for herself.

After just one night, he was in great danger of needing her in his bed, the way he needed air to breathe. He'd once felt that way about yachting and making money. Did that make him fickle or just too demanding?

~~~

BELL HAD YET to establish a good household routine in the aging family manse. When it came to dining, one room was as bad as another. She needed a raft of money and servants to put this place together as it should be, but she was oddly content to let her family shape the routine.

She followed the sound of her sisters' voices when it was time for the evening meal. Before she even entered the small breakfast parlor, their excited chatter warned that Quent had not left as she'd commanded. Not that she'd actually expected him to do so. He had a hide as thick as old leather.

She had to pinch the bridge of her nose to keep her eyebrows from flying off her face when she discovered her sisters and Quent tying knots with the old gold braid Kit had used to confine his tutor.

One of her well-trained footmen offered Bell a glass of her favorite sherry. She knew there was a reason she'd brought the servants, even if it wasn't for cleaning rafters. She took a sip before speaking a word. She didn't have to. Syd explained without asking.

"We are learning knots so we may go yachting on the river," she announced excitedly. "Isn't that absolutely famous?"

"Who's been teaching her to talk like that?" Bell wondered aloud, not offering her opinion on yachting—because she had none. She'd never sailed except for the wretched experience of crossing the Irish Sea after she'd married Edward. It was not an experience she longed to repeat.

"Mr. Penrose," Tess said, frowning worriedly. "Is his language not proper?"

"Cant seldom is, but I suppose that's mild enough. Why would one wish to tie knots for sailing? Isn't that what sailors are for?" Bell wondered if dealing with family caused an excess of nerves, thus bringing out her father's need for strong drink.

She set her sherry aside and tried to exhibit interest, but Quent's big body filled the small parlor. She was uncomfortably aware of him.

"For the joy of accomplishment," Quent said. "Here, I'll show you."

Bell studied the elaborate pattern he showed her with the gold braid and tried not to think about those long, capable fingers caressing her breasts. She picked up the sherry again.

"It's like learning to saddle your own horse," he added when she showed no interest in trying the knot. "One should know the sport from the ground up."

That made more sense, and she nodded agreement. Before she could speak, however, another footman arrived in the doorway.

"Mr. Acton Penrose and Mr. Carlyle Summerby have arrived, my lady," he intoned in disapproval.

Apparently neither man had presented his card, and their arrival time had warranted the city servant's disdain.

"Show them in, Vickers, and bring them a brandy. They must have had a hard ride out here." Bell turned questioningly to Quent.

He shrugged. "I told Penrose to follow with my horse if he wished. Perhaps Summerby sought me out for some reason, and they joined forces."

Summerby entered protesting. Apparently the earlier mist had turned to rain. Both men were damp and still wearing boots. Bell didn't think she'd ever seen her portly solicitor wearing boots. She hadn't known he could ride.

"My lady, I did not mean to intrude upon your dinner hour," Summerby said, attempting to right his damp coat and maintain decorum. "I can wait in an anteroom until you have a moment to spare."

Bell smiled at his ruffled dignity. She wielded her title and position to good effect when needed, but not with people she liked. "This entire house is an anteroom, Mr. Summerby. Until we have furniture that does not collapse when sat upon, we must be informal. The two of you shall join us for dinner. Vickers, please take our guests to dry chambers and let them freshen up and tell Cook we will be slightly delayed."

She tried to remain serene and perform her duty as the perfect hostess, but inside, she was panicking. Summerby would never ride out here unless the matter was urgent. He would have sent a messenger.

Quent looked as if he'd rather follow his aide out of the room, but he continued entertaining the girls. Bell wanted to be resentful of his presence, but instead, she was grateful to have someone she could rely on in case the news was bad.

Which was completely foolish because if the marquess was demanding delivery of his wards, Quent had no choice except to do so—unless Bell agreed to marry him.

In his own oblivious masculine way, that was what Quent was trying to protect her from by offering marriage. She had to accept that he was on her side.

It was very hard to do. In twenty-eight years of living, no man had ever been on her side before, unless she paid him. She kept waiting for Quent's real reason for being here to emerge.

The girls chattered through dinner, thrilled to have male company on whom to work their wiles. Bell attempted to steer the conversation in adult directions when she could. Quent was his usual taciturn self, joining in when business was mentioned, ignoring gossip. Bell sensed he, too, was worried about the abrupt appearance of their guests.

She wasn't about to let him receive the news before she did. After dinner was cleared away, she rose. "Gentlemen, in respect for the long ride our guests have made, I think we shall forego the usual brandy and cigars over the table. Syd, Tess, you'll need to entertain yourselves while Mr. Summerby and I adjourn to talk business. I assume Lord Quentin and Mr. Penrose have matters to discuss as well."

Her sisters frowned worriedly but obediently departed.

Quentin looked mulish. "If Summerby's news involves my family, I suggest that we all adjourn together. I don't need brandy and cigars."

Bell raised a questioning eyebrow at her solicitor. Summerby nervously toyed with his napkin—which indicated that Quent had guessed right. This involved the marquess.

Penrose confirmed her supposition. "The problem involves the Hoyt family as guardians. I think Lord Quentin's opinion would be useful, if you don't mind."

Bell resented her solicitor's nod of relief but grudgingly accepted it—for now. Men were strange creatures who feared a woman's reactions. They found safety in numbers, apparently. She ought to be cheered that it took three of them to deal with one of her.

She led the way to the library, wrinkling her nose in distaste at the musty air. She noticed with approval that the new staff had at least dusted out the cobwebs.

She eyed the array of cracked leather and worn upholstery and chose a wing chair near the cold fireplace, leaving the men to test the rest of the furniture. Quent, naturally, took a large leather chair and dragged it across from her. A footman set up a table with the brandy decanter near him. Penrose and Summerby carried smaller wooden chairs over to join them.

"Odd as it may seem, I did not think to acquire cigars," Bell said wryly. "May I now ask to what I owe the honor of your presence?"

Summerby clasped his hands nervously. More assured of his place, Penrose spoke for him.

"We've both had visits from a most... you will pardon my expression, my lady... obnoxious creature who claims to work for your family."

Belt felt the blood drain from her face. "*My* family?" She took a deep breath and acknowledged the possibility, although she hadn't heard from any of them since her marriage. "Since my mother was orphaned young, I suppose you mean my father's family. Did he give a name?"

Apparently now that the ice had been broken, Summerby recovered his poise. "He gave his name as Hiram Kennedy, and said he worked for the Earl of Wexford."

Bell almost spit out the sherry she'd been sipping. Recovering, she dabbed a handkerchief to her lips. "Hiram? *Hiram?* He used to be my father's stable boy. Does he claim to work for the dead then?"

"No, my lady." Summerby twisted his brandy snifter awkwardly. "If you will remember, you asked me to make inquiries. I sent an agent to do so. I fear he exceeded his boundaries and imparted information—"

Penrose interrupted. "Wexford's family had to be told he was dead. They would have learned it sooner or later since the marquess has sent inquiries to establish the extent of the estate. As the boy's guardian, it's Belden's duty to establish the condition of the lands the earl has inherited. Your agent wasn't at fault."

Bell had the sinking sensation she knew where this was headed. She refused to look at Quent, who had yet to say anything. She admired the way he waited until he had the facts before offering an opinion. "Go on, please, Mr. Summerby. What brilliant bit of blackmail has my uncle chosen?"

Summerby relaxed a modicum at her understanding. "I gather from my agent that your uncle's wife has taken to calling herself countess. My agent merely made inquiries into the object you sent us to retrieve. He assures me he made no reference to you or the children, merely asked after—" He tugged at his cravat and glanced toward Quent.

Bell grimaced. "It's all right, Lord Quentin is family. Quent, I asked Summerby to inquire into a mare of mine I had just learned wasn't sent to America with my father. I thought perhaps I could acquire her or her foals for Fitz."

She'd thought no such thing. She'd simply reacted with joy, terror, and panic, and this was the result. Dispassion and logic were far safer than overwhelming emotional reactions. One would think she'd have learned by now.

But they had Little Dream! She couldn't abandon her first love to her uncle's crude care. It was killing her that the mare may have been neglected... just as she and her sisters had been. She took a deep breath and blocked out what couldn't be changed.

She ought to be furious that the Scots marquess had poked his nose in where it didn't belong, but she was too accustomed to the high-handed methods of Beldens. And she could scarcely blame anyone for her father's relations being a pack of scoundrels.

Quent nodded and continued to wait without playing his hand— so very different from the quarrelsome men of her family. His composure helped maintain hers at times like this.

Summerby sipped his brandy and gathered his thoughts. "My informant tells me the mare lives, although it's malnourished and poorly treated. According to my sources, your uncle was unable to provide proof of ownership or the mare's breeding, so he couldn't sell her or the foals outright. The stallion she produced is a good prize winner, but the stud fees are minimal without the proper papers."

"And my uncle, him being the lazy sot he is, did not attempt to write me or mine, or even forge the papers, like any man with half a wit might have. He simply did what he's always done, racing the ponies and letting heads roll as they may." Bell bit her tongue. Her accent deteriorated when she was angry. And she was exceedingly angry despite her deceptively quiet tone. To mistreat an animal as brilliant and sensitive as Little Dream— It did not bear thinking on.

"What has this to do with the obnoxious personage?" Quent asked, sipping his brandy with every appearance of calm, although with Quent, it was hard to tell calm from furious.

He'd carried her through the house today as if she were a stuffed toy and had seemed to enjoy it. The man was dangerously volatile beneath that deceptive exterior.

"Lady Belden's aunt apparently made inquiries after we asked after the mare," Summerby explained. "At first, she was eager to sell. Once she learned of the earl's passing, she rejected the offer. She now insists she will only surrender the animals if her husband's claim to the title is uncontested. My agent assured her that was impossible. He left, giving her my address in case she changed her mind. The obnoxious Mr. Kennedy arrived soon after my agent presented his report to me. Mr. Kennedy repeated the... lady's... demands and apparently sought additional information on the children, which we did not provide, but we thought you should be warned."

Bell frowned in perplexity. She couldn't imagine Uncle Jim going out of his way to find someone to bully. What would be his purpose in sending Hiram to make inquiries? "I didn't even know Uncle Jim had married. Does he have children, perchance?"

Summerby made an expression of distaste. "Several children live in the house. One assumes they are his."

"And the name of this pristine example of motherhood and aristocracy calling herself countess before my father was even laid in his grave?" Bell asked.

"Mary Dolores O'Malley Boyle is all I know, my lady." Summerby looked hopeful, as if there might be some possibility that Jim had married someone important.

Bell knew better, and it took all her strength not to laugh hysterically. "My father's former doxy," she admitted.

And the whore had her hands on Little Dream and her offspring.

How did one hire an assassin?

Seventeen

"THIS IS THE reason I never married," Quent complained to Penrose, pacing the chamber he'd taken next to Bell's. "Women become embroiled in the most unreasonable tangles, and then they do even more inane things in ridiculous attempts to become unentangled."

"You never married because you wanted Bell and didn't have time or patience to court anyone else," Penrose countered rudely, studying the peeling wallpaper with fascination. He tore a strip and peered under it.

"It's a damned good thing you're more friend than aide or I'd give you your walking papers." Quent started to drop into a chair, then remembered the earlier debacle with the broken leg. He'd picked a chamber based on its closeness to Bell's, not the amenities. He tested the moldering upholstery before settling his weight into it. "Bell checks on her family for the first time in ten years because of a doddering old mare?"

"I heard the story on the way down here. Summerby is being excessively polite. By all accounts, the uncle has a reputation for brutalizing animal and people. Lady Bell has no reason to be fond of him, and she has every reason to be fond of the horse." Penrose warily took a seat at a desk with delicate legs and searched futilely for pens or paper.

Giving up, he dug his traveling desk from his baggage. "Her father's estate was entailed. It would never go to Bell but presumably to the uncle—if he can prove his parentage and legitimacy. She didn't have much reason to care what happened to the land. Since her father took her horses with him, she had no connection left to her home— probably Edward's intent. If Bell sent Summerby hunting for an animal that could be of little value now, it was clearly a much beloved pet."

"Thoroughbreds as pets! I hadn't thought Bell the sentimental sort." Which was the reason he was sitting here growling instead of heading for his yacht and Ireland.

He had to figure out what the devil he was getting into. He had never suspected the lady of being the maudlin sort—who would want children and pets and... family. Blast and bother, he hadn't been thinking at all except in terms of the lady's bed and the best way of negotiating himself into it.

"How many sisters do you have?" Penrose asked, driving the nail home.

"Six too many," he grumbled. "But they're not the sentimental sort. They don't treat their horses and hounds as *pets*. They're for hunting." Quent gave that a second thought. "Well, they won't allow the hounds to be put out at night, so maybe that makes them guard dogs."

"No cats?" Penrose asked innocently. "No favorite sheep?"

Quent pinched the bridge of his nose. "It's a moldering great castle. We used to live with the cattle not that long ago. I thought I'd escaped all that."

"You want a woman who dislikes animals and children then," Penrose said helpfully, again making his point. "I'll fetch Fitz's list. In the meantime, what do you intend to do about the obnoxious former stable boy and the doxy?"

Quent peeked warily from beneath the hand he was resting his head on. "Bell won't get sentimental over the pair if I have them spit and roasted?"

"That's between you and the lady. She may enjoy the thought of seeing you hanged." Penrose shrugged, obviously enjoying his predicament. "I should think a good magistrate and your father's name ought to pry the mare loose if the lady has some documentation of ownership, but spitting and roasting may be more satisfying."

"Courtship is a damned obstacle to accomplishing any business. I should be in Lancashire, investigating that steam engine." Quent straightened his legs and glared at his boot toes. "Remind me why I'm doing this."

"Because you're bored, making money isn't a challenge any longer, and you want in the lady's bed," Penrose recited promptly.

London was full of fair ladies. They all came with strings attached. Bell was the only one worth being tied in knots for, Quent realized glumly, transferring his glare to the gold braid he'd removed from Kit's depredations.

"I can't be in two places at once," Quent concluded. "My instinct says sail to Ireland and thrash the louts and come back with the mare, but my yacht isn't built for hauling cattle."

"A twelve or thirteen-year-old horse, or older, isn't worth the effort," Penrose agreed. "Stay here and go after the lady and let your minions take care of the spitting and roasting."

Quent tented his fingers and rested his chin on them. "You're looking at only the one small problem. The larger one is that Kit has a usurper sitting on his estate, one who apparently doesn't have his best interests in mind. We need Nick and his ship, and quite possibly whips and chains, to restore authority."

His aide's eyes gleamed with interest. "Atherton is back in the country, terrorizing Brighton at the moment. He and his bride are preparing to leave for Amsterdam on some diplomatic mission, but he's momentarily at loose ends. He'd enjoy threatening a few villains."

"What better man to send to terrorize a villain than a pirate?" Quent asked in satisfaction. "The heavens smile upon us. Do we have enough information to send him off to retrieve the lady's pet or do we need anything else?"

"Ask the lady about papers first. Nick is trying to be legal these days. He would prefer proper reclamation of the lady's property to actual abduction. Otherwise, we have everything else we need. I can go with him, if that helps."

Quent considered the offer. "Let me think on it. If I'm to pry Kit's guardianship out of my father's grasping fingers, I need leverage. This *is* more interesting than making money." Oddly, what he felt was anticipation more than dismay at discovering Bell had hidden facets to explore.

"Go find your own chamber," he told Penrose. "I'd advise looking on this floor and not the next where the tyrant dwells, unless you wish to wake up tied to your bed."

Penrose rolled his eyes. "And you're so besotted you haven't considered tying the brat to his own bed? I might as well hand in my resignation now. Good luck with whatever plot you're hatching."

He gathered his traveling desk and valise and departed—no doubt to ascertain where the girls were housed. Quent had no objection to marrying off one of Bell's sisters to a fine man. It saved the expense of a presentation. Bell might have other ideas—which was a great part of their problem.

Bell would not be the sort of wife who obediently followed his wishes. She'd defied him since the day they'd met. He had to start the foundation of dealing with what could become a life-long battle.

BELL SENT her maid off for a well-deserved rest, then sat at her vanity and brushed her hair, expectantly watching the door reflected in her mirror.

She wasn't disappointed. The latch turned, then rattled. Stupid man, thinking she would leave it unlocked. She'd made certain to claim a room with no other entrance, not even a maid's antechamber. And she had the key.

He scratched discreetly on the panel. She ignored him and braided her hair.

She trusted that Quent wouldn't shout at her with the girls sleeping just down the corridor. Summerby and Penrose were there, as well, since she'd had the servants find linens for their chambers.

She rolled her eyes at her reflection when he rattled something metal in the ancient lock and the tumblers fell. The same key unlocked all the doors, she assumed. If so, there would be more than one key. Or he'd picked the lock.

"Not invited, Mr. Hoyt," she admonished when he entered and closed the door behind him.

He leaned against the heavy panel, crossed his dauntingly muscled arms over his shirt, and watched her with admiration. A heavy hank of black hair fell messily over his brow. "If I waited for you to invite me, I'd die an old and lonely man. Or did you wish me to consider Lady Grace for my bed?" He named another of the available spinsters on his list.

He reminded Bell of that huge black Friesian he rode, all muscle and strength and sturdiness. Fortunately, the animal had been gelded—because stallions were damned dangerous.

She rose from the vanity and sauntered toward him, watching his gaze drift from her face downward. She wore only a diaphanous gown—because she was a self-destructive lackwit. "Lady Grace would spend your money on her charities and you would have to share her with Lady Charlotte."

She'd caught him by surprise with that, she could tell. He really did not pay proper heed to society gossip. Bell caressed his shirt, just barely skimming the heated hardness beneath. That apparently surprised him even more.

He caught his breath, then reached for her. "I suppose that would keep her occupied and out of my hair," he acknowledged.

She stepped back. "If uninvolvement is what you wish, then I'm not what you want. My life grows ever more complicated. Go home, Quent."

He crossed his arms again. "I don't wish to be *involved* with Lady Grace. You, on the other hand, require firsthand engagement."

She slid her palm approvingly beneath the open neck of his linen.

"Yes, I think I would like that." She grasped his hands, uncrossed his arms, and placed his fingers on her breasts. "Definitely, hand engaged."

To Edward's dismay, she had never been shy or even reserved. Quent, however, didn't seem to have any objections to her forwardness. Those long fingers she'd admired earlier cupped and caressed and aroused most deliciously.

"Not just once a week," he murmured, referring to the notorious settlement letter. He leaned over to kiss her cheek. "That is not negotiable."

His big body drew her as lodestone drew iron, which was why she'd added that clause, hoping to keep some distance between them. She tried to push away, but his lips were tracing swirls of desire down her throat.

"We are not foolish adolescents. We can restrain ourselves," she protested. "I don't wish to pretend we have a love match. This is merely lust."

"Not negotiable," he repeated, before kissing her to prevent further dispute.

She forgot the argument when he crushed her in those big arms and tantalized her with caresses. She'd never known a man could be so gentle, and so arousing. Her pulse raced. She stood on her toes and returned his kisses, plying them along his freshly-shaven throat, nibbling at his ear, until he leaned against the door for support.

She loved that she could have that effect on this arrogant man. "Separate residences then," she countered wickedly, shoving his shirt off one shoulder and tweaking his nipples.

"Right. You can have my sisters, your sisters, and Kit. I'll keep Penrose." He lifted her from the floor and carried her to the bed. "You get the screaming babes."

"Tess will marry and take Beebee with her," she said with regret, refusing to go further than the edge of the bed. She wrapped her legs around his hips and tugged his long shirt from his breeches.

"You're not too old to have your own. You could already be breeding." He unfastened the placket of his trousers. "One of the few advantages of marriage is that I needn't take care any longer."

She snorted rudely and rubbed the bulge behind his buttons. "You plow an infertile field. I do not marry for babes. If an heir is your desire, try the Widow Willington. She has a tribe at the age of twenty-five."

"My family is tribe enough. One old man is not the test of your fertility." He slid her gown up to her waist and rubbed her where she ached. "But I won't object to testing it regularly."

Just the talk of planting a child where there had never been one made her contrary body water. She didn't want to love again, not horses, not children, and certainly not a man. But one night of lovemaking hadn't been enough. She wanted what Quent had to offer again. With his buttons undone, he sprang free and eager, and she drew a sharp breath at the powerful sight of his aroused masculinity.

She tightened her legs around his hips and drew him closer, tired of the silly argument.

Quent disobediently dropped to his knees and held her thighs apart with his big hands. And then he lapped her with his tongue.

Bell shrieked. She grabbed his hair and tried to tug him away. He refused. And then she was utterly lost to a tidal wave of pleasure. She fell back against the mattress, weeping and rocking with the tremors he induced with just his tongue.

When she was limp and lost and confused, he stood, parted her thighs further, and rammed his reproductive organ deep inside her.

"Every night," he murmured, leaning over to kiss her.

Bell was in no condition to argue. In moments, he had her quaking again, milking him with her muscles, causing him to rear like a stallion and roar as he poured his seed into her womb.

Perhaps a marriage bed might be worth considering with a man like Quent in it.

THUNDER still rolled in the distance when dawn arrived. Quent didn't let Bell escape his arms until he'd had his way one more time. To his utter amazement and delight, she was everything he'd ever dreamed of and more—a wild mare in heat, a lithe acrobat, a daring lover. The proud dowager marchioness she presented to the world disappeared in bed, thank all that was holy.

"I hadn't dared imagine your lovemaking could be this good," he admitted when he lay limp and momentarily sated in the gray light. "I feared you might be frigid and in need of lessons."

She relaxed against his shoulder, drawing the sheet over them in the early morning coolness. "I know how to be frigid. Don't test me."

"You know how to be *angry*. That isn't the same. Let's practice dealing with anger. I'm sending Nick to Ireland to bring back your mare. Do you have any legal papers on it so he can pretend he's not a pirate?"

She yanked his chest hair and sat up, taking the sheet with her. "I saw them in my father's box. I did wonder why they were there but hadn't thought..." She swung her legs from the bed. "But you cannot simply take over my life. It's my mare, my uncle, *my* problem."

He hid his grin at her predictable response. "You can cede the mare to me in the marriage settlements. Unfortunately, you cannot cede your uncle."

Quent sat up, rubbed his stubbly jaw, and grimaced at the lack of pitcher filled with warm water. "I'll have to send for my carriage and valet if you mean to stay here. We can send Summerby for the papers at the same time."

Bell stirred the banked coals and added more fuel to raise the flames. Most of the fireplaces here had iron arms to hang kettles over. She swung the iron over the coals to heat the water the maids had carried up last night. "You are growing soft, Hoyt, if you cannot heat your own water."

Since she was delectably naked, his brain didn't register a word she'd said. Bell's waist was slender, but her hips were made for birthing babes and her bosom was ripe for feeding them. He'd never considered adding to his already ample family, but he suddenly had a possessive desire to know he'd planted his seed.

His father could take care of his own damned family. Quent wanted to start his own, to watch Bell swell with *his* child.

He was growing soft in the head, but not in other parts south. There would be children. Instead of rearing back in panic, he decided that was one more negotiating point in his favor.

Striding across the room to where Bell bent over the fire, he covered her breasts with his palms, and thrust his arousal between her legs from behind. Just to remind her that he wasn't a gelding, he nipped her shoulder as he lifted her onto him.

She cried out, writhed, and then gave him the ride of his life while the rain unleashed torrents outside.

"I'll send to have the banns read on Sunday," he said afterward, carrying her to the bed.

"Send all you like," she whispered sleepily, curling into the pillow. "I still won't let you have my money."

But this time, she didn't deny him her bed.

Eighteen

THE WIND and rain lashed and howled at the eaves, but Bell felt only a golden afterglow after Quent returned to his own chambers to dress. Still pleasantly sore from their vigorous lovemaking, Bell washed and strolled downstairs.

In the breakfast room, she discovered the entire household waiting for her— including the nursery set, the tutor, and Aunt Griselda, who never rose before noon.

"Roof's leaking. We couldn't leave anyone upstairs," Tess said in explanation.

"No, naturally not," Bell said faintly, attempting to adjust to this new routine. Even growing up, she'd grabbed food from the kitchen and ran. Dining *en famille* had never been part of her daily life.

She could be a *mother*. Could she put herself through that torment of hope again?

Kit was making sailboats of his toast in his hot chocolate. Beebee had been seated on a short foot stool on top of a broad chair and tied with a towel to the chair back to keep her from toppling. Spoons were beyond the infant's capability, apparently. She tossed bits of toast and eggs on the table, the floor, her lap...

Bell breathed deeply, and her frozen insides melted into warm and happy. She couldn't wait until orderly, proper Quent came down to see his reaction to chaos, family style. She helped herself to a cup of tea, removed a piece of toast from Beebee's fine golden curls, and returned a fork to Kit's hand when he attempted to imitate the toddler and use his fingers for the eggs.

"I apologize for the accommodations," she told Mr. Thomas, the tutor, and Aunt Griselda, who had insisted that as a mere companion, she ought to be housed on the third floor. "I'll have the staff find better chambers on the second floor until repairs are made. Perhaps the library might suit for a schoolroom. The beauty of starting a new household is that we can adapt everything to our needs and not adhere to tradition."

Bell had never thought such anarchy before, but she loved the notion now. Edward would have had a conniption fit if she'd changed one single piece of furniture. Now, she could gut the interior if she wished—Belden wouldn't know the difference, or care. She helped herself to tea and gazed out the tall windows, smiling even more broadly.

The rain had settled into a fine mist, leaving the grass and trees green and glistening like the hills of home. She was glad of the excuse to leave London and play house, but she wasn't in the habit of ignoring greater problems. Bell sipped her tea and pondered her next step.

She had no intention of being relegated to the position of ornament again. She would not let Quent take over her family's affairs.

As if summoned by her thought, he entered, dressed for travel in leather breeches and boots, with his dark stubble freshly shaved. Penrose was with him, but he was wearing country tweed and shoes. Interesting. Bell wondered what they'd planned without her. Not that she was any less guilty of planning without *them*.

"Good morning, gentlemen," she said smoothly, slipping into her seat at the head of the table. "What is appropriate yacht attire?" She was already wearing her travel gown.

Quent quirked an eyebrow and filled a plate from the buffet. "It's too muddy for the horses, but a good day for a sail. I thought I'd go into town and finish up some business."

"Similar minds and all that," Bell said airily. "I seem to have business as well. You won't mind if I travel with you, will you?"

He narrowed his eyes and set a plate of food down in front of her, as if this were a midnight buffet, and he was her courteous escort. "It's best if you stay here, out of sight, with the children."

Bell simply nodded thanks for the plate. She had no intention of eating if she was to go sailing.

"You promised to take us sailing," Syd reminded him. "I want to go, too."

Before Quent could object, Tess spoke up. "I think Beebee is coming down with a cold. I'd best stay here with her. But if you're going into town, perhaps someone could pick up the pelisses we ordered."

Bell smiled evilly at Quent over her teacup. He looked nonplussed by the various family demands. He was much too accustomed to his bachelor household, and her family wasn't as easily dismissed as his distant one.

"The water is likely to be a little too choppy for lessons," he said, filling his own plate and taking a seat at Bell's right hand—at the opposite end of the table from Kit. "I'll be traveling swiftly, in any case. We'll save the lesson for a sunny day."

Before Syd could offer another objection, Bell intervened. "Mr. Summerby might appreciate sailing with you. We can return his mount later."

"Actually, he rode mine," Penrose said, taking a seat at the center of the table, near Syd and Tess. "I rode Quent's gelding. I think Summerby would far prefer the yacht."

"Excellent. That's settled." Bell raised her teacup, and with a firm stare, dared Quent to object. "We can conduct our business on the journey. I think the girls have sufficient chaperonage and protection here. The only matter remaining is finding someone to repair the roof while we're gone."

"I can have that done," Penrose said without hesitation. "I acted as my family's steward until they sold the estate. I have a pretty good notion of costs."

Quent swallowed his coffee black, sat back, and frowned. "I'm leaving you here to act in my place, Penrose. You're to keep blackguards away from the family."

"Maybe I'll hire him as *my* steward," Bell said sweetly. Hiring servants and ordering a household about were accomplishments she had learned early on. "They're my family and not your responsibility."

"They're my father's wards," Quent countered. "Quit quibbling just because you can."

"Then don't quibble when I say I'm coming with you. This is what I've been trying to tell you— I am, at the very least, your *equal*, Hoyt. I am not a figurine to be set on the shelf until it's convenient for you to notice me."

He leered over his coffee cup. "Notice, I can do."

"Nice dodge," Penrose muttered, watching them with interest.

Bell ignored the male byplay. "Tess, I'll leave you in charge. You know where I keep coins if you need anything. I cannot promise I'll be back immediately. Help the housekeeper situate the children and the others to dry chambers. Tell her the new linens should be arriving shortly. Let the footmen answer doors. Mr. Penrose, don't allow strangers on the property, please. If you need help, both my grooms and my footmen know how to use firearms."

Tess and Syd stared at her. Bell shrugged. She didn't want to disillusion them about the disreputable elements of their family. Let them think she feared kidnappers on a general basis.

"Now that everyone is suitably terrified, including me, you had best have your maid pack bags. I might be gone for a while," Quent said grumpily.

"I am capable of returning anytime I like without your aid. I'm thinking of buying another carriage, and I know how to hire one," Bell said loftily.

She did, however, fret over what he had planned.

QUENT had wanted to catch the end of the turbulent storm winds and see what speed he could wring from his sleekly-designed ship, but his two passengers already looked a trifle green. Summerby was wrapped up in his redingote and just needed a muffler to complete the image of terrified hostler.

Bell, being Bell, carelessly wrapped an arm around a mast and strained to see the shore. She'd knotted her hem into a loop so the skirt didn't trip her up and wore a scarf around her hair and jaw, hiding her expression—not that she would allow anyone to see her distress. That she'd anchored herself to the mast instead of striding around, inspecting everything, told Quent all he needed to know of her fear.

With regret, he turned the wheel over to his first mate. Taking Bell's elbow, he pried her loose from the timber. "We can talk below."

Summerby willingly followed them out of the wind. The cabin was small. Quent had never meant it to be more than a place to escape the weather. He settled Bell on a cushioned bench and let Summerby take a seat across from her. Quent remained standing, lounging against the bulkhead.

He had no intention of discussing horse removal in front of a solicitor. Instead, he launched into the matter paramount in his mind. "I'll have the banns called *and* obtain a special license so we will be prepared to marry however you like and as soon as the settlements are signed. Summerby here can arrange it so what's yours will remain yours, but prohibiting me from investing your funds is foolish. I can advise you better than Summerby. I can probably increase your income faster than you're currently spending it."

Bell glared. "I am not a risk taker. You are. And it's not as simple as that. We have two separate townhouses, Belden Hall, Kit's estate, your father's monstrous castle, plus all the costs of our various families. It could take years to settle all our differences. I simply don't see the point in marriage. Tell your father that I can take care of my family just fine, if he'll leave them to me."

Quent hated reducing marriage to a quarrel over funds, but at least he understood the basis of her fear. He resented that she thought him no better than Edward, but she had no way of knowing differently.

If their problems were limited only to money, he knew he would ultimately win. But the obstacles between them were much more challenging. She had a place in society that she would have to give up if she married him. He had a bachelor life that he preferred. Each day, more subtle complications raised their ugly heads. She had a right to be afraid—he was terrified.

But he'd negotiated himself through worse predicaments. All he had to do was keep his damned obstinate father in line.

Quent braced his legs against the sway of the ship and met her glare without flinching. "You may declare yourself my equal, but all of Parliament and most of England would disagree. You cannot be named guardian. I can. And we can sell all the unentailed property and build a castle, if that's what you wish. I don't know how many more reassurances I need to give you."

"Perhaps, my lady," Summerby said pacifyingly, "you could let me speak directly with Lord Quentin's advisors, and the settlements can be drawn out without the emotional attachments. I'll give them your requests concerning expenditures, but we cannot resolve differences on who makes the decisions. I fear that's a problem all marriages face."

"I want a legal statement from Lord Belden that he will appoint Quent as guardian upon our marriage, and I want a statement from Quent agreeing to let me make decisions about my family's future," Bell said adamantly.

Quent hid his grin. He was finally turning the corner—she was admitting that she *might* marry him. The statement from his father... might take sabers and dirks.

"Then I'll have to insist on making all decisions for *my* family's future," Quent said silkily. "If my sisters want to throw themselves away on penniless suitors, I stand in my father's stead and can reject their offers."

"Don't be ridiculous. If they're good men—and your sisters would never choose otherwise—I'll simply fund them as I have my other protégées," Bell said belligerently.

He could tell the instant she realized she'd just agreed to dower his penniless sisters. She frowned and quite wonderfully shut up.

"Let's start there, Summerby," Quent told the solicitor. Taking a page from Bell's book on a silent ending to an argument, he refrained from crowing over his skills as a negotiator. "My lady, would you like a stroll about the deck now that you have your sea legs?"

She eyed him suspiciously but took his hand.

"I don't know if I qualify as having sea legs," she protested. "We are still only on the river, aren't we?"

Quent shrugged. "On a day like this, the river qualifies. Mostly, it's a matter of accepting that you can't bridle wind and water as one does a horse."

"But the sails do that, do they not?" she asked, emerging on the deck and looking about with more interest than earlier. "Ropes and canvas are a form of bridle?"

"And the rudder, yes, I suppose." Leaving the solicitor safely ensconced in the cabin, he found a spot where the wind didn't blow Bell's hair about as much and bluntly launched into the next argument. "I understand the horse is important to you, but you do agree that Kit's future is more important than a horse?"

"Of course," she said with irritation. "I simply don't intend to give in to the demands of a bully and a whore on either matter. I had no objection to my uncle living in that hovel and eking out a living as best as he could. He *is* family, after all. But I will not tolerate being threatened."

"We don't know that your uncle is the one doing the threatening, since his wife could have sent the stable hand to do her bidding without his knowledge. Women are capable of almost anything in the interest of their children. She presumably wants better for them than she had." Quent was merely testing Bell's knowledge of the people she'd left behind so he could arrange his plans to suit. He had no illusion that a woman demanding a title that wasn't hers had Bell's finer sensibilities.

Bell wrinkled her delicate nose. "I cannot imagine Dolly as anything other than self-centered. If she wants her children to advance in the world, it will be because she wants them to take care of her. But really, I need to talk to any of the remaining tenants. They can tell me more of Dream and her offspring then Dolly is likely to acknowledge. Da was daft but never mean. He left me Dream's papers. He wanted me to have my horse if she was still alive, if Edward ever relented. Jim can't keep her from me."

"He can if he hides her. And if you want the offspring as well, the matter grows more complicated." Quent concealed his alarm behind calm reasoning. He didn't want her traveling to Ireland and confronting dangerous relatives, but denying her would only make her more determined. "Nick is practicing to be a diplomat, and his wife is quite good. Let them assess the situation."

Despite her finely sculpted features, Bell managed to look mulish. "I want *all* Dream's offspring. Jim shouldn't be left with animals, much less people. We don't need drawn-out court battles. I can buy him off."

Quent's alarm escalated. He tamped it down behind cold logic. "Let Nick scout the territory first. Once we know how the ground lies, we can storm the castle. A little planning will clear the field and achieve everything you seek."

She continued scowling. "This isn't war. This is a usurper who needs his head removed."

"And you're not a medieval queen who can shout *Off with his head!* Besides, any queen who wanted to keep her own head didn't shout that unless she'd already planned and plotted and knew it was safe to do so. Admit that Nick is in a better position to go in as a stranger and do the planning for you." Quent loved the way her eyes shot fire as she considered his advice.

"I don't like it," she fretted. "I know these people. Nick doesn't. I want it ended once and for all. I want my horse back now. Any claim to Kit's title is spurious. Dolly simply wants to make trouble and money."

"I agree," he said reasonably. "But I think if we simply go about our normal business, pretending she and her bully don't exist, we'll drive them to commit more foolhardy escapades. We can call in the authorities once we have all the facts in hand."

Her scowl disappeared, and Quent almost shuddered in expectation.

"You're right! They'll come looking for me. *Then* I can cut off their heads," she said in bloodthirsty delight. "That makes sense, thank you. Let Nick find my horses. I'll take care of Dolly and her cohort."

Quent heroically refrained from bashing his head against the mast.

Nineteen

BELL CLUNG to her bloodthirsty vow to slay anyone who stood between her and her horse. The determination helped her stay composed while Quent assisted her into a rowboat to take them to shore near Whitehall. With her horse as her goal, she would take on hurricanes. A rickety little rowboat and filthy water wouldn't daunt her.

On shore, they parted ways with Mr. Summerby, who hurried off to his office in the city with his head undoubtedly spinning with all their instructions about the marriage settlements. Without asking what she wanted, Quent hired a carriage to take them to her townhouse in Mayfair.

The stomach-churning exhilaration of sailing combined with Quent's potent presence and her own fierce resolve succeeded in keeping Bell too off balance to protest. She didn't *want* Quent helping her. She didn't want to be dependent on his aid. But she liked having his competent assistance. She was a turmoil of confusion.

At home, Butler greeted them stoically, without complaining that she'd removed all his underlings to the country. Even though they'd left Aunt Griselda behind, Quent insisted on entering the house with her, and Bell couldn't find the wit to argue. He took Edward's chair in the study, which should have left her uncomfortable but didn't. More important matters had disrupted her orderly life, and she didn't have time to fret over chaperones and who sat in what chair.

How odd that small matters disappeared when confronted with life-changing events.

A decade ago she had lacked the confidence to believe she could overcome society's gossip. These days, she knew she could stare down any biddy daring to criticize her behavior—and They Would Wilt beneath her scorn.

She felt lighter discovering that freedom.

"Do you have anyone to send to Nick in Brighton?" Quent asked, removing pen and paper from the desk as if it were his.

Scanning through the notes and invitations that had arrived since she'd left, Bell held one up. "The Athertons are in town. I can send one of the kitchen boys over."

"Excellent. Wonder if Fitz would be interested in going with them to Ireland? He could handle the horses while Nick commands the crew. Do you know where the mare's papers are?" He didn't look up from his writing.

Bell really wanted to resent him taking over *her* study, but she hated this gloomy bookshelf-lined room. Once upon a time she'd attempted to persuade Edward to share their correspondence here as she and Quent were doing now. But she'd been a young country girl, unfamiliar with London society, and he'd disdained her offer. Since then, she'd used a sunny office on the next floor.

She left Quent to his note-writing. The chest containing all her father's possessions had arrived shortly after the girls. She'd poked around in it and knew what she needed.

She dug out the box in which her father had always kept important papers. Inside, she located the yellowing document she'd seen earlier and unfolded it, smoothing her fingers over the fading ink. Little Dream had been sired by a descendant of Eclipse, one of the greatest race horses of all time. Her birth had been properly registered in the General Stud Book under the Wexford title. Once upon a time, her family's stable had been respected.

She dug further into the papers and found the one wrapped in faded blue ribbon—the certificate her father had presented to her for her sixteenth birthday, giving her ownership of the foal she had raised. Tears slid down her cheeks as she remembered how proud she had been that he'd recognized her hard work.

She'd raced the two-year-old that day and won her first prize. The prize had paid the taxes and bought Easter dresses for Tess and Syd. She had some good memories of home—few, perhaps, but some. She had tried to set all her memories aside when she'd married and her family had departed. It had been less painful to look forward instead of backward. But maybe now that she had her family again... she could let herself remember the good parts.

If she could have Little Dream back... her heart might be whole again.

She carried the documents down to Quent, who studied them with interest. When he looked up at her, he must have seen the tears she'd tried to wipe away. He came around the desk and wrapped her in his arms.

"We'll retrieve your horse, *ma belle*. I'll send troops to hunt her down, if we must."

She wept harder then, and buried her face in his broad shoulder. "It's just so hard to trust anyone else—"

"Someday, you need to tell me your story," he murmured, stroking her hair. "Or maybe it's better if you don't because I can't strangle the dead. I'll just show you that I'm not Edward or your father or any of those other men who failed you."

Bell lifted her head and shoved away, swiping angrily at her tears. "They failed me because they wouldn't *listen* to me! Just once, I want a man who acknowledges I am as capable as they are."

She tried to walk away, but he caught her arm and hauled her back. He was so damned big and competent, and she was small and dressed in frills. She wanted to stomp her heel on his boot to prove she wasn't helpless. She simply froze and looked down her nose at him—an expression that had served her well these last years.

Impervious to her ire, Quent studied her through serious dark eyes. "I *am* listening. I am trying very hard to hear what you aren't saying very clearly. If I have learned nothing else from my sisters, it's that men and women don't speak the same language. So if you try to communicate with me, you need to help me out until I learn what tears and anger really mean."

Shocked, Bell quit fighting him. "You would listen if I said I should go with Nick to Ireland?"

"I would listen, but I probably wouldn't agree," he said with a wry smile. "Not because I don't believe you're capable, but because I would die a thousand deaths should anything happen to you. That's not easy for a man to admit, so don't expect to hear it again."

His admission caused a wriggly, almost pleasant sensation in her middle and tamped down her temper. "And you don't think women die a thousand deaths just *worrying* over their stupid men who insist on doing reckless things?"

"*Touché,*" he acknowledged with a nod. "I'll try not to do reckless things, if you'll promise the same. Although what we both deem reckless may not be the same. Will you explain your anger?"

Forced to examine her reaction, Bell sighed in exasperation. "I'm not angry with you but men in general. And you do not need to hear the pathetic litany of very good reasons I have for despising the male of the species. Just do not deny me in your decision-making is all I ask. If Nick agrees to sail to Ireland, then I must be present when you talk with him to tell him what to expect."

"Very well, I think I can do that. I'm not much accustomed to allowing anyone—not even my family—into my decisions, so you may need to remind me." His eyes danced with an interest that had little to do with the topic under discussion.

Bell patted his cheek. "Certainly, my dear. If you leave me out of your decisions, I will leave you out of my bed. Perhaps you will remember then?"

Feeling oddly comforted by the argument, Bell left him to his note writing while she sent servants to pick up packages for her family.

Once Quent discovered how much a second family would cost, he might change his mind about the efficacy of marriage. Until then, she would enjoy the prospect of another night of sharing her once-lonely bed.

She would be concerned that becoming the Wicked Widow instead of the Virgin Widow might harm her sisters' chances with society, but marrying a Scots tradesman would cause worse damage. She wasn't worried about society anymore. She knew how it worked. Money always cast a favorable light, and she meant to find *good* men for her sisters, not simple-minded idiots who listened to gossip.

THE HONORABLE Nick Atherton and his wife Eleanora—who refused to use her Mirenzian title of princess—filled Bell's parlor with their larger-than-life presences.

Quent had once thought brown-wren-like Nora to be a quiet, unassuming seaman's widow—until she'd displayed her talent with swords and sailing. She'd routed villains and Nick's demanding father and brought incorrigible Nick into line, all within the space of a few weeks. If dashing Nick could find happiness with such a formidable personage, then Quent thought he should be able to deal with a dignified lady like Bell. He hoped.

Today, the demure princess was wearing a sophisticated blue silk afternoon gown with a sash that looked as if it ought to hide a pistol.

"Bell, I hope we can help," Nora said in greeting, hugging their hostess. "And I want to meet your sisters and brother before we leave for Amsterdam! I cannot imagine how it must be to suddenly have a family!"

"Since you only recently acquired a few royal cousins you didn't know about, I think you have some idea," Bell said dryly, gesturing for her guest to take a seat.

"But my cousins don't live with us!" Nora laughed. "I would most likely kill them if they did. I'm sure your siblings are much more reasonable."

"Only younger," Quent said grimly. "But it's not the young ones causing trouble. It's the old ones."

"Shall we take this to the study and leave the ladies to exchange notes on new family?" Nick suggested. Tall, blond, and garbed in the height of fashion in his dark blue fitted tail coat, starched linen, and Hessians, Nicholas Atherton looked the part of genial diplomat and earl's son. Only those who knew him well knew the ruthless history concealed behind his indolent facade.

Quent didn't have to look at Bell to know her reaction to Nick's suggestion. "You really do like living dangerously, don't you?" he asked.

Nick chuckled. "It was worth a try." He bowed over Bell's hand. "My lady, we would protect you from the evils of the world. You deserve only sunlight and roses."

Bell slapped his hand. "Flattery will get you nowhere. I would sail with you, if Quent would let me."

Nick looked mildly alarmed. "That shouldn't be necessary. My crew would no doubt faint at the prospect of accidentally flapping their vulgar tongues in your presence. Even Nora agrees she's better off staying here. Fitz has agreed to handle the cattle. We'll pick him up on our way back to Brighton."

"Let the men play their games. We'll play ours," Nora said, comfortably settling on the sofa and taking the teacup Bell handed her. She glanced up at Quent. "Sit down, sir, and quit hovering. We want to hear Bell's side of the story first. She'll know her family better than you."

Quent appropriated the cushion beside Bell, establishing his territory. He felt like a destrier in a ladies' closet. He was unaccustomed to sharing tea and discussing business with females.

He'd learn, if he had to crush all Bell's china in the process.

"Summerby's clerks have drawn up notarized duplicates of the mare's papers so Nick will be removing the horses with all legalities covered," Quent told them. "We just don't expect it to be as simple as walking in and taking the animals."

"They'll hide them," Bell acknowledged. "I'm amazed they haven't forged papers and sold Dream already. Or maybe they've been thinking about it since she's growing older and worth less for racing and breeding. You can offer money for her past upkeep. I know she would have earned far more than her feed over the years, but I don't want to dicker. I just want my horse."

"And your aunt wants your brother's title," Quent reminded her. "You can't dicker with that. We'll have to leave horsenapping to Nick and Fitz and hope for the best." He could tell she didn't like it, so he distracted her. "We need to decide on wedding plans."

As expected, Nick and Nora exclaimed in excitement, and Bell's glare warned he'd feel the brunt of her wrath later. But for the moment, she was neatly diverted from fretting over the horse.

"Horsenapping, really?" Nick murmured to Quent a little later while reaching for a tea cake. "How dangerous are these people?"

Bell and Nora were arguing over the advantages of a quiet ceremony over a public one. Pretending to lean over and choose a delicacy, Quent bent his head closer to Nick's. "Boyles are bloodthirsty and reckless, but I suspect this branch is most likely lazy and incompetent. Threats should do it."

Belle leaned over and handed him a wafer with green paste on it. "Uncle Jim was six-feet tall and burly when I saw him last. He knows how to use a musket but not a sword. I have good ears, so stop shutting me out."

"And the doxy?" Nick asked, eyes dancing with amusement.

Quent fumed but let Bell have control of the conversation again.

"Mary Dolores used to live in the village and make her living on her back. She's bigger than I am, but she's far more likely to use her blunt wits than her brawn. I doubt she knows which end of a weapon is which. That doesn't mean she hasn't hired people who do." Bell wrinkled her nose in thought. "Or seduced them into helping her."

In any other company, the ladies would be fainting in shock at Bell's crudeness. Nora and Nick merely looked fascinated.

"Very well, we'll go in peace and carry heavy arms," Nick agreed. "My gang can handle anything up to and including a pirate crew. They have few illusions about females. If your horse is there, we'll retrieve her."

"Scout first, make sure the mare is there," Quent warned, wishing he was going with them to make certain it was done right. "And ask about foals. We understand there's a valuable stallion."

"Fitz will handle that," Nora said serenely. "You can be certain he'll have his eye on the stock. He's nearly frothing at the mouth at the prospect of acquiring descendants of Eclipse."

Quent squeezed Bell's hand, and she sent him a look that he interpreted as gratitude—although he wasn't entirely certain for what.

Until these last weeks, he'd never realized that she lived in fear—but he understood it now. When one was raised among bullies and thieves, the fear never quite goes away.

She needed him, even if she wouldn't acknowledge it.

And if he wanted his future wife to accept that he wasn't one of the thieves and bullies, he'd have to exert himself to prove he could be trusted in more ways than commerce.

With only his tyrant of a father as an example of a family man, Quent was traipsing dangerous ground. He tugged at his neckcloth and slanted Bell a glance. Unlike his sisters, Bell would stab him with a pitchfork if he resorted to bullying.

Twenty

AFTER THE Athertons departed, Bell was too anxious to settle down. Glancing at the long clock, she decided she had time to run to the shops for a few additional purchases. She donned gloves and hat before realizing she had neither footman nor personal maid to accompany her. She'd sent everyone—plus the carriage—to Essex and left them there. She could take a parlor maid with her, but Butler was likely to snarl.

Frustrated, she vowed to go on her own. It wasn't as if she wasn't capable of walking a few blocks carrying packages. She'd simply grown pampered these last years.

Before Butler could open the door for her, Quent materialized. She'd thought he'd left with the Athertons.

"Going for a walk? May I join you?" He took his walking stick and hat from the servant before she could reply.

"Have you moved in?" she asked suspiciously.

"You have no footmen, so yes, I'm moving in. It's not as if Butler is capable of holding off your obnoxious relations," he said unrepentantly as they strolled down the street. "And as far as I can ascertain, you don't know how to wield a sword or pistol."

"I should learn," she muttered. "You don't really think Dolly and her cohort are so diligent as to be watching the house, do you?"

"They were in London just a few days ago, so I'm hoping they are," he said with relish. "That way Nick and Fitz can retrieve your horses uninterrupted while I have the pleasure of beating your relations to a pulp. Once all that's settled, we can marry in peace."

"And you call me bloodthirsty! You do realize I haven't signed any settlements yet, don't you?" she asked, trying to maintain her hauteur while perfectly aware every neighbor was watching them. She swung her parasol as if she hadn't a care in the world.

"Our men of business haven't quit arguing, true. That doesn't keep us from going for the special license tomorrow." He patted his pocket. "I'll drop the betrothal announcement at the newspaper while we're out. That should shut up any cackling." He nodded at the windows they passed.

"I don't know what you think marriage is," she said grimly. "But it's not all smiles and kisses. I'd like to keep you as a friend, but I just don't see that happening. You'll grow bored once you've won your goal. You'll look for other challenges, and I'll have to throw things at you to catch your attention."

He glanced at her in surprise. "Is that what you think? You believe I could ever forget your presence?"

"Edward did," she pointed out. "Sometimes, I used to sit in his study and read while he worked on his Shakespearean folios. A few times, he'd find places where the text didn't agree with the original, and he'd comment, but I'd never read Shakespeare, and it took me too long to find the passages. I tried reading the plays he was working on so I'd know more, but I didn't have his education, didn't understand the language, and he looked at me with disgust if I asked questions. So after a while, he forgot I existed. I don't think he missed me when I quit sitting with him."

"And you think that's what I'll do?" Quent asked, shaking his head in amazement. "I can't even imagine *seeing* those folios with you in the room, much less concentrating on the text! I'm not certain I could accomplish anything meaningful with you to distract me. That's what worries *me*."

Bell wanted to preen a little at that admission, but she was determined to be practical. Edward had turned her silly head with his initial attentions, but she knew better now. "Lust wears off," she reminded him. "You'll be doing business in my drawing room and forgetting my existence in no time at all."

Quent walked beside her silently for a few minutes, apparently mulling that over. Then he grabbed her arm as they reached the shops on Bond Street and steered her down an alley. "I have the remedy for inattention."

She wanted to laugh, but he seemed quite serious. With Quent... it was so very hard to know what to expect. She respected his intelligence, though, so she followed.

He stopped at what appeared to be a small wholesale shop, the sort of place where milliners might purchase their feathers or shoemakers might go for leather. Opening the door, Quent waved at a clerk behind the counter, who nodded as if he knew him. Without explanation, Quent drew her deeper into the shop, amid crates and bolts of fabric, until he reached a dark corner in the very back. He shoved boxes and barrels aside until he found what he sought.

"Here," he said in satisfaction, holding a container out to her. "Every time you fear you've lost my attention, you may hit me with one of these. I'd much prefer that over denying me your bed."

In the dim light from a single dirty window, Bell couldn't tell what she was holding, other than that it was gritty with dirt. Grimacing at what the dust would do to her gloves, she pried open the top, and still wasn't entirely certain what she held.

Quent grabbed an item off the top and spread it open for her.

"A fan!" she exclaimed. "You want me to hit you with a fan?" She handed him the box and tried to study the delicate silk and fragile wood. "It's so light! It would shatter to pieces."

"Exactly," he said in satisfaction.

Carrying the entire box, he steered her toward the front of the store where there was more light. "They're worthless. We can't even give them away, so why not shatter them for a good cause? I thought they would sell fabulously, but they're Chinese. Ladies didn't take to the foreign designs."

Bell halted by the front window and studied the watercolors on the cream silk. "Are these cherry blossoms? The tree looks ancient and gnarled, but the pink is so lovely!" She looked closer, then carried it outside where she could see the odd figures more closely. "Look, they are wearing the most wonderful tunics. The detail is exquisite! I can see the dragons on his... skirt? I wonder what that's called. Kimono? And look, she's hiding behind a tree and laughing. And who is this gray beard on this round mountain? How clever! I want to know the story!"

"That was my reaction," he said, pleased. "But everyone else turned up their noses. They're not terribly costly, so if you smack me with one, it will hurt my pride more than my pocket."

Bell laughed in delight, opening and closing the fan, making the figures peer from behind bushes and bridges depending on how far she unfolded it. "I'd rather smack you with my hand than break this."

With the box under his arm, he took her elbow and steered her toward the shops. "Your hands are for more pleasant purposes. That is the reason nannies use switches. One associates pain with switches and pleasure with hands. Unless you wish to carry a switch about the house, use the fan."

"I shall wrap the string around my wrist," she assured him, laughing. His mention of her hands producing pleasure thrilled her and inspired wicked images of how she could touch him. She was eager to return home to show him just exactly what her hands could do.

Her heart lightened that he'd actually considered her complaint, thought it valid, and produced a solution, no matter how silly. Unlike

Edward, he was *listening* to her worries.

She feared that wouldn't last past the honeymoon period, but it was so very refreshing to know that he was trying. No man had really tried to consider her opinions before. Perhaps she needed to try equally hard to consider his.

"I think I shall start carrying my fan about and create the sensation of next season," she declared. "Let us take this box to my modiste and make them exclusive, so very rare and precious they can be found in only one place. We'll pay for my sisters' wardrobes with the sale of fans by this time next year."

"Save several for shattering," he said wryly. "Because I'm now kicking myself and wondering if I should have consulted you about the fans earlier. Your knowledge of fashion and society might sell the rest of my unsalable stock and raise cash for my father's roof."

"That's the solution!" she crowed in delight. "Let me help you sell your strange shipments, and we'll have things we can talk about together."

She let the mention of his father's need for a roof sail right past her.

Instead, she basked in the way Quent looked at her as if she were a goddess descended from the skies. It wouldn't last, she knew, but she could enjoy the novelty while it did—and while keeping her family safe.

QUENT sent for his own carriage to transport the packages that Bell accumulated at the shops. The sun was low in the sky by the time he assisted her into the interior.

He'd never been a man who enjoyed shopping. His tailor knew his size, and he simply sent for a new coat when he needed one. The man came to his house and fitted it, and the package arrived the next day—no wasting time idling in shops.

But perhaps he'd been wrong to avoid this part of Bell's world. For hours now, she had been teaching him things he hadn't known. The fans had been a fascinating revelation. Her modiste had instantly seen what Bell had seen and had started matching the various fan colors with bolts of fabric in dramatic fashion. Customers had begun to inquire as he watched.

He usually dealt in wholesale goods like grains, wool, and spices. He was a trader and an investor, not a merchant. Selling bulk wasn't the same as retail.

His captains sometimes suggested oddities like the fans, but Quent didn't have much patience with selling to shops. His tastes were not that of the general public. Indomitable Bell opened new possibilities.

Once inside the carriage, he tugged her closer and pressed a kiss to her temple. "You are the epitome of public taste, you know, the grand dragoness of society."

She tilted him a puzzled look. "Am I? I've always thought myself quite ordinary."

Which was one of the reasons he admired her. Despite the dignity with which she carried herself in public, she was approachable, as many women in her position weren't. And, he realized, that's what made her successful.

"I've lived in London for the same amount of time as you have," Quent tried to explain. "In all that time, I never learned how modistes create fashion or why ladies follow it. You, on the other hand, have spent your time studying what makes society work. That is the key to how a rural Irish girl became an effective marchioness and leader of the *ton*. You are quite astonishing."

"Well, it only makes sense to learn the rules of the realm in which one lives," she said crossly. "I see nothing astonishing about that. You have done much the same in your man's world."

Quent bent to kiss away her frown but a glance out the window caused him to hesitate. The carriage was just rolling past the stately mansions on Bell's street. He brushed his kiss across her brow and touched a finger to her lips. "Shhh, do you recognize that tubby fellow leaning against the lamppost?" He indicated a disreputable character who looked out of place among fashionable ladies and nannies walking their charges to the park.

Bell looked where he pointed and paled. "Hiram," she whispered. "What can he gain from watching the house?"

Hiram, her father's stable hand, the one who had been making demands of Summerby, Quent recalled. He would have a word with the fellow and not a polite one.

Quent knocked on the driver's door and ordered him to go around to the mews before he sat back and addressed Bell's question. "One assumes he's looking for you. It's hard to say until we ask."

"And we'll ask?" she asked.

"Oh, yes, we'll ask," he replied dangerously as the carriage rolled down the alley.

He escorted Bell through her kitchen garden and up the back steps. Her husky young footmen weren't here to guard the portal. Damn.

"Lock the doors," he told the startled butler who hurried to assist them. "Post servants with blunt instruments at the lower windows. Send someone to stay with the lady upstairs until I give orders otherwise."

Bell shook off his hold. "Don't be ridiculous. It's just Hiram. I can swat him with a fan and bring him to his knees."

"Not if he has hired help. Let me test his defenses first, then you may swat him as much as you like, although I suggest an iron poker." Leaving Bell still protesting, Quent loosened his neckcloth, handed over his expensive hat, and stalked out the front door.

He'd grown up wrestling with three strong brothers and a herd of cousins. He regularly worked off his frustrations at Gentleman Jackson's. Tubby, aging, stable hands didn't stand a chance against brute strength.

The man looked startled when Quent marched down the front steps, but he didn't have the sense to run. Hiram continued picking at his broken fingernails as if he were waiting for someone. Which made Quent hesitate.

What if he could catch the notorious dollymop as well?

Deciding a bird in the hand was better than two thugs on the loose, Quent strolled past the lout, flicked open the blade on his walking cane, and spun about. With the knife end at Hiram's back, he murmured, "You'll be coming with me, sir. Walk slowly or I might slice out your liver."

Twenty-one

NERVOUSLY peering from behind the front window draperies, Bell watched as Quentin marched her father's former stable boy toward the back alley. Lifting her skirt, she raced down to the kitchen door she'd entered just moments ago. It was all very fine for Quent to say he was taking care of her, but she damned well wanted to know what was happening so she could defend herself. And her family.

She'd spent her youth protecting her family. The instinct did not go away with disuse, she realized with disgust.

She was waiting in the tiny garden by the time Quent prodded Hiram through the gate. Hiram fell to his knees at Quent's shove. He looked startled to see her, but his bulging eyes always looked surprised. He'd apparently tarted himself up in a shiny frock coat and threadbare linen from the second hand store for this visit.

"My lady, I didn't do nothin'!" the ruffian pleaded, recovering quickly from his surprise. "Tell this rapscallion to back off, that I'm just an old family friend."

"You were never my friend, Mr. Kennedy," Bell retorted, keeping a stiff distance and wearing the expression of disdain she'd perfected for just such occasions. "You toadied to my father, perhaps, and sometimes Uncle Jim, but never me."

"That's cause you were just a youngster! But it's different now, ain't it?"

"How is it different, Hiram?" Quent asked menacingly, leaning against the gate so his prisoner couldn't escape. "Threatening the lady's solicitor sounds like business as usual in the Wexford way."

"Didn't threaten," Hiram countered mulishly. "The countess just let him know we got the estate in hand."

Quent—blessedly—held his tongue and let Bell address this one.

"The countess, is it?" Bell asked coldly. "And Uncle Jim has filed his papers claiming the title with the English court, all right and proper now, did he? Will he be taking his seat now that he's a lord?"

Hiram grew sullen and tugged at his soiled tweed vest, which hung well below his frock coat waist. "He's like your da, not much on court and such. But that don't make him no less an earl."

"Well, yes, I'm afraid it does," Bell said with insincere sympathy. "It would have behooved Uncle Jim to stay in touch with my father instead of pretending da was dead all these years and usurping his title. Because my father has an heir, and my brother's guardian is quite a stickler for legalities. But that doesn't explain your presence. What do you want, Mr. Kennedy?"

"Don't want nothin'," he protested. "Just standing by, waiting for someone. You got no cause to be treating me like this. There's laws!"

Waiting for someone. Bell exchanged a glance with Quent, who nodded to show he understood.

"Well, no, actually," Quent offered nonchalantly. "The lady owns the property and if you don't have her permission to be loitering outside her gates and you can't show you have business here, then the law will throw *you* in gaol, not us. So perhaps you'd best start stating your business."

Persuading information out of a hired hand was a waste of time. She wanted the real offender. Bell feigned a yawn. "Just tie him up, dear. We'll wait to see who else shows up. Perhaps we can have a small soiree."

"My pleasure, *dear*," Quent said with a wicked grin. "Shall we let him shout so the rest of the party knows where to find him?"

Bell pretended to ponder. "It's a little late for a tea party in the garden," she said, noting the darkening skies. "Perhaps we could simply truss him up until morning, and then let him call to his fellows."

"A nice night for the stable," Quent agreed. "We'll give your family time to show up."

Bell hid her grin. So, he understood who Hiram was waiting for.

"Excellent." Without a backward glance to the cringing man on his knees in her garden, Bell swept inside.

Once there, she hurried to the front window again. As suspected, Hiram hadn't been outside her door to catch some sun.

She smirked in triumph as she noted a plump female wearing gaudy, wide pink skirts from her mother's day—possibly from the countess's wardrobe—standing on the corner, looking puzzled. The woman paced back and forth, peering up and down alleys, ignoring the curious stares she drew from street urchins and passersby.

Bell didn't have Quent's swordstick. Not knowing who might be lurking in the shadows, she didn't dare make a target of herself. She needed to hire more footmen.

No, she didn't, not when she had Quent. Happiness surged through her at the sound of his boots in the back part of the house. She opened the front door and pointed out the figure in pink. "Dolly," she murmured. "Will you use a sword on her?"

"Come along." He caught her elbow and led her out. "Let's have that tea party."

NOT SEEING any threat in a pair of brass-faced *parvenus*, Quent was almost enjoying himself. He hoped Nick and Fitz would find the uncle in Ireland as simple to deal with as Dolly and Hiram.

The pink-garbed female turned and noted their approach with alarm, but Quent caught her elbow before she could decide which way to run. Bell graciously linked arms on the other side, and they dragged her, protesting, toward the house.

"Honestly, I can't imagine what you're about, accosting a lady just walking! It's above enough that I can't stroll down a London street—"

Bell raised her eyebrows, snickered, but held her tongue.

Quent followed her up the front steps, where her butler held open the door, his dignity entirely undisturbed by their ranting guest. It may have helped that Quent had greased Butler's conscience with a purse of coins earlier.

"Well, I never..." the frump was protesting. "It's not as if I meant to *intrude*..."

"Then just what did you mean to do, Mrs. Boyle?" Quent asked, relishing the moment as the would-be countess halted to take in Bell's elegant parlor. "In society, one waits for an invitation before appearing on someone's doorstep."

With her overlarge breasts spilling from an old-fashioned bodice that was meant to be accompanied by a modesty piece, the faded beauty flung back her wilted bonnet. Her once blond hair had lost its luster and looked more haystack than crowning glory, but then, Quent allowed that he might be prejudiced. Next to Bell's dignified beauty, any woman would fade away.

"Fat chance that Miss High-and-Mighty would invite *me* inside," the blonde declared irately. "Not once did she ask after me or her ailin' uncle or any of the rest. But now there's somethin' in it for her, she sends her sneaks around, lookin' to see what they can steal."

Behind the woman, Bell looked amused. She gestured at Quent to continue.

"If you're referring to Lady Belden, might I introduce her?" Quent suggested.

"Lady Belden!" Mrs. Boyle looked as if she might spit. "That imp from hell ain't no lady, for all she was born into the family. Who are you and what are you doing in her house? Hires servants to do her dirty work, does she?"

Quent lifted his eyebrows, understanding Bell's amusement. He gestured for her to take the next act.

"Why, Dolly," Bell simpered, "I'm that hurt that you've forgotten me. I hadn't thought I'd harmed your hard head when I brought that vase down on you. How sorry I am that you've lost what little brain you possessed."

Bell had smashed a vase over the head of her father's mistress? Quent would have liked to have seen that. He eyed her with appreciation, realizing the depths he had yet to explore.

The appalled Mrs. Boyle swung around and glared. "*You*? That can't be you. Don't play me for a fool, girl. You're no lady. Anyone can see that. Where's your jewels, I ask you? And look at that gown! It looks no more than something that should be worn to bed. You're his lightskirt, no doubt. What kind of shady goin's on am I caught up in?"

Quent feared Bell might double up laughing. So much for protecting her from fearsome relations.

"Be that as it may," Quent said solemnly, "may I present my fiancée, Lady Isabell, dowager marchioness of Belden? Or was there another lightskirt who hit you over the head with a vase?"

"Izzy?" the creature screeched in disbelief, realizing her error. Then feigning a faint, she staggered backward toward Quent.

He stepped aside and let her stagger a little further so she collapsed on a sofa.

"Izzy?" he murmured as Bell wrapped her hand around his arm. "Do I get to call you Izzy when you swat me with a fan?"

"Calling me Izzy will earn a swat," she murmured back, admiring the performance on the sofa. "Do you think she will slide off for effect or call for her smelling salts?"

Quent tapped his finger against her lips to silence her and addressed the problem. "Dear me, Mrs. Boyle, where is your maid? I fear the household isn't in the habit of carrying smelling salts. My Izzy never suffers from the vapors."

Bell pinched his hand but snickered.

He hadn't enjoyed himself so much in ages.

The mop-haired Dolly straightened and attempted to regain some of her lost dignity. She tugged at her pink silk and glared. "How'd ye know my name?" she demanded.

"Providing you actually have a marriage certificate to prove the name is yours," Bell said with exasperation, "it's the name you gave my solicitor. It was not very difficult for me to deduce who had come to town asking after me and for me to point you out to Mr. Hoyt. Again, what are you doing here?"

"I could do with a cuppa tea," their guest said petulantly.

"We could put her in the stable with Hiram," Quent suggested, losing his patience.

Mrs. Boyle's faded blue eyes grew wide in alarm. "You ain't hurt him, have ye? He be the only one worth anythin' 'round the place now that Jim's down with the ague and dropsy all the time."

"You're right, this grows tiresome," Bell said in her world-weary voice, expressing no sympathy for her supposedly ailing uncle. "She's looking for excuses and doesn't have any, which means they were up to something nefarious. My guess is that they hoped the house was empty so they could break in and look for Dream's papers. The horse would be worth considerably more with those. Let's call the watch."

"I'd do no such thing," Mrs. Boyle said in indignation. "Hiram said he'd just scout about a bit if I'd keep an eye on his back. We just wanted to talk to ye, all pleasant like."

This time, Quent snickered. "By Jove, I can imagine how pleasant it would have been for Bell to come home and find the two of you sitting in her parlor. You do know her servants are hired pugilists who use their fists as weapons? Did you think we'd leave my lady alone?"

Dolly paled more, if that was possible. "Izzy ain't never been one to need servants," she complained. "We thought she'd be about the countryside on her horse."

"You have my horse," Bell snarled.

Which was when Quent finally grasped some portion of Bell's refusal to ride again. It didn't make logical sense, but as an eighteen-year-old, she had been deprived of the animal that had been her mother, father, home, and source of income for years. She was clinging to a memory while avoiding any new attachment—*just as she avoided attaching herself to him.*

If he considered how she'd turned to Edward and been cast aside... her rejection of all emotional connections almost made sense.

He was finally beginning to understand the woman. He knew she was loyal. He hadn't understood how deeply her feelings ran. Her defensive tactics had new meaning... and the ability to shatter his soul.

"I'll sell ye the horse," Dolly offered. "Just let me and mine have what's rightfully ours."

"And what is that?" Quent demanded. With his new

understanding of Bell, he struggled with panic. If Nick didn't find the mare—*he could lose Bell.*

"Jim's got to be the earl so he can keep the estate. He worked all his life for that bit of rocky land. It's his. No young upstart can have it." Dolly crossed her arms defiantly over her ample bosom.

"That's impossible," Bell said in frustration. "The law dictates inheritance, not us. You and Jim can continue living there as always. No one's denying you that."

"If my young 'uns can't count on that land as theirs, you'll not ever find your damned horse," Dolly retorted. "That's that, and I'll be leavin' now."

She struggled to rise from the low settee. Quent left her there. He wrapped his arm around Bell's shoulders, but they were as stiff and unforgiving as fortress walls.

"You've moved the horse?" he asked.

Dolly pushed herself to her feet and adopted a mulish expression. "You think I'm stupid? The old nag is all I got to bargain with, her and her expensive get we can't even sell. But I found a Gypsy what will take them if you don't. I'll guarantee you'll never find them unless you give us what we want."

She stalked toward the door, where Butler waited to let her out.

Quent held Bell and let the harridan go. Even if Mrs. Boyle was a thief and a blackmailer, he wasn't in the habit of beating up women.

Twenty-two

BELL TRIED to let Quent comfort her that evening. But as much as she loved him for keeping her company and for distracting her with kisses, the polite lady she'd been had vanished. She could no longer bury years of fury and fear under the artificial dignity of her title, and she couldn't sit still now.

Uncle Jim had made his bed. She felt no sorrow over his illness or the probable faithlessness of his choice in wife. And if he'd been passing himself off as earl all this time, she had even less sympathy for his poor choices.

But dumb animals shouldn't have to suffer for what their human owners did.

Her skin stretched tight and thin over all her roiling emotion. She'd wanted to pummel Hiram until he told her where Dream was. Instead, she'd let Quent bribe him—not anywhere near as satisfactory as kicking sense into the clown. She needed to run, to ride, to shout and scream.

Only it was much too late in the evening to dash across town to verify Hiram's claim that Dream was here, in London, close enough for her to touch. She'd pleaded with Quent to be taken to the docks, but even she knew it was a ridiculously dangerous idea.

Instead, they'd sent word to Nick and Fitz to stop them before they sailed in the morning as they'd planned. Sending messengers just wasn't enough. She was about to come apart attempting to contain her frustration. After all these years of cool composure, she felt as if she would burst at the seams.

Bell wrapped her arms around Quent's broad, comforting chest, and let him carry her off to bed. He made love to her with heartbreaking tenderness, and she clung to him afterward, as she'd never clung to Edward—and Quent let her. With her head resting on his broad shoulder, feeling him breathing evenly, she could appreciate having a partner to lean on occasionally.

She still didn't sleep well. She had nightmares most of the night—horrifying visions of Dream breaking her legs trying to escape, of Kit riding off and falling to his death, of her sisters screaming. Even Quent's comforting arm didn't protect her from dreams. This was the reason she'd learned to bury fear and anger—they were unproductive.

And still, she couldn't let them go.

In the morning, she rose at the break of dawn to gather her riding habit.

"What the devil?" Quent grumbled from beneath the covers when she stumbled over a chair leg and woke him. Looking surly with his square jaw darkened with beard stubble, he surged from the bed in all his naked glory. Seeing that she was already half dressed, he growled and grabbed for his own clothes.

Bell wasn't so far gone as not to appreciate the ripple of abdominal muscle when he reached for yesterday's linen. Nor was she blind to the fact that he had to struggle to don his breeches over his morning erection. She just refused to act on lust when she had other matters on her mind.

"You're not going to the docks, Bell," he grumbled. "I'll hire a few grooms, bend Hiram's arm, and we'll spring the horses from their pens before breakfast. There's no need for you to dirty your shoes. The wharf is no place for a lady."

She continued pinning up her hair. Arguing was pointless. If Dream was stabled in some run-down pen, in danger of being sold at market, Bell would find her. She had been stunned that Dolly would have gone so far as to bring the horses across the Irish Sea to hide them from her. She feared Hiram was lying, but she would take no chances.

"We should wait for word from Nick that he's on his way," Quent said, yanking on his waistcoat. "We can find the animals and take them to Wyckerly for you. Taking a carriage to the docks is foolish, Bell. Let me ride down with my men."

Bell pinned her hat to her hair and yanked on her spencer. Giving him a steely look, and picking up her gloves, she merely replied, "I'll send Butler to hire a carriage for me. You do as you like."

She didn't expect him to understand that she was holding herself together with pins and string. She didn't precisely understand it herself. All these years, she'd told herself that a horse was a horse, a beast of burden, and she ought to be missing her father more.

She was pretty certain now that she'd been lying to herself. Her father hadn't been there to comfort her when she cried. Dream had. Her father hadn't provided the prizes to feed her sisters. Dream had.

Taking her sisters away had ripped out her heart. Taking Dream had seared the wound and made it certain that she'd never love anything again. Abandoning Dream when the mare needed her... wasn't worth thinking about.

She was not her father. She could not desert her family as he had done. And family included her horses.

Behind her, Quent struggled with his boots. Bell drifted down the staircase, looking for Butler.

He was oddly unable to be found. The buffet had been set as usual, so he had to be about. Bell caught a maid carrying in a platter of sausage and asked her to send Butler up. The maid curtsied and ran down to the kitchen.

Butler still didn't appear.

Fretting, Bell was about to pull on her gloves and find a carriage on her own, when Quent clattered down, still unshaven but ready to ride. He grabbed a cup and poured coffee, swallowing the steaming liquid in a few gulps that made Bell wince.

"You win," he said. "I've sent Butler for a carriage. We'll stuff Hiram in it with you, and we can let him go once we find the horses."

Bell stared at him in shock. "*You* sent Butler for a carriage?"

"Naturally. I sent for him the instant you made your preference clear. Are you going to eat any of this food or are we heading out now?" He grabbed a piece of toast and folded it around a handful of bacon.

"Naturally?" she asked dangerously. "What do you mean, *naturally*? Butler is still my servant, is he not?"

Quent raised the slash of his dark eyebrows and finished chewing before replying. "He'll soon be *our* servant, unless you want to bring my people over here. Sharing is what marriage is really about, dear heart, not who spends funds on what." He looked up as Butler arrived in the doorway. "All set?"

The taciturn servant bowed respectfully. Quent grabbed her arm and dragged Bell toward the door, unaware that he was within an inch of being stabbed by the knife Bell snatched from the sideboard.

"You do not know who you are dealing with, *dear heart*," she muttered.

"I'm very afraid that I do," he retorted. "But that's not stopping me now. Let's test our mettle by stealing stolen horses, shall we?"

QUENT was almost reassured that Bell had grabbed a knife as they left the breakfast room. It was a nice sharp meat knife and should intimidate Hiram nicely if he developed any ideas of escaping once they let him out of the stall.

Not that Hiram seemed in any hurry to run. Their prisoner had been bribed with a healthy purse, given good food and ale, luxurious blankets, and a roof that didn't leak, even if he had been in a locked stable. Quent had arranged for servants to deliver warm water and clean linen so the man almost looked respectable when he climbed up on the driver's seat. Quent lashed Hiram's fists behind his back and tied him to a rail, but it was an open carriage. Bell could still hear him if he cursed.

Since he'd left his horse back in Essex, Quent had asked for a loan from the Duke of Fortham's stable. Lady Anne, the duke's daughter, kept a formidable array of animals and grooms and had gladly loaned him what he needed. It had been all Quent could do to persuade Anne to stay home and not come rescuing horses with them. The duke would remove his head if Quent had taken his only child down to the docks.

Trailing a train of rough grooms, Quent rode beside Bell's carriage. He tried to ignore her furiously stiff posture as they progressed past farm carts entering the city to sell their wares and servants hurrying to market. At this hour, most of Mayfair's fashionable residents were sleeping. Quent hoped her ire would disperse once she had her horse in hand.

The fishermen and sailors on the dock were up and about as the strange progression of grooms and carriage wended its way down the cobblestones. Rude whistles and calls followed Bell, and Quent had to grit his teeth. Bell seemed impervious.

She had *raced* horses—as an innocent young girl, riding astride, surrounded by drunken gamblers. Quent still had a hard time grasping that the Virgin Widow standing on a pedestal well above the rest of London could be that reckless girl. But he'd seen glimpses of the hellion lately. He had to adjust his mind to the notion that he wasn't wedding a lady who would sit properly in her parlor where he put her.

At this point, he was so far gone that he might even adjust to the thought of Bell wearing men's breeches. But he was a selfish, primitive male. Letting other men see her magnificent limbs was a different matter entirely.

As they drew closer to the warehouses and animal pens, Quent leaned from his horse to consult with Hiram and confirm their destination. Quent kept his hand on the pistol hidden beneath his coat while he scanned their surroundings. He wanted anyone watching to know they were armed. He simply didn't want Bell to see it. Foolish of him, probably, since she was the one carrying a knife and hiring armed footmen.

At a nod from Hiram confirming that they'd arrived at the proper location, Quent directed his men to surround a paddock filled with horses to be sold at market. The stench of dung was so thick, it was hard to breathe. Quent cast an anxious glance to Bell's ramrod straight figure on the carriage seat before sidling his horse up to the side.

"This the place," Hiram said. "They buy up all the sad cattle in Ireland and haul them here, where the wealth is. Dream's get should fetch more than we got paid for 'em."

"You mean the horses have already been sold?" Quent asked in shock, not looking at Bell for fear he'd lose his temper.

"We couldn't pay to transport them now, could we?" Hiram asked indignantly. "And the doc was refusing to physic Jim unless we paid his bill, so we needed the ready."

"And you thought you'd sell Dream and grab your money before I claimed what was rightfully *mine*," Bell added with dangerous sweetness.

Quent held up a cautioning hand to her.

Hiram just glared. "They're there. Just go buy 'em back. You got enough blunt to buy the lot."

Quent dismounted hurriedly, catching Bell before she could climb down on her own. "We'll find them," he reassured her, swinging her down from the carriage. "And if we don't, we'll hang Hiram, how's that?"

"Not good enough," she muttered, stalking toward the nearest building, leaving Hiram volubly protesting that he wasn't a thief.

QUENT hunted down the man in charge of the paddocks, but as Bell had feared, the records were incomplete and on the verge of illiterate. One did not deal in undocumented Thoroughbreds without blurring a lot of lines. Stalking out of the grubby office, Bell returned to the paddocks.

Heart in her throat, she climbed up on the rail to better see the animals milling in the filthy pens. The odor of horses and manure, the nickering, and anxious side-stepping, brought back memories both good and bad. She fought tears and heart-pounding hope as she scanned the collection.

Ancient nags ready for the glue factory mixed with yearlings, underfed mares, and temperamental geldings. In a different pen were the stallions. She wanted to adopt them all. Damn blasted selfish men, treating intelligent animals like insects to be walked upon. She'd take any one of those horses before she'd take a man.

Quent climbed up beside her. "What am I looking for?"

Perhaps she'd keep this man, though. His calm rationality steadied her shameful temper. Bell enumerated Dream's markings, from the white arrow on her forehead to the darker brown patch on her left haunch. Quent climbed down and spread the word with the grooms they'd brought with them.

The stable manager ambled out and Quent enlisted him in their search. The man cast a glance to Hiram, simmering on the carriage seat, and nodded. "Stolen, is she? The owner will still want his costs plus transporting."

"He'll get it," Quent agreed without twitching. "And we'll give you coin for your time, if you help us search."

Bell didn't care how he spent her money in this case. She climbed down from the fence and entered through the gate as if she were a proper lady, although the wild Irish rebel threatened to emerge as the animals pressed around her. She wanted to scream her fury and send the lot stampeding into the street.

It was akin to hunting a needle in a haystack—worse, because the horses shifted as they walked through them. Her damned long skirt was a nuisance in the filth. She wanted her riding breeches.

She couldn't wear breeches anymore.

If she was carrying Quent's child, she wouldn't be able to ride either.

She nearly tripped and stumbled with the shock of that thought, which did nothing to pacify her pounding heart.

A sharp note whistled from outside the pen, but Bell only dimly registered it. She'd spotted a white arrow on a skinny bay to her right. She smacked a black rump out of her way, nudged past a gelding that didn't want her to pass, and chanted over and over, "Little Dream, come."

The mare finally lifted her bony head and looked. Bell wanted to weep at the mare's frailty. She elbowed the gelding until it sidestepped, and then she was there... in front of her baby.

So many memories... so much pain. She almost didn't dare touch. But how could she not? It would be like refusing to hug an infant.

She took off her glove and stroked Dream's nose, letting her sniff. The mare nickered and tossed her head, then sought the caress again, accepting her. Weeping, not caring how mad she appeared, Bell flung her arms around the mare's neck and buried her tears in Dream's thin coat, a coat that had once been glossy and thick, not patchy and rough.

The mare tried to eat her bonnet, and Bell chuckled through her tears. "We'll find you some proper feed soon, dear one. Do you have babes here? Where are they?"

The mare nodded her head as if she understood, as she'd always understood. Tears streamed down Bell's cheeks, unchecked, and her heart cracked wide open.

When Quent approached with bit in hand, her cracked heart welcomed him. She didn't have words for what he'd done for her. Finally feeling free to express all her roiling emotions, she flung her arms around his neck as she had the mare's, whispered nonsense endearments, and kissed his ear. He hugged her back with a ferocity that steadied her, and aroused her at the same time. For the first time in ages, hot blood instead of ice water flowed through her veins.

Passion burned behind his dark eyes, exciting her even more than his strength. He reluctantly set her back on the muddy ground when the whistle sounded again.

"Fitz and Nick are here," he told her, his voice low and husky. "Since they were probably at Wyckerly, I think you'll owe Fitz a mare and Nick a new pair of boots after an all-night journey, especially if they have to turn around and sail right back."

"Not to Wyckerly, to Belden Hall," she said in excitement. "Can they sail her?"

Quent rubbed Dream's neck but watched Bell. "Are you sure?"

If he understood her as well as he seemed to, if he realized how much this horse affected her—he was a man beyond all men, and her blood raced with excitement. She nodded. "I'm sure. Let's see if we can find her offspring."

She was risking her heart all over again—for Dream, for *Quent*. She must be mad. But she could no more part from her horse again than she could let Quent go. And she would marry the damned man to prove it.

She was no longer a terrified, helpless eighteen-year-old. This time, she knew the flaws of the man she would be marrying. And she still wanted him, even if Quent was likely to usurp her household and run rampant over her wishes, unless she kept him well in hand—like a wild stallion. He'd given her confidence that she could do it, although it might take snapping a thousand fragile fans to make him listen.

The stallion in him would make it worth the effort. She could scarcely think straight for thinking of ways to make him as happy tonight as he was making her right now.

Leading Dream to the gate, she greeted a rumpled, unshaven earl and diplomat. Fitz and Nick studied Dream's protruding ribs as if Bell had lost her mind.

"This is what we risked life and limb for?" Nick asked dubiously.

"Good conformation," Fitz said, although his expression agreed with Nick. "Out of Eclipse, you say?"

"I do," Bell said in a tone that brooked no argument. "Hiram says there is a filly and a colt with similar conformation. He says the filly has the white arrow and the colt has the black patch and a white foot. But Summerby had word of a stallion." She smoothed the hair over Dream's haunch, showing the color oddity. "She's not good for show, but if Dream's offspring race as she once did, they should run like the wind."

"I'll keep an eye on this one," Nick said, taking Dream's bridle. "I'm not a horseman. Go forth and find your babes," he told her.

Leave it to a man with too many sisters to know she thought of the horses as babes. Bell stood on her toes and kissed his stubbly cheek, then let Quent tug her impatiently back to the pen. She understood. She'd be impatient if he kissed another lady's cheek, too. What they had was too new and precious to share. But she rather liked that he was jealous of her affections.

Fitz was already scrambling through the smaller stallion pen. Within minutes, he was whistling for their attention.

"Look at this one," he crowed. "Perfect conformation, white foot, better than the rest of this glue factory. He's not more than a three-year old! What a looker." He held the stallion's halter as it shook its dark mane.

From beside Bell, Dream nickered approvingly. Bell laughed, feeling more light-hearted than she had in years. "Hiram lied. A stallion, then, and not a colt. Let's find the filly." She petted the mare, then dived back into the pen with Quent at her heels.

Fitz led the whinnying stallion from the pen while Bell and Quent scanned the horses nearest to where they'd found Dream.

"I can recognize good bones and muscle when they're led out one at a time," Quent complained. "But trying to see legs among a sea of tails isn't easy."

She kissed his bristled cheek, too, just because she could. "You just look at their asses, dear."

He laughed and hugged her. "I think I like the Irish imp as much as the lady. How much do you trust Hiram?"

"Not at all," she said, coming down off her cloud. "He's already lied about the colt, hoping we wouldn't search the stallion pen. If he stands to earn anything from the sale of my horses, he'll hide anything he dares. He'll need to. Dolly will have his carcass gutted if she learns he's told us where to find them. He's probably planning on profiting enough to run and hide."

"Then is there some chance that the filly we're looking for may not have the white markings?"

Bell shrugged. "Possibly, although without the markings, it will be harder to prove she's out of Dream. Should we torture him to find out?"

"Bloodthirsty wench. I only ask because I see a filly over there with a dark patch on her haunch but no white arrow." Quent nodded to a smaller horse on the far side of the paddock.

Bell set off in that direction without a second thought. Not until Quent pushed in front of her did she realize it made far more sense to let his larger size lead the way. She was simply accustomed to doing everything herself. Learning to share tasks could be complicated... but pleasurable.

Quent held the filly's head while Bell examined her. The black patch was a positive sign. The shape of her head, her stance... Bell's heart nearly exploded in her chest.

"She's magnificent! Just look at her! Legs like that will eat up ground. Wonder who the stud was? It's not as if Jim could afford a Thoroughbred."

The filly tossed her head restlessly and stomped. Bell dodged her hooves and let Quent yank the halter to keep her head down.

Having secured the stallion, Fitz was now making his way through the pen to meet them. His eyes gleamed with admiration as he studied their find.

"My word, I need to start looking here more often! None of these would have made it to Tattersall's," Fitz exclaimed when he reached them. "I wonder if there are more like yours in here."

"Ask for the Irish loads," Bell told him dryly. "We breed them and lose them all the time for lack of funds. But I'll be having these back, I think."

Fitz and Quent glanced at each other and grinned. Bell ignored them. She had *all* her family back.

Twenty-three

THEY SPENT half a day hunting for the missing animals, hiring grooms, buying feed, setting up stalls on the ship, and waiting for Nick's turn at the dock so he could load three horses.

Quent knew he should be gnashing his teeth with impatience. He expected to find another irate letter from his father waiting in his office. He should be taking up unfinished business instead of spending coins like water. And they still needed to obtain the special license.

But the transformation of a decorous marchioness into a woman who smiled and hugged and laughed and teased was too miraculous to miss. To hell with his office. Bell's ladylike graces had vanished. In their place was a real woman, one unafraid to show her excitement and joy. He might regret that later when she unleashed her temper instead of happiness, but his heart grew lighter every time she held his hand or kissed his cheek. Even Nick and Fitz were staring at them in surprise and awe.

Quent hadn't done a blamed thing, and his betrothed still made him feel as if he were ten feet tall and invincible. She made him *feel*. Common sense said he needed to run right now. But all sense fled every time she laughed.

He did have the presence of mind to set one of the grooms to following Hiram once the man was released. Like Bell, he didn't trust the former stable hand, but Quent had no authority to hold him any longer, and no evidence to prove that Hiram had stolen the horses. They didn't even have documents on any of them except Dream to prove whose horses they were. Hauling Hiram to the nearest officer of the law would be an effort in futility.

"I have to stay with Dream," Bell told Quent earnestly once they had the horses loaded on Nick's ship. "Older horses don't fare well with change, and she's been through so much these past weeks! I can sail on your yacht anytime, but this time, I have to sail with Dream."

"Fitz is perfectly capable of seeing to the animals," Quent argued, heart sinking. He'd hoped for more time together in the peace of the city, where he belonged. But he didn't want her sailing off without him. "We could stay in London, obtain the license, close up our houses." Finish up some business, answer some correspondence, make love without family about... "We don't need to race out of town yet."

"Fitz needs to go home to his wife and children. The horses are my responsibility, not his." She threw an encouraging look to the auburn-haired earl lounging against the railing, waiting for the argument's conclusion.

"Nick can sail around to Brighton, and I can take the animals up to Wyckerly and feed them," Fitz suggested. "It would just require a little more riding to my place than to yours."

"Offloading is bad in either place," elegant Nick offered unhelpfully.

"Dream goes where I go, and I'm going home to my sisters," Bell insisted stubbornly. "We can't be sailing them all over the Channel, so they go with me until they're healthy again. Then Fitz and I can talk about breeding the younger ones."

Starting a breeding program did not sound promising for life in the city.

"I'll leave my yacht docked and go with you," Quent agreed in resignation. He glowered at his so-called friends. "Do either of you ever win an argument with your wives?"

Fitz grinned. Nick whistled and admired his sails.

Bell hugged Quent and kissed his neck. More than his spirits rose to the occasion. He captured her waist and held her close, fair compensation for business lost.

Taking this as answer to the discussion, Fitz offered his farewells and strolled back to the dock to find his own way home. Nick signaled for the ropes to be untied from the moorings and the anchor weighed.

Quent resigned himself to a long ride in a dark hold with three nervous, highly-strung animals. "Do I need to slay any dragons while I'm at it?" he asked, following Bell down the gangway.

"Your father is the dragon. If you could just stifle him..." She let her voice trail off suggestively.

He smothered the fear of the angry letter no doubt waiting at his office. In his frenzy for cash, his father would be selling off his sisters and Bell's both if he didn't act soon.

"We haven't even agreed on the settlements yet," he said without revealing his concern. "Hard to stifle him until then. I take it we're renovating Belden Hall if you're keeping horses there now?" He helped her remove her confining jacket in the heat of the hold. The little slip of nothing she wore beneath it had *him* perspiring.

She knotted her long skirt high enough that he could have seen her ankles—if she hadn't been wearing boots.

"Renovating the Hall is probably best," she agreed. "We'll need a steward to return the land to use so expenses won't eat us up. I don't think either of us will succeed as farmers."

Ah, another negotiating point in forcing his father's hand. "I can bring down one of my brothers to act as steward. And there are bound to be more female relations who will gladly take up residence at the Hall as caretakers. Both should please my father, although that won't be enough to persuade him to give up guardianship."

Knowing his father, it would only make the old man eager to see what other income he might generate from the unused estate. He had to apply his business perspective to that and not his despair at being inundated in family. "I see no point in renovating a house that will be empty most of the year unless we put it to good use."

Quent took the anxious stallion's bit and rubbed the animal's nose as the ship swayed into the current.

"Since Belden Hall belongs to the marquessate, I certainly don't mind it being used by Hoyts," she said. "I dislike waste and always thought it a shame that Edward denied the Hall's use to your family."

"Does this mean there's some hope of peacefully settling our family disagreements?" Quent hadn't really doubted that Bell would be more reasonable than the late marquess, but differences lingered in many matters.

"My family will be living there also, and they're seldom peaceful," she pointed out with a laugh. "I'm not sure how long I want to be in a household with your stubborn but polite sisters and my stubborn but obnoxious siblings. If I have a vote, I'd vote to leave them all in the country to fight it out, while we retreat to the city. We can invite them to visit one at a time."

His optimism rose considerably. "Then you will not mind if I maintain an office in town?" he asked. "I can't neglect my business simply because I've married a wealthy woman."

"And you think I do not have business to tend?" she asked loftily. "You will notice I have not spent these last years frivoling my wealth away."

"A matter of opinion," he reminded her, "but you are entitled to use your funds as you deem best. I would not have offered for you if I thought you were an inveterate gambler. If you wish to spend your funds on horses and the Hall and our families, I have no objection. Give me some credit and don't be so defensive, Bell."

Through the darkness, he could see her hugging her mare's neck. She'd been badly damaged, but he knew she had the strength to overcome anything. She had already overcome her past, but now... she could be so much more. It was almost as exciting to watch Bell emerge from her chrysalis as seeing what steam engines would become.

"I'm trying to be more confident," she said with a hint of sadness. "I know you're a good man. But so was Edward once. People change, and that's what scares me."

"We'll change together," Quent suggested, hiding his hope, as he'd hidden it from the day he'd met her. His longing had been a part of him for so long that he didn't dare confess how much power she had over him.

She considered his suggestion far longer than he could hold his breath. "That could be nice," she finally answered. "We're both a bit old to change, though, aren't we?"

"When I was your age, I was sitting all night in coffee shops, spending my days in counting houses, burning candles at both ends. I think I've changed," he said with a grin.

"You were wenching and studying the marriage mart at the same time," she reminded him. "I remember seeing you haunting the back of the theaters and the ballrooms. You were so gorgeously frightening, all thick glossy curls that needed cutting and smoldering dark eyes that pierced to the bone."

"It wasn't your bones I was seeing," he retorted, unreasonably pleased that she remembered the yearning youth he'd been. "But I'd sworn off marriageable women then. It was you I was studying."

"Me?" She actually sounded shocked.

"You." He flashed a smile, hoping she could see it. "I expected you to be another Camilla, and I waited for you to start playing fast and loose on your elderly husband. You never did, to my vast disappointment."

"No wonder Edward hated you! Good heavens, I really had no idea. I was very young and very lost and very careful to do nothing that would make him take a dislike to me. That still doesn't mean I can change now," she warned.

"We're smart," he assured her. "We'll change."

"Mostly, we need to be determined to make marriage work," she said warily. "Do not think I have any illusions. I know you want to be off about your business and that you're fretting because you haven't had time to obtain a license and for half a dozen other reasons. I appreciate that you understand how much my horses mean to me. But somehow, we have to learn to continue living our own lives instead of in each other's pockets."

"Right now, there is nowhere else I'd rather be than in your pocket," he asserted, and realized he meant it. "Business can wait. The license is a nicety. I don't think our reputations will be lost if we have simple banns posted. I can't imagine the settlements will be completed in three weeks, anyway. Just as long as I'm welcome in your home while we wait, I'm content."

"No, you're not," she said with amusement. "You're simply doing what a stallion does, not that I mind at all. But let us at least pretend to be respectable."

And being welcome in her bed would have to satisfy him for now, because Quent was certain they hadn't seen the last of her conniving relations. Now that the Boyles had an estate in their sights, they'd be after Bell until they had what they wanted. Or he strangled them.

And then he had to find some way of making his father see reason or tell him to jump off a cliff. Which would mean severing relations with his entire family. That would be a trifle more difficult, akin to saying he'd cut off his right arm to keep Bell. No matter how much he complained about his many siblings, he knew his protective instincts wouldn't allow them to suffer—and his damned father counted on that.

IT WAS the early hours before dawn by the time Nick moored his ship at the small village near Belden Hall, a time when Bell would normally be arriving home after a ball. The emotional day had been much more exhausting than dancing. Wearily, she waited for the all-clear before leading her horse out of her stall.

Quent's stalwart presence kept her on her feet, but she was ready for their bed. She didn't care what the household thought, she needed his strong arms around her, reassuring her that all was well.

The horses were as weary as she was—and undernourished despite the grain she'd bought for them. They didn't protest too vigorously as she and Quent led them up the ramp and out of the hold.

She kissed Nick's cheek as he held the wheel steady. "Will you come with us or sail straight back to Nora?"

"I'll wait here until the tide changes," he told her. "With your permission, we'll come back to visit and see how you fare in your rural abode before we leave for Amsterdam."

Bell smiled at his hint of doubt. "Quent and I are very civilized. You will not find us reduced to rags and ruin any time soon, although there may be heads upon poles if our families should interfere. Will you be here long enough to attend our wedding breakfast?"

He bowed over her hand. "Of a certainty. Nora would never allow me to miss it. Try to arrange it before the winter winds fly," he added with a laugh.

He slapped Quent on the back and left them to find their own beds while he returned to his comfortable bunk.

"I sent a groom into the village to secure a room for us," Quent told her. "Let's not wake the household at this hour. Besides, you're dropping with exhaustion."

Bell hugged him again. "No sisters demanding our attention or brothers scalping tutors. A few civilized hours alone, perfect!"

"You're sure you don't want to send them all to Scotland?" he asked with a note of hope in his voice.

Bell laughed. "Not for the world. Perhaps this is one of the ways I'm changing, but I love having people around me again."

Quent heaved an exaggerated sigh. "And here I escaped too much family to find peace in London."

She leaned wearily on his arm as they walked up to the inn. "You still have time to bow out. I'll not hold you to any promises you made in rash lust."

"No, my promise to you is a sacred vow. As long as you will have me, I will be there. This is one way that I will not change, and that's another vow." He kissed her head and led her into the inn.

It wasn't a promise of undying love, Bell knew, so much as a vow not to let her out of his sight, but that was pure Quent.

Reassured, Bell hid her laughter as Quent dickered with the landlord over accommodations. He ended up promising to pay a monthly stipend in return for improving a chamber just for them and their guests. The landlord was thrilled to think the Hall would be opening and bringing in more paying customers for the tavern and stable as well as the inn. She was amazed that Quent actually remembered she was waiting and didn't linger to argue details.

"You would have made a fine marquess," she murmured as they traipsed the stairs to their chamber. "You have a habit of taking charge."

"I don't think parliament would appreciate that habit," he said dryly. "And I know I would not appreciate their dithering. You must accept me as the untitled tradesman that I am."

"I do," she murmured with enthusiasm, throwing her arms around his neck after they closed the door behind them. "A title doesn't keep me warm in bed."

He slid his broad hands under her spencer and cupped her breasts. "There's my Irish lass speaking."

"Does that make you my Scots lad? No titles at all, sir, just you and me and that lovely bed, please." She tugged off his loosened neckcloth.

"I am happy to oblige."

With a tenderness that belied his size, he began removing her clothing with more efficiency than her maid. Bell tried to return the favor, but she had less experience. She fumbled the buttons of his breeches, possibly because he pressed impossibly large against them.

Her need for him was almost frightening. After years of distancing herself from others, she felt the old urge to pull away, but Quent gave her no opportunity. He was there, big and demanding and... too heart-racingly tempting for words.

He kissed her into nakedness. He stroked her into bed. When she was sprawled wantonly over the sheets, he shocked her into surrender by kneeling between her legs and plying her with fingers and tongue until she cried out both release and demand for more.

Wickedly, unrelentingly, he returned to her breasts, spreading kisses in search of all her weaknesses. When she could tolerate no more, Bell shoved his shoulder, forcing him back to the mattress.

"I have always wanted to do this," she said with glee. And with no other warning, she settled over his loins and took him deep inside her, where she could set the pace.

"By the devil, Bell," Quent cried, "you'll be the death of me yet."

As their bodies took over, no further words needed to be said—that was the best part of lovemaking, Bell decided. She didn't need to think at all, just let him love her—*as she loved him.*

Twenty-four

As LONG AS Quent had Bell at his side, he didn't doubt his decision to marry.

The moment Bell disappeared into the bowels of Belden Hall—and her sisters descended on him—he had the urge to flee for town, just as Bell had predicted.

"Where will the wedding be held?" Tess demanded. "You have the license, do you not? Should we be writing invitations to the breakfast?"

"Will there be any eligible bachelors?" Syd asked eagerly. "And will your family be there? What about the marquess?"

Quent shoved his hand through his hair and tried to glare down their eager questions, but these were Bell's sisters. They deserved answers. He didn't have any. "Where's Bell?" he asked in desperation. They'd only just arrived an hour ago. How far could she have gone?

"In the stable, of course," Syd said with exasperation. "That is why we're asking you. We can't pry her away from her horses long enough to be sensible."

"Then I suppose I'll have to leave the planning to the two of you," he suggested.

"Don't be ridiculous! We know nothing of your friends or customs. Have you even set a date?" Tess asked.

They hadn't even agreed on the settlements yet. Or obtained a license, although Quent had managed to send a note around to the church to have the banns read. Not that there were many people in town to hear them in August, but that was legal enough. It simply took longer and limited options for the ceremony.

"There are many agreements to be worked out first," he said evasively. "I'll have my sisters come down to help and all of you can work out the details."

"They probably know as much as we do if they live in Scotland," Tess said with scorn. "You *are* planning to marry, aren't you?"

"Definitely, but we've waited this long, we can wait a while longer to do it properly." That sounded like a good enough answer, but it didn't satisfy Quent much more than it satisfied the girls. Life had too many interruptions. Anything could happen before he marched Bell to the altar.

Quent hunted down his assistant for male support. Penrose seemed to be in his element, interviewing roofers and gardeners and tenants. Quent knew nothing of renovating houses. He supposed he could set up the estate books and examine the agreements Penrose was leaving on the desk in the unused study.

Was this how Bell had felt when she'd been dumped into society without any preparation?

He really needed to be back in the city, in familiar surroundings. He was an investor, not a steward. Show him what was needed to build a steam engine, and he'd set up an entire production industry that would feed his family into the future. Give him a horse... and he rode it. The country held no interest for him.

Restlessly, with nothing else to keep him occupied, he went in search of Bell to reassure himself that he was doing the right thing.

The stable was hot and musty and for horses, not men of business. Quent acknowledged the necessity of animals, but then, outhouses were a necessity, and he didn't feel inclined to spend much time in them. Bell, on the other hand, was developing a decided tendency to emulate the duke's horse-mad daughter and live in her stable.

He found his wife-to-be instructing the head groom on the proper diet for her neglected animals. Her riding habit was the worse for wear. He had a suspicion she would prefer breeches, but he wasn't ready to relent that far on the proprieties.

"They won't be ready to ride for a while, will they?" Quent asked, stroking Dream's nose.

"Probably not until spring," she said absently, checking the horse's hoof.

"Do you mean to stay here all winter to tend to them?"

She glanced up and blinked in surprise. "I hadn't thought about it. It would be pleasant to have Christmas in our own home. But you have business in town, don't you?"

"Christmas is a few months away, and your sisters have made it plain that we have a wedding to plan—which needs to be in our parish unless I obtain a license."

She grimaced. "I suppose we should be back in town before the end of September anyway. It will be cooler and people will be returning for the short session. It would be easier on our wedding guests if we wait until then."

At least she wasn't putting off the wedding to December, Quent realized in relief. But he needed to be in town before then. "I don't like leaving you alone out here, but I have business that requires my attention. If Penrose is turning himself into a steward, I'll have to think about hiring another assistant."

She patted her horse's rump and moved on to another hoof. "Any of your brothers inclined toward business? If not, then you'll need to drag Penrose back to town and hire one of your brothers to work here."

"If I take Penrose, there would be no one out here with you." And he wasn't about to suggest that his father send any of his family until the knots were tied. If nothing else, he needed to check his office for his father's latest demands. "I can set up the estate books, I suppose." Estate books were child's play. He needed to be in the city—with Bell.

This was the least romantic courtship he had ever heard of, which left him frustrated for no discernible reason. Had he expected anything different? Bell had agreed to be his. Shouldn't his triumph be sufficient?

She must have heard something in his voice, because she set the horse's hoof down and emerged from the stall. Straw dangled from her skirt, and she had a smudge of dirt on her nose, but her cheeks were pink and her eyes glowed. She was the most beautiful sight Quent could imagine, and he loved that she was paying attention even when it seemed she wasn't. He was being churlish to disturb her. He bent and pressed a kiss on her cheek that promised more in privacy.

"Surely there is some business in the country to keep you entertained?" she asked. "We could buy the inn or the dock or the butcher shop or something to make you happy?" She caressed his cheek and offered one of the glorious smiles that stopped his heart and made him lose his mind and want nothing more than to please her.

"Or we could set up a blacksmith shop for all your horses or a feed and grain store," he said dryly. "Not precisely the same as investing in steam engines and shipping lines, but they'd serve their purpose. If Essex had anything worth transporting, I could open a carriage trade."

She laughed. "All our profit would go into transporting our families back and forth." She looked past him to the long carriage drive winding up the hill toward the house. "And it looks as if one of them has found their way here already, unless the neighbors have taken to traveling coaches."

Quent turned to examine the intruder and cursed. "That's my family's barouche. I haven't invited anyone."

"Well, I can't imagine anyone but your sisters leaving Scotland, and they will be far more pleasant visitors than Dolly and Hiram," she said cheerfully. "I'll need to change. Let's send my sisters down to entertain them and make them wait," she said wickedly, catching his hand and racing toward the side door.

His heart lightened just considering how long his family could be made to wait—and what he could do with Bell while their uninvited guests cooled their heels.

BELL THOROUGHLY regretted her overly optimistic declaration that Quent's family couldn't be any worse than hers.

The Marquess of Belden sat upon the largest chair in the ancient hall, glaring at the company much as Henry VIII must have done when displeased with his queens.

Lord Belden wasn't much smaller than the Tudor monarch in his later years. No wonder the marquess didn't travel often. Even a barouche would be uncomfortably small after a few hours. Bell was pleased to note that, unlike the Tudors, Quent's father maintained most of his thick hair, although it had turned a distinguished gray.

"This is a surprise and an honor, my lord," Bell said dryly, dropping her best curtsy.

"Surprise being the foremost description," Quent added, not bowing. "What the devil did you think, risking your life with a journey like that? I could have sent my yacht if you had simply let us know you wished to visit."

"And given you time to whisk everyone out of sight?" the older man grumbled from the high-backed armchair he'd appropriated. "I'm not an idiot. I've given you sufficient time to respond to my command to bring my new wards to me, and you have failed to do so. I thought it my responsibility to present myself to them. Where are they?"

"Hiding," Bell responded pertly, before Quent could draw his ire. "They are wary of strangers, and apparently your entrance was... less than agreeable. We have not invited guests for a reason. The Hall is scarcely habitable."

"That damned carriage drive nearly broke every bone in my body! I had reason to complain. Now bring them out of hiding so we can be on with this."

"We'll discuss matters in my study like civilized gentlemen and leave the ladies out of it," Quent said, quashing Bell's temper as effectively as she'd halted his.

Bell started to object, but Quent shot her a warning glare. Well, fine, she didn't want to deal with the ill-tempered old goat anyway. She smiled sweetly and dipped a partial curtsy. "As you say, sir, I'll talk to Cook and the housekeeper and see that all is prepared to your satisfaction."

Her sarcasm was rewarded with Quent's swift grin, but he responded in his normal businesslike manner. "If you find Penrose in your wandering, send him to join us. His penmanship is better than mine."

That sounded ominous.

Bell told herself that the marquess was an old man, set in his ways, and that he simply wasn't willing to deal with a female. Quent would know how to cope with him. Surely, the old Scot could be made to see reason.

She told her sisters the same, but they didn't seem convinced.

Tess was packing a valise and hastily ordering the nursemaid to pack Beebee's things. She shook her head at Bell's argument. "I will not go anywhere with that mean old man. Nowhere," she insisted. "I will walk back to town, if I must. I will hide in barns. I will return to Ireland!" She nearly shouted this last.

"We aren't that desperate," Bell told her, feeling desperate despite her plea. "He can't kidnap you. He brought no bailiffs. We can argue your marriage negates the age codicil of the will if we must go to court. Quent will make him see reason before then. You must at least present yourself so he sees you as a young lady and not an irrational child."

"I feel like an irrational child," Tess wailed, turning and flinging her arms around Bell. "I want a home. I want Jeremy. I want daddy. Why can't anything stay the same?"

Caught unprepared, Bell hesitated, then wrapped her arms around her grieving sister and hugged her. "I will always be here for you. I won't let anyone take you where you don't wish to go. Do you understand me?" She pushed away enough to meet Tess's eyes. "You go nowhere you don't wish to go, I promise. I will have Summerby arrange it so that even over my dead body, you will have a home of your own."

Tess took a steadying breath and nodded. "I know you believe that. I just can't trust fate anymore."

"I understand, but you have to trust *me*." Bell knew what it was like to be tossed by the winds of fate. She'd already given Summerby changes for her will. She would rush him.

"Maybe I haven't earned your trust yet," Bell continued, "but I'm trying. I know next to nothing about the marquess except he's in need of funds, and I have what he wants. We'll work it out. Leave your bag packed if it makes you feel safer, but come down to dinner dressed in all your finery. Show him that you're a confident young woman who doesn't need his guidance."

"What about Syd and Kit?" Tess whispered anxiously.

"We ought to let Kit loose on him," Bell said without remorse, "but we'll pretend we're a proper household for just one night. After that, it depends on how the marquess behaves. I think Syd should come down and play the demure miss for now. We'll see how that goes over first."

"All right, but I still want horses saddled and waiting," Tess retorted.

"Make sure you have coins in your bags before you go," she warned, just to show she understood.

Not feeling any relief, Bell departed to hunt down Syd and tell her the same. She felt as if her life had become a perpetual sail across the Channel, all stomach-churning dips and swells.

Quent's roars from the study did not reassure her. She wondered if she could kidnap her own sisters, but she knew she wasn't being reasonable. Except for the domineering old marquess, Quent's relations were perfectly lovely and would welcome her family with open arms. She simply didn't want to let them go now that she had them back. Was that selfish of her?

Putting her heart on the table for her family to cut up was probably a mistake, but Quent was right. If she couldn't take chances now, she would never move ahead with her life, and she would be forever lonely. Family was worth the risk of another broken heart.

She made certain the marquess was given the next best bedchamber and the new linens. She had a maid set coal to burning to take out any lingering must. Perhaps if he understood that she knew how to manage a household, he would soften a bit.

Quent's father had despised Edward. She feared revenge was his motive in demanding the guardianship.

And since Bell hadn't given him access to any of Edward's funds, perhaps he despised her too. That just made her more angry than fearful. Lachlann Hoyt, fourth marquess of Belden, had not once made himself known to her, even when she'd been a grieving widow. She owed Quent's father *nothing*.

But she dressed in the only decent dinner dress that she'd brought with her, kissed Quent's cheek when she entered the parlor where he waited, and bobbed a brief curtsy to the grumbling marquess. Pretending she was in complete control did little to settle her anxiety.

"I didn't know we would have visitors so we haven't stocked the best brandy yet," she said apologetically. "I'll have someone run into the village tomorrow to see what's available there."

"I brought my own whisky," the marquess growled, holding up a flask. "The English never stock the good stuff."

Edward had despised Scots whisky, but Bell refrained from mentioning anything that might anger their guest. "I'm sure Lord Quentin will arrange to have the best he can find on hand the next time you visit. Did the two of you have a good talk?"

"We did not. Where are my wards?" the querulous old man demanded.

Bell glanced questioningly at Quent, who shrugged and looked indifferent—not helpful. She continued smiling. "Lord Wexford is in the nursery at this hour, of course. He's only six. Mrs. Dawson and Lady Sydony will be down shortly. You should have brought Lady Margaret and Lady Sally with you. My sisters would enjoy their company as much as I do." She reminded the old goat that she had been sponsoring Quent's sisters these last couple of seasons.

"I'm not frittering another farthing on the chits," Belden grumbled. "They've been offered positions as teachers at that school they attended, and they'll take them. The family is large enough as it is. They don't need to marry and bring home more hungry mouths to support. Tell the fillies to hurry and let's be on with dinner." He heaved his girth from the chair.

Bell bit down hard on her fury and glanced at Quent. Had he known that his father didn't mean to let his sisters have the come-out she'd planned? Quent remained stoic and didn't look at her, which didn't aid her anger.

She knew exactly what the old curmudgeon was about. She and Edward had had these power struggles frequently over his last years. It had taken much practice, but she'd learned to retain her composure. She knew the countermove and it did not include cracking a porcelain shepherdess over anyone's head.

"My household, my hours," she said sweetly, tightening the golden reins to remind him of who was in charge. "The dinner bell will sound at six as planned, and my sisters will be down then." She could have added *You will remember I am the marchioness and this is my home until I die*, but she was still trying to be polite for Quent's sake.

The marquess sent Quent a hard look. "And this is what you're signing up for—wedded to a hen who rules the roost? You'd better think again, boy."

Quent, damn his leather hide, merely sipped his whisky and raised his magnificent eyebrows. "You think I should prefer being under your thumb rather than that of a beautiful woman's?"

Bell didn't know whether to conk him or kiss him.

Twenty-five

IF HE ONLY HAD Edward's most excellent brandy, Quent thought, he could easily drink himself under the table. He wondered what Bell would think of public drunkenness.

That was a stupid question and proved he was already half-foxed on bad wine. Bell would despise a drunkard like her father.

Resolutely, Quent dug into the fine potato dish the cook had provided to accompany the roast beef.

The interview with his father had not gone well. His father was quite convinced that with Sally and Margaret out of the house and supporting themselves, and by marrying off Tess to the cousin with all the children so Bell's dower money would support them, he could save enough to buy his own damned roof. The promise of a stewardship for one of Quent's brothers did not take the man's eyes off possible income from rents from the earl's Irish estate.

The old man was a product of a different place and time. And a product of poverty and injustice, which had made him bitter, ruthless, and, yes, occasionally cruel—or in best case, just thoughtless. Bell wasn't likely to appreciate the problem of dealing with him.

Quent had kept his two lives separate for good reason. It was a given that fiercely independent Bell and his dictatorial father would despise each other on sight. He feared the old man was likely to antagonize Bell into refusing marriage.

Sitting at the head of the table where Bell had placed him, Quent signaled the footman to fill his water glass. Best to keep his head while Bell and his father did their best to rip off each other's. Bell, at least, bit with socially acceptable politeness.

He'd feel more comfortable with Bell at his side. Unfortunately, Bell had chosen to distance herself in the role of dazzling society hostess tonight. She was seated at the opposite end of the table—next to his father. She was incredible, adorned in pearls and silk, directing the conversation with the skill of a dowager marchioness—and smothering his father in the most insincere smiles Quent's imagination could conjure. She was formidable—and so very much out of his plebian league.

The dowager marchioness side of her was capable of burning acid with her tongue. Bell could give lessons to the queen on subjugating pretension. His father had better be careful or he'd be fortunate to come away with his skin intact.

Which was when Quent realized that Bell's exquisitely dignified behavior was leading the marquess down the garden path, and chances were very good, right over a cliff. His hopes for keeping relations amicable between Bell and his father plummeted to nil.

She was forcing him to choose sides.

"You are kind to consider the welfare of my sisters," Bell was saying in that false tone she'd employed dangerously all evening. "But they are newly bereaved and need close family for comfort. When we're ready, we'll certainly consider a good school for Lady Sydony."

Sitting on either side of the table, Bell's sisters sat blessedly mute, toying with their food and sending the marquess glances from beneath their lashes. Gauging from their unusual lack of smiles and chatter, Quent would have to say the girls weren't thrilled with his father's blustering autocratic habits.

Since they'd been raised by a dissolute Irish rebel in the freedom of American society, Quent was fairly certain his father's iron-fisted imperialism would not bend them to his will any better than it would bend Bell. Quent would wager they were already plotting. The sisters merely waited to see if he and Bell stood up for them. Quent reached for his wine glass again.

His family had been his reason for existence for most of his life. His siblings needed him as much as Bell's needed her. If battle lines were drawn... He didn't want to choose sides.

"Nonsense," his father declared. "Your sisters don't know you any more than they know me. And they certainly don't know my son. Marrying just to take them as wards is asking for trouble. They'll be fine once they're settled."

Quent almost spurted his drink in surprise. The old man, in his curmudgeonly way, was trying to *protect* him from marriage—to a woman the marquess thought was a manipulative harridan. His father's old-fashioned defense of his family was the reason Quent couldn't tell him to go to the devil. He himself was guilty of a little too much of the same.

If Quent judged Bell's rising color at all, his father was about to learn how the Virgin Widow protected her own. Battle lines were being drawn as he watched.

"I told you the subject was not open to discussion," Quent warned, stepping in to prevent his intended bride from pushing his father over the cliff. "I am marrying Bell, and that's final. We will sue for the guardianship of her family, if necessary. Without my funds, you cannot afford an English barrister to fight us. So let's have a decent family meal and speak of more interesting topics. I believe Lady Tess can tell us more of American shipping concerns."

The girls gazed at him with awe and admiration. Bell looked as if she might slap him. Bell was the smartest person at the table tonight. She knew he'd just set off the old man's stubbornness. But sometimes, a man could only take so much.

"My sister's boy, your cousin Gareth, is clerking with a barrister," the marquess reported in triumph. "He will have my case heard."

With all the regal dignity and grace only a woman with one of the highest positions in society could command, Bell rose from her chair. Even the marquess hushed. Pink stained her cheeks. Her eyes flashed emerald fires. Quent could swear her hair gleamed with more red than russet, and had there been a sword at hand, she would have held it.

Well, he had warned the marquess to try to keep the peace. For the sake of family harmony, it had seemed best to maintain a respectful dialogue.

His father had been the one to break the rules.

As much as he feared the result, Quent refused to follow Edward's path and deny Bell her chance to speak.

Leaning back in his seat, he crossed his arms, nodded, and let her loose. Very few ever stood up to his intimidating father's authority—especially when the old man was legally in the right.

Quent anticipated the fireworks with trepidation.

BELL DIDN'T NEED Quent's approval for what she was about to say. She'd been struggling all through dinner, trying to be polite and reasonable—just as she'd used to do with Edward. That had grated badly.

Then she had tried a subtler approach, showing the marquess that her sisters were grown, with minds of their own, and not in need of an oppressive guardian. But if the irascible old codger could diminish the prospects of his own daughters— obviously, he was the sort who thought women were mindless tools to be used for his own benefit. His suppression of Quent's requests did not bode well for dealing with headstrong Kit.

She had wanted to be generous for the sake of the children. Hell would freeze over now before she left them in his hands.

"My lord," she addressed her dinner companion in her best dowager frostiness. "You and my late husband have far more in common than you can possibly know."

The marquess harrumphed. "Edward was a clutch-fisted, obstinate bigot. There isn't a man alive who could call me that."

"Then this *woman* will call you so," she said coldly. "All that matters to you is how much coin you have and how you can acquire more. Women are no more than pawns on your chessboard—proving your bigotry. The one honest thing Edward ever did in his life was to respect me enough to marry me. And it turns out that he even did that for selfish reasons—just as you are forcing my sisters into servitude for your own selfishness. My father was in no position to protect me, but by all that is holy, I *will* defend my sisters!"

"Servitude!" the marquess bellowed. "School isn't servitude!"

"It is when all you think of is how cheaply you can push them out of the house until you can marry them off to the highest bidder without a bit of consideration to their happiness! You are doing the same thing to your own *daughters*! How can I possibly believe you have my sisters' happiness in mind when you are making your own daughters miserable? Quent and I shall invite them to stay with us. You cannot force them to become spinster teachers if they wish to marry. Sally and Margaret are of legal age—they can choose to leave you anytime they like."

At the far end of the table, Quent gave a muffled cough that might have been objection, but Bell was too furious to care. "Women are too valuable a resource to be thrown to any available man or cast aside as worthless dependents," she continued, not letting the marquess speak. "We have minds and abilities and are your *equal*—unless you're such a coward that you fear we're better than you and seek to suppress us.

"If you attempt to force my family from my care, you are a bigot, a coward, and far greedier and more spiteful than Edward ever was. I will not hear you speak another word against me or mine when you sit there like a fat cockroach, feeding off your young. Quent could be racing yachts and horses instead of working himself to the bone trying to keep you in comfort. You have smothered his life just as you would your daughters. Did you ever consider their happiness? Or were you hoping to force me into paying your expenses so Quent might pursue more grandiose projects than your roof?"

Quent rose, ire flaring in his eyes and his fists knotting on the table. "That's going too far, Bell. You needn't defend me along with your sisters. You're hurting yourself as well as them to speak to my father in such a manner."

"Someone needs to speak plainly to him," she threw back. "And if you won't, I will! I have no intention of politely obeying still another tyrant wearing the bedeviled Belden title—if I have to haul the girls back to the Americas to stop you."

"I'll go to Ireland before I'll go back to the Americas," Syd protested.

"Beebee and I'll go with you, and we'll take Kit with us," Tess agreed stoutly.

"You won't go anywhere without my permission," the marquess roared. "The Irish estate is under my authority until the lad comes of age."

"You can't earn enough to keep a roof over your own head," Quent shouted, as Bell had never heard him shout before. "I told you we'll fight you. You accomplish nothing by antagonizing the ladies."

"You *owe* me a roof," the marquess shouted back. "I paid for your education so you can provide what the cattle cannot. And you owe *me* respect. You don't owe Edward's doxy a second thought. What's the matter with you, boy? I've come to set you free from her clutches."

"I don't owe you a spot of respect when you behave like a tyrant," Quent said, pounding his fist on the table until his water glass jumped. "You're ruining everything."

Bell waited for Quent to say he didn't *want* to be released from her clutches, but he was too caught up in his power struggle with his father.

"You wanted your fancy city life," the marquess countered. "Are you giving it up for this moldering piece of expensive rock? Is that what you want?"

"Of course not! I told you, we'll find a place for Stuart to work here, and possibly Elizabeth, if she would like to take charge of running the place. That's two more of your dependents off your hands. Then you can buy your own roof. Bell and I prefer the city."

She didn't remember discussing where they'd be living. She hadn't even agreed to a settlement yet, and he was catering to the damned marquess, directing her life—as she had vowed never to allow another man to do again.

"What the devil does the roof have to do with it?" she cried over the men's bellows.

"The roof damned well has nothing to do with it!" Quent roared, sounding very much like his father.

The marquess finally dragged his bulk to his feet. "And is this how you plan to raise the bairns then? Shouting and roaring over their heads?"

Bell shot him a look of incredulity. Then cast her glare to her no-longer betrothed.

He didn't even notice her horror.

Quent was just like every other Hoyt who'd ever lived—concerned only with himself. She didn't need to hear more.

Heart crumbling to ashes, Bell coldly interrupted the tirade. "Edward's *doxy* will buy your foolish roof if you'll simply assign guardianship to me, my lord," she said sardonically, with all her foolish hopes crashing around her. She cast Quent a deprecating glance. "Then you can keep this puppet of yours and let him dance to your tune in his lonely tower for the rest of his years."

Looking stricken, Quent started after her. The marquess yelled at him in Scots, then collapsed heavily into his chair and grabbed for his whisky glass.

Uncaring, Bell nodded at Tess and Syd. "Come along, we'll leave the men to finish biting off each other's heads."

"This is not over!" Quent shouted after her.

QUENT FEARED it was very much over. Bell's horror-stricken face would be etched into his worst nightmares for years to come.

"You've just destroyed everything I've worked for these last ten years," he said heavily, shoving away his wine and glaring at his unrepentant father.

"No, lad, ye did that yerself. Ye don't love the lass. Let her be. Find yerself a good woman who'll knit your sweaters and warm your bed, not a flighty Thoroughbred who skitters off at every loud noise."

"What the devil do I want with a woman who knits?" Quent asked in disgust. "If I want sweaters, I'll buy them!"

And if he wanted a woman to warm his bed, it was Bell, but even he refused to discuss some things with the bully. Besides, he greatly feared he'd seen the last of the beautiful, laughing woman who had adorned his sheets these last nights.

Pain crushed him.

Worse yet was the agony of knowing there was a certain truth in what his father said.

He didn't know how to raise a family. Or to argue without creating a gale storm of the likes his family created over every dinner table. All he knew how to do was negotiate a business deal.

As he watched his entire precarious house of cards crumble, he shoved up from the table and glared at his self-satisfied parent.

"If love is what you feel for me and the reason for driving off the only woman I've ever wanted, then you can take your love and shove it into the frozen loch of your damned heart," Quent told him. "I'll not be your *puppet* a day longer."

The marquess raised his flask and drank deeply.

Through an open window, the wild cry of a terrified horse blended with Kit's furious screams of outrage.

QUENT DASHED for the nearest exit. Bell had already lifted her skirts and was racing through the hall. He stopped her sisters from doing the same. "Wait here until we know what's happening. You'll need to direct the servants." With longer strides, he sped after Bell.

He'd spent the last ten years building up a sturdy fortress of civilized behavior to hide behind while he acquired a fortune.

The proper, dignified mate he'd chosen had obliviously shredded every ounce of his civility in less than ten days. He was prepared to crush heads with his fists and stomp her enemies with his boots.

The madwoman evidently thought she could do it on her own. Quent ran faster, catching up with Bell outside in the side yard, hauling her up by the waist until she kicked his shins with her slippers.

"That was Dream's call," she said fiercely. "Put me down."

"First, we—" He didn't need to finish the sentence. One of the new mares cantered through the open stable door, with Kit on her bare back, clinging to her mane.

The boy was weeping and screaming obscenities no six-year-old should know and so focused on his target that he didn't even notice Quent and Bell in the shadows of the house.

Turning in horror, Quent glanced down the carriage drive in time to see a dust cloud of horses galloping away.

"They've stolen Dream," Bell cried in horror, picking up her skirt and sprinting for the stable.

"Or your damned brother let them loose," Quent muttered, but he was hot on her heels and not prepared to argue.

Inside Dream's empty stall, Quent hauled a dazed groom to his feet. The filly and stallion were gone as well. He was amazed the thieves hadn't taken any of the other horses, which were in far healthier shape.

"This is Hiram's doing," Bell called from another stall, as if she understood his thoughts. "He's taken the horses he knows."

"What the devil was Kit doing out here with them?" he yelled back, flinging a saddle on his Friesian.

"Feeding his pony," the groom said, rubbing his injured jaw. "They didn't even know he was here until one of them planted me a facer. When he came out squalling and swinging a pitchfork bigger than him, they shoved off right quick. They mighta taken more animals if he'd not screamed like a banshee."

Damnation, but the Boyles had more courage than brains sometimes. Quent was almost proud of the lad—except if the thieves had known he was the earl, the boy could have been kidnapped.

Irrational panic set in at that thought. He had to reach Kit before the boy caught up with the raiders.

"Go up to the house," Quent shouted at the groom. "Tell them to send for help, then saddle up as many men as you can to follow us."

"Aye, sir. I'll fetch t'other grooms. We'll be arfter them horses. I never seen such bloody bold thieves."

"I'll introduce my family before I hang them," Bell called furiously over the stall wall.

What the devil was she doing in there?

Adding a whip and stout stick to his arsenal on the saddle, Quent mounted up and looked over the panel to where Bell was yanking on a groom's boots over a pair of men's breeches. She had her evening gown hiked nearly to her waist while she assembled her unseemly attire.

The damned woman could distract him even when he was murderously furious. Her legs in men's breeches were a sight to behold. He shook off his lust to concentrate on the moment.

"You're not going anywhere," he warned. "I'll fetch Kit home. The thieves won't travel far on those malnourished nags."

"They don't need to travel far if they have friends waiting down the road. Never, ever underestimate an Irish horseman." Boots on, she stood and yanked down her skirt over the breeches.

"I don't have time to argue. Just use your head for once and stay here. Don't make me tether you like a mare." Impatiently, Quent kicked his gelding into action. The Friesian wasn't a race horse, but it could last all night, if needed.

Bell caught up with him a few minutes later—riding astride the bare back of one of Fitz's mares with her evening gown hiked up to her hips. The breeches were too baggy for her slender thighs or Quent might have expired from lack of blood in his head at the sight.

"Devil take it, Bell," he shouted in fury and utter fear. "Go back to the house! Don't make me have to look after you as well as the boy."

She saluted him and kicked the mare into a full gallop.

Cursing, Quent pushed his mount faster. And he'd thought he wanted to settle down to a civilized life with...*a mad Irishwoman*?

Moments later, Bell's horrified scream sliced through his gut worse than any sword.

From the road, Quent watched Kit's small body fly over the head of his balking mare. It had to be the most appalling sight Quent had ever faced in his life, and his heart nearly stopped in his chest. He kicked his horse into a full gallop across the pasture as that sturdy little body splashed into the pond the mare had refused to enter.

Quent choked on terror and guilt as the boy sank—and didn't come back up.

He'd considered the lad no more than a nuisance and an obstacle to work around, but he was a damned plucky brat and would make a good earl someday. Losing him like this... wasn't happening on his watch.

Bell reached the pond first, but even as she reined in her mount and leapt down, she hastily grabbed the bridle to steady herself. What the devil was the woman thinking? It had to have been ten years since she'd been on a horse.

Quent reached her just as Bell stumbled toward the brackish pond. He doubted that she even knew how to swim. His terror doubled. Rather than try to tussle with her, he leapt off his horse and ran past, wading into the mud and water to where the surface rippled.

With no thought to his expensive clothes, he dived beneath the dark waters. They weren't deep, thank all that was holy. He found the struggling dark shadow and filled his hands with whatever he could grab.

He came up for air, hair and water streaming down his face. But over his shoulder he held a soggy, limp bundle of clothes. Bell had waded in after them, weeping as Quent had never seen her do. Her sobs of relief and panic shattered what remained of his poise. He bit his tongue to prevent shouting at her to get her damned derriere out of the water and back to shore, where she belonged.

Still suppressing his rage and panic, Quent whacked Kit's back with his hand as he strode from the pond, hoping Bell had the sense to pry herself out of the muck because his head was too jumbled by *feelings* to think clearly. Before they had reached solid ground, Kit was coughing and crying and starting to kick.

Weeping, Bell lifted him from Quent's arms the instant they hit shore. She cradled Kit's heavy weight and stumbled to her knees, hugging her sobbing little brother.

Still too shaken for rationality, uncertain whether he had the right to comfort either of them any longer, Quent grabbed his gelding's reins. He'd almost lost a spirited, courageous little boy before he'd recognized the value of the boy's character. How had he thought he would make a good guardian if he didn't grasp that the children were more important than his father's damned roof?

Distraught, he lingered a moment until the pair were in a state to listen and obey. He might be damned useless for all else, but he wasn't having any more women and children drowning if he could prevent it. The thieves could go to hell first.

"They stole your horses," Kit hiccuped, trying to wiggle out of his sister's arms.

"But they didn't steal you, and you're far more valuable," Bell asserted, refusing to let him go. "Don't ever, ever do that again. You will make an old lady of me. Lord Quentin will drown trying to save you. We thank you for what you tried to do, Kit, but..." She broke down weeping again.

"Can you even swim?" Quent asked, wringing out his coat.

"Of course," Kit replied, belligerent now that he wasn't as terrified.

"Bell, can you?" Quent demanded, stomping his boots in an attempt to empty them.

She looked up, dazed. "Swim? No, I don't think so. What does it matter now? You saved him, and as much as I want to hate you, I can't. You have my undying gratitude, if only for this."

Gratitude wasn't what he wanted, but he'd take what he could get. "Devil take it then, don't dive into any more ponds if you can't swim. Even if it makes me an odious tyrant, I insist that you take Kit back to the house. Let me follow the thieves, and for once, give me some credit and don't doubt that I can catch the bastards."

He was still steaming over their quarrel. He had no experience in settling irrational arguments, but he'd damned well better learn. When Bell opened her mouth to protest, he leaned over and shut her up with a rough kiss. Tearing away, he glared at her. "Go home. This time, you can't do it all yourself."

"I'll arm the grooms," she agreed with obvious reluctance. "Don't do anything I'd do until they arrive."

In his current state of agitation, the thieves would be lucky he didn't rip off their heads. Quent didn't make any promises.

Twenty-six

CRADLING a soggy Kit, Bell barely managed to hold her seat on the mare after Quent boosted them up. Her brother was unusually quiescent as she arranged her skirt and kept him close. She couldn't shake her fright at nearly losing this precious life. How could she think she was capable of keeping her siblings safe all on her own? Hadn't she proved her incompetence in anything except giving orders?

Before she could knee the horse into action, a sharp whistle warned they were no longer alone. She shuddered and clutched Kit, swinging her mount in the direction of home and safety.

Two men on stocky ponies blocked her path. Beside her, Quent cursed and grabbed the cudgel from his saddle.

"Thought we heard some'at," one said. "Would that be the earl who'll be stealin' folks' homes?"

Oh, botheration. Hiram had brought his bully boys from home.

Raising his cudgel, Quent placed himself and his big horse between her and the thieves. "That's my spoiled rotten nephew. My men are right on our heels, prepared to hang horse thieves. You'd best move along."

Bell prayed they believed him. Her heart quailed at the possibility that they would harm Kit for a ridiculous title.

In alarm, she heard a splash behind them. Holding Kit tight, she tugged her mare to a right angle from Quent's.

Hiram was riding Dream through the muddy pond, holding a pistol.

He was riding *her* horse. Dripping wet, terrified beyond measure, she still had the sense to savor a flash of triumph. If she accomplished nothing else, she'd show one damned man not to mess with what was hers.

She hugged a sniffling Kit and whispered in his ear. "Don't say a word. Listen to Lord Quentin, pretend you're his nephew, and if anything bad happens, listen for me to say *síos*. If I do, start kicking and screaming for all you're worth. Understand?"

Kit hiccuped and nodded.

"Less likely to shoot us if we got a hostage," one of the thieves concluded. "Hand him over."

"That will not happen," Quent asserted. "You have a head start on my men already. We have to take the boy home before he catches cold. You don't need him."

Hiram splashed through the low-lying water. "It's the boy or the woman. Hand him over, milady," he ordered. "That bloody man of yours would have us killed for certain elsewise. We'll set him down once we're safe."

She wouldn't have Quent attempting to fight off three brutes if she had any choice at all. "Remember what I said," she whispered to Kit.

Bell held up her hand before anyone came closer. "Hiram, I didn't want to see you hang, but I'll have you drawn and quartered for this."

"Not likely," he said with a shrug. "We used your coins to buy fares to the Americas, and those horses you're on will pay our way once we're there. Get down from that one and make your man do the same."

"That's double-dealing, Hiram!" she protested. "We paid you for finding Dream, and now you're stealing her back."

Her knees ached, and she was losing her grip. She couldn't hope to race for safety. It was only a matter of time before she fell with Kit. She hugged him close, resisting releasing him, praying the grooms would arrive first.

Quent idled his gelding into place between Bell and Hiram's pistol, but he couldn't be in two places at once. Protecting her from a pistol opened them up to the two rogues on the road—who kneed their ponies into action, riding at them from two sides.

Quent swung his cudgel at one, but the other pony rode close enough for its rider to grab Bell's reins. Her mare reared in fright, and her weak knees gave out. Rather than harm the mare's mouth by yanking back, Bell slid backward, hitting the ground but clinging to her brother. The rogue leaned over and snatched Kit from her arms.

Kit cried out, but then abruptly shut up. She could see his pale face straining to watch her while his captor galloped toward the road. Hiram held his pistol on them, giving the kidnappers time to escape.

"Bring that mare over here, milady. I be needin' her more than you," Hiram ordered. "I sure don't want to be puttin' gunshot in you."

"I'm fine, Quent, stay seated," Bell warned. Pulling herself up, she led her mare straight at Hiram. "*Síos*, Dream," she shouted at the top of her lungs.

Blessed Dream, with Hiram on her back, responded to the command *down* that Bell had taught her years ago. The horse kneeled in the mud—and Hiram tumbled over her head.

Bell cracked her crop across Hiram's gun-holding arm once he hit the ground. For good measure, she stamped on his fingers with her boot. He hollered, and she kicked the pistol into the brackish pond.

Bless his Irish heart, Kit did what came naturally. At Bell's shout, he screamed and beat his heels into the escaping pony as his captor tried to escape back to the road.

"Brilliant," Quent acknowledged curtly, kneeing his massive mount after a screaming , squalling Kit and his would-be kidnapper.

Bell was shaking so hard, she wanted to collapse in quivering fear, but now was not the time. She clung to the reins of Dream and the two mares, stomping Hiram's hand every time he tried to get up.

With Kit wailing like a banshee, kicking his heavy boots, and thrashing about as only a holy terror could do, the thief holding him could barely control his pony, much less force it to run. Quent would be on him in seconds.

Swallowing back her fear, Bell clung to Dream's neck. Her heart throbbed in terror, but she had to admit that she would be useless chasing after thieves. She had to admit that she couldn't do it all.

She prayed and watched over her shoulder as Quent performed a circus maneuver worthy of her own father. He leaned over and swept Kit from the terrified pony, heaved the boy over his saddle, then spun his war horse on a dime, and hurtled back to her while the thieves raced away.

He might call himself a tradesman, but Lord Quentin Hoyt was a warrior through and through.

Not even breathing hard, he dropped Kit on Dream's saddle. "Good work, lad, hold on." He held out his hand to Bell. "Don't worry about that bastard you're kicking. He can't go far on foot. Take Kit home. I'll go after the other horses."

Once upon a time, she would have argued. That time was not now, while she was shaking too hard to climb into the saddle.

Bell set her overlarge boot in Hiram's too-long stirrup. With a boost from Quent's big hand on her posterior, she managed to throw her breeched leg over the man's saddle. Dream stood still like the dream she was, letting Bell struggle astride while taking Kit into her arms. Choking back tears, she settled Kit in front of her, clutching him with one arm while she took the reins of both mares in her free hand.

"The horses aren't important. Come back with me," she pleaded with Quent, too weary and wrung out to fight.

"I don't let horse thieves go free," he said with finality.

Her heart wept over this man she'd thrown away less than an

hour ago. He was an obstinate Scot, a tyrant in the making, but he had the courage of Robin Hood and King Arthur rolled into one.

Arguing would be futile, but he was only one man. She couldn't let him risk his life for what was not his battle. "I can't bear to see you hurt. Please don't do anything until the grooms catch up with you," she asked. "We don't know how many thieves there are."

"Take him home," Quent said curtly. "I'll be fine if I know you are."

That was as much of an admission of his concern for her that she would ever wring from him, Bell suspected. As much as she wanted to weep and tell him not to go, she'd reached her limits.

She didn't have his physical strength. To help him, she must find someone with more stamina and weapons.

Cradling a soggy but now-boisterous Kit, Bell barely managed to stay in the saddle on the ride back to the house, trailing Kit's mare as well as her own. Despite the brat's bouncing and excited chatter, she didn't want to release his small body. Her heart still raced, and she shivered with fear and damp. When they reached the front steps, a footman ran out to take Kit from her, and she nearly tumbled off.

"I kicked him!" Kit shouted the instant he hit the ground. "I kicked him and he let me go."

Wearily, Bell embraced Dream's neck while Tess and a maid ushered their little brother into the house, still shouting his triumph. He'd have nightmares later, no doubt.

She would have nightmares. Right now, she couldn't even dismount.

Syd was wearing her habit, pacing up and down, and swearing, because the grooms wouldn't let her saddle a carriage horse. At sight of her own mare, she brightened.

"I have a sword," she declared murderously. "Let us go after them."

Humbling herself, Bell untangled her feet from the stirrups and slid ungracefully from Dream. Once her feet hit solid ground, she grabbed the saddle and hung on to keep from sinking to her knees. "Where is Penrose?"

The elderly marquess limped from the shadows. "He and the grooms took off across the fields. There is apparently a bend in the road they mean to cut across. Where is my son?"

"He saved Kit, then rode off after the thieves. One of them is still in the pond. We'll need to fetch the scoundrel before he does anything else stupid." With her damp clothes clinging, Bell risked releasing the saddle to climb the steps. "Syd, call for the carriage. You can't possibly catch up with the men, but if they corner the thieves, they may need help transporting them or the horses. I'll be dressed by the time the team is harnessed."

"There are no grooms to harness the team," the marquess argued.

"I can harness a team," Syd said scornfully. "Where do you come from that you can't pull your own weight?" She stalked off, leaving the marquess silent.

"Do you really want my siblings in your household?" Bell murmured wearily. "Kit just chased horse thieves and drove off a full-grown kidnapper. Tess will soon come down, dressed for riding and probably carrying one of the medieval sabers from the hall. And I have absolutely no doubt that Syd can use the sword she was wielding. What can *you* do?"

"I can harness a team," the marquess snarled, before hobbling down the stairs after Syd.

BELL PERSUADED Tess to stay home, wielding an ancient pistol, and standing guard over Kit. She let Syd carry a blunderbuss and ride with the carriage driver as lookout. In dry travel gown, Bell climbed inside and took the carriage's forward-facing seat, as she always did.

Looking miffed, the marquess did the same, forcing her to squeeze to one side. Apparently title and age had precedence over gender, Bell concluded wryly. She refused to shift sides but stared stonily out the window, praying for Quent's safety.

She despised being weak, but she had to accept the fact that Quent was stronger than she in many ways. She could not say the same for the marquess.

Her rambunctious siblings *needed* Quent's forward thinking. They needed his strength and understanding. And she'd flung him away.

"I have reconsidered," the marquess said flatly as the carriage rattled down the rutted drive.

Bell bit her tongue and strained to see ahead, although she had little hope that Quent was already riding back to her.

"I will grant you guardianship of your family if you will release Quentin from his vows," the marquess continued.

Bell almost choked. She swung to glare at the old man in the gloom from the dim carriage lamps. "You have wanted Edward's money for decades. Why change your mind when your son almost has access to it?"

He gripped the knob of his walking stick and stared ahead. "Much as you think otherwise, I love my children and want what's best for them. I am well aware that Quent left home to escape the chaos and responsibility of a large and fractious family. He prefers his peace and solitude. He will be miserable living with your... belligerent... siblings."

That possibility gnawed at Bell's insides. Despite her fury, despite everything she'd learned over the years, she still *loved* the damned man and wept at the pain of losing him. But even her stupid, worthless heart knew that if you love someone, you want them to be happy. Quent was happy when surrounded by books and papers—not chattering females and boisterous children.

He didn't deserve complete and utter chaos for the rest of his days.

The marquess was offering her everything she had wanted—her family and freedom to keep her own wealth. And Quent would be happier for it.

She should be triumphant. Why then, did it feel as if her world had just crumbled into dust?

DREAM'S OFFSPRING might run like the wind, but they were limited to the speed of the ponies to which the thieves had tied them. Carried on a storm of fury, Quent soon found the trampled copse where the thieves had camped. In the moonlight, he followed a trail of broken branches and horse droppings. It was easy enough to see where they'd returned to the road and in which direction they rode.

That a hired hand like Hiram had dared treat Bell with such disrespect not only infuriated him, but ripped at his insides. How could people who had known her not see beneath her feminine exterior to what a brave, strong, intelligent woman she was? That trick with the damned horse was proof enough for the smallest mind. She'd taught the horse to throw off a thief! Hiram had to be a beef-witted bastard not to have known she could do that.

She'd looked so exhausted, Quent had almost surrendered the hunt just so he could hold her. But he didn't want these mindless villains thinking they could come after her again. She might have taken him into dislike, but she couldn't stop him from arranging it so there would be no more depredations like this one.

His gelding followed the road in ground-covering strides until he heard noises ahead. He slowed to a walk and took to a hilly field.

From this higher viewpoint, he could see Penrose riding hell-bent down the road with his band of grooms. Help had arrived. He no longer had to wait. His fury surged now that it had an outlet.

Quent didn't bother to conceal his position any longer but whistled in a manner that Penrose would recognize. He gestured ahead, then struck out in pursuit.

With Penrose and the grooms riding up the road and Quent thundering down the hill from in front, the thieves didn't stand a chance.

Quent lashed his whip at the first raised pistol, disarming the ruffian before he could aim. The weapon hit the ground and detonated, terrifying the stolen Thoroughbreds into rearing and sidestepping in protest. Without Hiram to give orders, it was all over but the shouting after that.

The grooms galloped in and secured the frightened horses, leading them from the fray. Penrose ran down a thief who tried to escape on foot. After leaping from his horse and knocking off the bounder who had tried to kidnap Kit, Quent trussed him up with sailor's knots.

With the thieves secured, he returned to his mount and went in search of Hiram—not difficult since Bell had unhorsed the old stable hand.

By the time the carriage lumbered up the road, three thieves and Hiram had been gathered and bound, prepared for transport.

As his father climbed down from Bell's city carriage, Quent nearly fell off his gelding. Concealing his shock, he rode over and snatched the blunderbuss from Syd before she could accidentally shoot anyone. He nodded in surprise at his father but didn't dare hope that Bell would have deigned to travel with him.

His eyebrows nearly flew off his head as she climbed down next. His father and Bell in the same carriage for miles... did not bear considering.

"Where's Dolly?" was the first thing she asked.

No one answered. The thieves' silence was telling. They knew the name. The harridan still had to be around. Quent turned to Bell's head groom. "Check at the inn. Who is the magistrate here?"

"Used to be Belden," the groom answered. "Squire's been doing the work these last years."

Quent didn't bother glaring at his father, the absentee landlord. It wasn't as if the law would allow a woman to act as magistrate—even though Bell had to be equal to any man he'd yet to meet.

With some understanding of all the frustrations she faced as a female, Quent swung down from the saddle. Without asking her permission, he gathered Bell in his arms. He needed tangible proof that she was well and unharmed by the evening's escapade.

She resisted his hug—proving his rebellious Bell was alive and strong.

He narrowed his eyes when she stepped away the instant he released her. "How's Kit?" he asked warily.

"Acting as if he's as big and brave as you," she retorted. "He's well and with Tess. Shall I go with you to find Dolly?"

Quent glanced to his father leaning on his walking stick. "I'd thought to use the carriage for transporting the thieves to the magistrate. My father has complicated the issue."

"Yes, he seems to have a habit of doing that," she agreed coldly. She nodded toward a neat farm on a slight rise ahead. "Perhaps you could lock the men in that barn over there and fetch the squire in the morning."

Taking Bell's hand to reassure her—and himself—that all was well, Quent ordered one of the local men to run up to the house and inquire. She disentangled her hand and stepped away.

Irritated by Bell's coolness when his own blood was running red hot, he regarded her with caution. "I can take Penrose and go into town for Dolly. Do you want to return to the house with my father?"

"No, I want to go after Dolly with a whip," she grumbled, finally showing some spirit.

"We didn't bring any side saddles," Quent warned, eyeing her trailing skirt.

With a sign of resignation, she leaned against him for just a moment, letting him wrap his arms around her. "I know my limits. I'll ride back with your blasted father. I'm sure you and Penrose are quite capable of trussing Dolly and dumping her in the river where she belongs."

Quent held her tight, knowing everything was all wrong but not knowing how to make it right, not while he had a troop of men and thieves waiting on him. "I'll carry you home myself and let the others sort themselves out," he suggested.

She shook her head and pushed away. "No, I'll be fine. I'll try not to stab your father until you're there to witness it."

He snorted and let her walk away, but his heart had taken a dive to his boots. He would have enough difficulty sorting through the mess he'd made. If his father had said something to Bell to make her react this way, he'd have to wait and whip the marquess in the morning.

Twenty-seven

IN A BIT OF luck, Quent discovered the squire in the village tavern. He'd left Bell's grooms at the farmer's barn, guarding Hiram and the thieves. He and Penrose sat down beside the tall, saturnine landowner who had assumed the Hoyt family responsibilities as magistrate. In a few curt sentences, they explained the situation.

"Horse thieves ought to be hanged," Squire Blackstone said. "Simple enough and saves His Majesty the expense of transportation."

Quent certainly agreed after they'd kidnapped the boy and nearly given him failure of the heart. But aware that he'd already trampled all over Bell's authority, he preferred not to issue any death sentences in her name.

"One of them is an old retainer of the marchioness's family," Quent warned. On his own, he'd have the gang drawn and quartered—but there were children and an old man back in Ireland who would be badly affected by a public hanging. He had to think in terms of Kit's future and not just himself. "And the female upstairs is a childhood acquaintance. I'd rather not upset Lady Belden if it can be avoided. Remand them to assizes and let the court take them off your hands."

They might still end up hanged, but it would be on the court, not him.

"You'll provide the transportation?" the squire asked warily.

"I'll pay for it and send guards, if needed. I don't know how you want to deal with the one upstairs." Quent laid coins on the counter for the squire's drinks. He wanted this over quickly so he could return to Bell. Negotiating his way back into her life might not happen, but he was constitutionally unable to give up trying. Now that he'd recognized his sentiments, he realized Bell had meant too much to him for too long.

"We'll just lock in the thief until morning," the innkeeper said cheerfully, reaching for a key ring. "Won't be the first time."

"I'll verify that it's her," Quent agreed in resignation. "It's likely to be a scene."

"She's had enough blue ruin that she'll be no problem," the innkeeper assured them.

And so it was. Dolly opened the door with an air of triumph. She tottered in the entrance, regarding them through blurry eyes. Before she realized that her visitors weren't a victorious Hiram and gang, Quent identified her and walked away, leaving her in the capable hands of the squire and innkeeper. He'd lost all sympathy for her long before she'd hired kidnapping thieves.

If the court ruled on transportation because she was female, he'd have to hire an agent to travel to Ireland to ask Bell's uncle if he and his family would like to travel with Dolly to New South Wales.

He couldn't trust his father to care about the people on Kit's Irish estate, he realized. There was far more to this guardianship business than handing the children over to chaperones and tutors. Bell understood that as he had not in his single-minded pursuit of her bed.

He had to accept all of her—bag and baggage. That's what she and her father had been trying to tell him while he'd been building his precarious house of cards, thinking he could deal with family as if they were business.

As he and Penrose rode back to the Hall, the fury that had driven him this far died to weariness of mind and soul. The world was full of terrible people. Quent had a need to cuddle Bell and tell her he would protect her from all woe, even knowing she'd hit him over the head if he said any such thing. After the childhood she'd endured, she deserved a future of happiness and carefree laughter. One way or another, he was determined to see that she had it.

He didn't push his fancies any further than that. He wasn't a fanciful man. He had a goal—Bell's happiness. He'd find some way to attain it.

Penrose took their horses to the stable. Quent climbed the Hall's interior stairs in the light of a single candle, loosening his neckcloth and waistcoat. A bath would have been nice, but it was late, and the servants would be abed. He should have brought his valet with him.

He hesitated outside her bedchamber, not wanting to wake Bell. But he couldn't help himself—he opened the door.

She wasn't there.

Unaccustomed to being swept on the storm of emotion he'd suffered this day, he panicked. He had to furl his canvas and tighten the lines to regain control. The carriage had been sitting outside the stable. She was here somewhere.

He turned to his own chamber. The fire was lit and water was heating in the kettle. Bell would have seen to that. In relief and gratitude, he stripped to wash.

By the time he'd scrubbed and donned a dressing gown, Bell still hadn't arrived. She was still angry. He couldn't let her finish all the gains they'd made this way. He dragged on clean breeches and found slippers and went in search of her.

Not wanting to wake her sisters, he started at the far end of the corridor where they'd moved Kit and his retinue. Quent wasn't entirely certain which door was which, but a footman stood guard near the back exit.

"Lady Bell?" Quent inquired.

The footman nodded at the door on his right.

Quent cracked the door to peer in. Bell sat in a wing chair beside Kit's bed. Her hair tumbled over her brow and her head leaned at an uncomfortable angle, indicating she slept. In the bed, the boy slumbered, motionless for a change.

He ought to walk away, but he couldn't. After years of living alone, he'd let this pair attach themselves to his insides. Heartstrings, his mother had called this connection. To walk away would be to sever them. He would most likely die if that happened. He'd never lied himself. To deny his attachment would be a weakness.

He slipped in and lifted Bell into his arms. Kit was well-guarded and sleeping soundly. The boy didn't need him. Bell did. She stirred in his arms, started to push away, but settled again when Quent reached the corridor. He nodded approval at the alert footman, then carried his intended to his chamber, where the linens would still be warm from the fire.

She didn't protest when he removed her dressing gown and slid her under the covers. She wore a nightshift. He removed his breeches and wore nothing.

After this past night, he wasn't letting any chance to hold her go. She turned to him with kisses, and that was all the encouragement he needed to seek the bliss she offered.

BELL WAS GONE from Quent's bed when he woke the next day. Would the day ever come that he could count on waking beside her?

He told himself it was his usual restlessness before closing a deal that had him climbing out of bed at dawn to search for her. Their lovemaking last night should have settled the quarrel. It hadn't. He needed the words said and the license signed before he'd believe fate would finally reward him.

As long as his father was here, he wouldn't be traveling into the city for business. Quent dressed in boots and a tweed jacket and the last of his clean linen, then walked down the corridor to be certain Kit had recovered from his adventures.

The boy was bouncing on his cot, refusing to let his valet wrap his neckcloth. He shouted in glee at sight of Quent and dived at him.

With a laugh, Quent caught the boy, winked at the valet, and let Kit ride on his back. "I'll carry you down to the breakfast room, just this once," he said sternly. "Only because your sisters will worry if you're not at the table on time."

The boy blew a rude noise and tried to kick with his boots. Quent imprisoned his ankles in his grip and held him until they reached the small downstairs dining table the family had adopted for breakfast. There, he leaned over and dumped Kit, laughing, to the floor.

His father glowered from behind the newssheet. "The boy needs to learn restraint, not to behave like a hooligan."

"The boy needs love and laughter and his family, which is why I'll sue you before I let you have him," Quent said without rancor.

His father paled. He was definitely up to no good.

Bell's sisters stared over their teacups. Bell was nowhere in sight. Filling his coffee cup, Quent gestured it in salute, then headed for the stable.

When in doubt, always look for Bell in the stable. He was a quick student.

He found her in a morning gown and shawl, standing at the paddock, stroking Dream's head and feeding the horse from her palm. At least she wasn't dressed for running away. Breathing a little easier, he strode across the gravel.

"Dolly and Hiram are in the hands of the authorities. I'll send a man to Ireland to talk with your uncle." He leaned against the fence, sipping his coffee, and studying Bell. "Arrangements should be made to look after Kit's holdings."

She didn't look at him. The stone in his stomach doubled in size.

"I received word from Summerby yesterday," she said matter-of-factly. "He has been making inquiries. Uncle Jim has been ill and confined to bed for a while, just as Dolly said. That's why our agents haven't spoken with him. Hiram has been acting as their steward. If Dolly and Hiram are transported, there will be no one to look after her children or Jim or the estate."

He should have known that Bell's quick mind would have already anticipated the problem and probably considered a possible solution. Why had he even thought this was his burden to bear?

Because he wanted her to need him as he needed her.

Irritated despite himself, he asked, "You've inquired with the local church to discover if they have other family?"

She nodded, brushed off her empty palm on her gown, and turned to face the Hall—again, not looking at him. "Summerby has also looked into Kit's mother's family. They're Irish, poor but respectable, as I suspected," she said without inflection. "It's possible they might be interested in moving in. Kit ought to know all his family."

"The poor lad," Quent murmured, "a passel of ill-bred cousins on his father's side and who knows what starving aunts and uncles on his mother's side. He'll have to find gold in Africa to support them."

"Taking care of extended family and tenants is what having a title and land entails," she said sadly. "Edward refused to acknowledge that. I'll teach Kit differently."

"*We'll* teach Kit differently," he said, narrowing his eyes in suspicion. "You needn't do everything alone anymore, and I needn't fight my father's whims by myself. You've cowed him nicely."

That statement surprised him. He'd been thinking marrying Bell would add to his responsibilities. He hadn't quite adjusted to the notion of a woman who would actually *help* him. But he already knew that Bell was just that sort of woman—if he'd let her. Maybe he was a slower student than he'd thought.

Bell turned glistening green eyes up to him. "Your father has agreed to grant guardianship of the children to me. You're a free man."

Her tears registered first. The impact of her statement took a moment longer.

A free man? Quent thought he quit breathing. He nearly crushed the cup he was holding while he gasped for air as if the breath had been knocked out of him.

"You won't have to give up your peaceful bachelor life," she continued, not acknowledging his reaction. "There will be no need to decide how to combine our households. I will be forever grateful that you were willing to help me, but now I will return the favor. I'll call off the banns. Everyone will place the blame on me. I hope we can still be friends."

She really was crying off! After everything that had happened last night... Why had he thought he could mend irreparably damaged fences?

Quent struggled with the war exploding inside him. Fury fired cannons. Grief performed a mournful bagpipe dirge. Desolation lamented his lost soul. He thought his heart quit beating.

He'd no notion that all that tumult could *still* roil his insides. Maybe she was right. Maybe he needed to return to his orderly... solitary... life. It certainly seemed as if love might kill him.

"My warrior instincts don't lend themselves to swords and pistols in the manner of our ancestors," he heard himself saying. He'd never tried to explain himself before, but desperation required that he try now, if only so he understood what was happening while his complacent world drowned in tidal waves of despair. "I'm better at winning economic battles. I established my small shipping company in Edinburgh straight out of school."

She leaned against the fence and glanced at him with curiosity. "I understand that. The term 'gentle giant' was made for you. But when you roar, people listen."

"It wasn't always that way," he said, thinking back. "Back then, I was still a student of business and learning the ways of society and discovering women. When Camilla came to town for her debut, she encouraged my attentions and introduced me to the rarified atmosphere of her father's wealthy, aristocratic company. I made acquaintances at her soirees that I could never have made without the duke's invitations."

Beside him, Bell almost growled. "We were all young once. You didn't need them. You would have won them on your own."

"Perhaps." He shrugged, still struggling with his inner turmoil and trying to pour it out in an orderly manner to better examine his devastation. "I was arrogant. I thought Camilla's attentions meant she would welcome my suit. I courted her. I'd been raised in a large family, where a wife and children were part of being a man. I was perfectly confident that I would be wealthy someday. I assumed she thought the same."

Bell took his hand, pried his fingers out of a fist, but didn't interrupt, even though she had to know the rest of the story.

"When I went to the duke to ask for her hand, he laughed at my pretensions, said he was doing a favor for my father by inviting me into his circle, that his daughter would only marry a title. Who or what I was or would be meant nothing to him." Quent hadn't replayed the painful humiliation of that scene in years. It didn't hurt as much now as it had then.

"Foolishly, I demanded that he ask Camilla. She'd allowed me favors that only a couple with an understanding should have indulged in." Quent sighed and rubbed the back of his head. "It's hard to believe I was so young and stupid. Camilla laughed, of course, told me I was lovely. And then the pair of them hit me with the truth... Belden had just married a young Irish bride, and my father was no longer heir to a wealthy marquessate. In their eyes, I had become nobody but an impoverished younger son of a younger son."

"Mea culpa," Bell whispered

Quent refrained from doing more than holding her hand. "Not your fault at all. It was a good lesson. My fury and humiliation pretty much diluted any heartbreak I might have suffered. I packed up my bags and business and rode to London. My first sight of you nearly brought me to my knees, but I persevered. I had every reason to hate you. I had you investigated. I watched you like a hawk, waiting for you to fail Belden. And while I waited, I built my business on my own terms."

"While I tried to build a marriage," she murmured.

"Which is why I learned to love you from afar," he said, admitting what he'd only just recognized himself. He was ready to cry and fall to his knees with the pain of genuine heartbreak. "Despite every reason to hate you, I learned to admire your strength. You were lost and naïve and you bravely faced society's contempt, learning how to speak properly, learning the ridiculous etiquette of precedence, and demanding respect as the wife of a powerful man. You forged connections that helped Edward, even if he never bothered to tell you."

She tilted her head thoughtfully, and her bonnet brushed his jaw. Just that touch made his insides clutch.

"I wanted to be useful," she said sadly. "I was used to doing everything for my family. I would willingly have conquered Spain if he'd asked it of me."

"And you would have," Quent said with certainty, understanding now how deep her courage ran. Holding his heart in his hand, he touched a finger beneath her chin, and still, she did not notice. He tilted her head so he could meet her eyes. "You're not hearing what I'm saying again, *ma belle*. I have loved you from the first time I laid eyes on you. You were married, and I wasn't worthy. But these past weeks, you've given me reason to believe that perhaps I've at least earned your respect. Don't make me beg."

Her eyes widened. Her lips parted, but words didn't emerge.

Taking that as a good sign, he wrapped his arms around her and lifted her into his kiss. She hesitated, for just a fraction, and then she flung her arms around his neck and returned his kiss with all the passion of which she was capable. He nearly staggered under the immensity of her trust.

And then she pulled back to meet his eyes. "I have loved you for so long that I could not begin to tell you how it came about. You are just always there, a sturdy presence inside my soul, a trusted friend, a shoulder to lean on, and a man I admire above all others. How could I not love you? And loving you, how could I burden you with my quarrelsome family while keeping you from your own? I love you so much, I had to let you go free so you could be happy!"

She almost wailed this last.

He chuckled and held her close, so she could feel his heart clamoring. "I know I have a lot to learn about families, but I'm confident you can teach me what I need to know. I could never be happy without you, and I could not live if you took my heart and left me nothing."

"You have a heart to go with all that formidable brain," she said in wonder. "I had never dared hope you would condescend to open it for *me*."

"I give you my unworthy heart for safekeeping," he warned. "You have the power to destroy me as others never have."

"I will take very good care of it," she assured him. "After all, you have told me I am strong. I shall be a fortress in your defense."

He laughed. "And here I thought I would be the one to protect you!"

Twenty-eight

MID-SEPTEMBER sunshine beamed through the cathedral windows. The bright rays through the stained glass mellowed the old oak benches and slate floors. Oddly, a white banner bearing an Irish crest rippled on one side of the nave. A red banner with a Scots crest hung unobtrusively on the other side.

Both sides of the aisle were unfashionably filled.

Bell peered from around a door at the rear of the church and bit back an inappropriate whistle. "My word, did Quent invite all London?"

"No, all London invited themselves. You did announce the date, after all," Jocelyn Montague reminded her. "Here, let me adjust the lace. You have too much hair for that little scrap."

"It's Belgium lace. Quent imported crates of it years ago. I'm about to make it fashionable again," Bell declared. "A large audience will help."

"You are marrying to increase his profits?" Tess asked with a grin, tucking a white rose bud into Bell's primrose-colored sash.

"We are marrying because it is easier than fighting over who pays for what," Bell said airily. "And because he will keep you and Syd on tight strings where I will not, and I will introduce his sisters to society where he will not, and for all sorts of very practical reasons. I have *loaned* the marquess money for his roof, with good interest. We are also investing in steam engines together."

"She lies," Syd said with assurance, holding a bouquet of white and yellow roses and lavender phlox and prancing in front of a mirror as if she were the bride. "It's all very romantic but neither of them will admit how smitten they are."

Abigail Wyckerly and Nora Atherton looked at each other and laughed. Bell cast her former protégées a disparaging glance, but a smile tugged the corner of her mouth. How could she do anything else except smile when she had friends and family around her and the most wonderful man in the world waiting for her?

"You will see," Bell said sternly. "We shall establish a dynasty that will rule all London. And maybe Ireland," she added as an afterthought, hearing Kit's familiar shouts from the cathedral.

"I swear, you and Quent will compete on your death beds to see who gets to heaven faster. I'll have to loan you my husband to work out a diplomatic settlement." Jocelyn quit fussing with hair pins and lace and stepped back to admire her handiwork. "Really, there should be more purple, but you'll do."

"Blake would just drive a dirk through their hearts to speed them on their way," Abby said with a laugh, knowing Jocelyn's husband for the warrior he was.

Ignoring the byplay, Bell spun around in her striped lavender and yellow gown, letting the silk train swish for the benefit of her admirers. "I'll wear a lavender spencer to the breakfast. Will that suit?"

"Most excellently. Is that a bagpipe I hear?" Jocelyn peered around the doorway and the others jostled to see. "Oh my word, one of them has a bagpipe—and he's wearing a kilt!"

"I suspect that's the marquess's call to arms. He's tired of waiting. He'll have us all arrested as traitors to the crown if they're wearing kilts." Bell peered with them, but her gaze was only for the striking man waiting at the altar, looking harassed, impatient—and most elegant in his dark coat and crisp white neckcloth.

"Yes, I think we've dallied as long as we can," Bell murmured in amusement. "Fitz and Nick appear to be betting on something. Quent may strike them dead with his glare at any moment. Blake looks as if he's sizing them up for coffins."

Abigail smiled with confidence. "My husband only bets on sure things, so Nick is about to lose more of his gold, not his life. Perhaps we should go out there before Fitz bankrupts anyone else."

"I'm amazed Quent and Blake aren't persuading the duke to invest in fashionable weddings while they're idling their time," Bell said dryly. "I don't know which is worse, your noble rakes or our less-than-noble tradesmen. Out you go," she said to her sisters, pushing them toward the door. "Let all society admire your charm. Try not to let Kit trip you."

Her sisters strolled out with the confidence of young women who *expected* all of society to admire them. Boyle arrogance came naturally. For a moment, Bell wanted to weep. Her sisters would be married with families of their own shortly.

A sea of handsome dark male heads on Quent's side swerved to admire the sight.

Nora leaned over and kissed Bell's cheek in the Italian fashion. "They are beautiful. You will be proud of them. And you will make a wonderful aunt for all their beautiful babies. Come along now, it's time."

Taking a deep breath, Bell sent her friends ahead of her to find seats in the first pew on her side of the nave. When the horrendous bagpipe hit a high note, she stepped out after them.

QUENT CLENCHED his gloved fingers and tried not to make a fool of himself in front of his entire family. *Entire* family. The marquess had dragged every last one of the lot to London to see him marry the dowager marchioness. If Bell decided to take flight... he'd have to emigrate.

"That noise machine is bound to send her raving for the exit," Nick said cheerfully, hitting on Quent's worst fear.

"The lady is smart," Fitz asserted. "She'll marry him first, then run for the exit, leaving Quent with both their families."

Quent wondered if he could slam his friends' heads together.

Diplomatic Blake appeared to be studying the crowd for politicians whose arms he could twist later at the wedding breakfast. Quent understood Blake's need to further his causes better than Quent understood his own anxiety. He knew Bell wouldn't desert him. But this moment had been ten damned years in the making. He expected the world to end before it happened.

On the verge of strangling his uncle and setting fire to the bagpipe, Quent finally noticed Bell's sisters emerging from the rear. They didn't appear to be anything other than delighted to be the center of attention, however briefly. He unclenched his fingers and took a deep breath but kept his gaze fixed on the rear of the church.

Bell's friends emerged next. He scarcely saw them—until Abby, Lady Danecroft, caught an escaping Kit and steered him back to a pew. Once in the pew, the boy's tutor removed what appeared to be a Chinese firecracker from the young earl's grip.

Fitz, watching his wife with delight, laughed. "Oh, you will have your hands full with that one," he whispered. "Think about sending him to the Navy."

"Nora's family sent over the fireworks," Nick said with a sigh. "The Italians love gunpowder. I can't believe she let the boy have one. I assume it's one of the small ones that won't blow off his fingers."

Quent quit listening. His bride had emerged looking like a spring garden, although Bell had assured him that she was wearing sedate autumn colors. Her russet hair was the only autumn color he noticed.

The yellowed Belgium lace allowed her spectacular tresses to gleam in the light from the stained glass.

Even the bagpipe shut up.

She looked happy, and he finally breathed freely again. Reaching for his bride's hand once she reached him, Quent held her close as the vicar finally spoke the words making the dowager marchioness, the Virgin Widow, the beautiful Lady Bell just plain Lady Quentin Hoyt.

LATER THAT EVENING, after their guests had bedded down in both townhouses, the Hall, and in the homes of their friends, Quent carried his new bride onto his yacht.

Bell laughed at the quantities of lace adorning every inch of the cabin. "You mean to sell your cargo to Cyprians and bordellos?"

"Excellent idea, although I'll have to find more bachelor friends to do the selling." He lay her on the lace-adorned bed. "But tonight is reserved for just us. No arguing siblings, no complaining nannies, no papers to be signed."

"No bagpipes," she added teasingly, sitting up to remove the pins in her hair.

Quent pushed aside her hands. "Allow me. I've been wanting to do this all day." He removed the lace, and with satisfaction, set a gloriously silky tress free. "I am tempted to set sail for parts unknown and come back in ten years to see how they all managed without us."

"They would, you know," she said seriously, tugging him down beside her. "Our families are intelligent and capable. We need only let them intrude as far as we like, if you will only give up on trying to protect them from the consequences of their rashness."

He kissed the side of her neck and her shell-shaped ear and began unfastening her spencer. "You are a dreamer, my dear, but I love you anyway. Champagne now or later?"

"Later," she agreed, to his happiness, reaching for his neckcloth. "My courses were due a fortnight ago. You may have nine months of uninterrupted lovemaking in your future. After that, I make no promises."

Quent choked and ripped off his own neckcloth while staring in incredulity at his amazing bride. "You cannot know for certain this soon," he said warily.

"Of course not." She started on his waistcoat buttons. "In life, nothing is certain. But just keep in mind black-haired, green-eyed chubby babes when you feel the need to drag me off to bed."

"That is most definitely not on my mind now," he said firmly as he yanked off his tailored coat. "Off with that bodice, woman. My only purpose tonight is to make you the happiest bride this world has ever seen."

She laughed and smothered his face in joyful kisses. "And how do I make you the happiest groom? You know I will not stand in your way if you wish to take Nick up on his challenge of a yacht race to Amsterdam."

Finally conquering the pearl buttons of her bodice and the lace ties of her undergarments, Quent bent to lavish her curves with kisses. He lifted one beautiful breast from its confinement for further ravishment before responding to her question.

Caressing her peaked nipple, he met her gaze. "You challenge me more than any race. If we need the wind in our hair occasionally, we'll choose the means together. But for now, *you* make my heart race. I do not need wind and speed. Tell me you feel the same, and you will make me the happiest of men."

"I do not need wind and speed," she agreed. "I need you. I need you more than rain and sun, more than air itself. And I am ashamed to be so slow at admitting it."

"As long as you admit it now, I am happy. Kiss me, wife, and let us try harder for green-eyed babes in our future."

If the yacht rocked harder than the tide that evening and the cries of the gulls found human accompaniment, there was none to notice.

Author Bio

WITH SEVERAL million books in print and *New York Times* and USA Today's bestseller lists under her belt, former CPA Patricia Rice is one of romance's hottest authors. Her emotionally-charged contemporary and historical romances have won numerous awards, including the RT Book Reviews Reviewers Choice and Career Achievement Awards. Her books have been honored as Romance Writers of America RITA® finalists in the historical, regency and contemporary categories.

A firm believer in happily-ever-after, Patricia Rice is married to her high school sweetheart and has two children. A native of Kentucky and New York, a past resident of North Carolina and Missouri, she currently resides in Southern California, and now does accounting only for herself. She is a member of Romance Writers of America, the Authors Guild, and Novelists, Inc.

For further information, visit Patricia's network:

http://www.patriciarice.com
http://www.facebook.com/OfficialPatriciaRice
https://twitter.com/Patricia_Rice
http://patriciarice.blogspot.com/
http://wordwenches.typepad.com/word_wenches/
http://patricia-rice.tumblr.com/

About Book View Café

Book View Café Publishing Cooperative (BVC) is a an author-owned cooperative of over fifty professional writers, publishing in a variety of genres including fantasy, romance, mystery, and science fiction.

In 2008, BVC launched a website, bookviewcafe.com, initially offering free fiction and gradually moving to selling ebooks of members' backlist titles, then original titles. BVC's ebooks are DRM-free and are distributed around the world. BVC returns 95% of the profit on each book directly to the author. The cooperative has gained a reputation for producing high-quality ebooks, and is now moving into print editions.

BVC authors include New York Times and USA Today bestsellers; Nebula, Hugo, and Philip K. Dick Award winners; World Fantasy and Rita Award nominees; and winners and nominees of many other publishing awards.

CPSIA information can be obtained at www.ICGtesting.com
Printed in the USA
LVOW10s0919120415

434269LV00002B/490/P